ALBERT

or

THE BOOK OF MAN

by Perry Brass

Belhue Press

Belhue Press second printing
Copyright ©1995 by Perry Brass

Published in the United State of America by:
Belhue Press
2501 Palisade Ave., Suite A1
Riverdale
Bronx, NY 10463

Cover and inside photos by Anthony Colantonio
Cover and overall book design by M. Fitzhugh

LIBRARY OF CONGRESS CATALOGUE NUMBER: 94-74524

Publisher's Cataloging in Publication
(Prepared by Quality Books Inc.)

Brass, Perry.
  Albert: or the book of man / by Perry Brass.—Bronx, NY: Belhue Press, 1995
  p. cm.
  Preasigned LCCN: 94-74524
  ISBN 0-9627123-5-3
  1. Gay men—Fiction. 2. Fantastic fiction. I. Title. II. Title: Book of man.

PS3552.R336A53 1995   813' .54
                      QB195-20120

To the memories of my friends Jeff Campbell and Michael Dash; for Marc Collins, Christopher Berg, Hal Kooden, and my other friends who are only visiting here from Ki. And always for Hugh.

Other books by Perry Brass:

Sex-charge (poetry)

***Works* and Other "Smoky George" Stories** (short stories)

Mirage, a science fiction novel

Circles, the sequel to *Mirage*

Out There, Stories of Private Desires. Horror. And The Afterlife.

". . . may my soul go forth to travel to every place which it desires. . . ."

The Egyptian Book Of The Dead
from the papyrus of Ani, translated by Dr. Raymond Faulkner

There is always that need in human beings to create the Other. To create it, worship it, and destroy it.

It may be true that each man is his own worst enemy; but once he realizes the power within himself and learns (because this knowledge is not innate) to act on this power, he becomes his own best ally.

INTRODUCTION

This story begins on *Ki*, a small planet associated with the distant star cluster the Pleiades, within the constellation Taurus. Ki is a beautiful primitive place with very limited resources. To keep its human numbers from overwhelming its size, thousands of Ten Moons ago—the Kivian reckoning for years—the population was divided into three groups: the Off-Sexers, warlike tribes composed of dominant males and submissive females; the Same-Sexers, nature-worshipping homosexual men who are aligned with the Temple of Ki; and the Sisters of Ki, renegade women who periodically break away from their Off-Sex families and are taken in by the Temple. There they devote themselves to the service of the Goddess Ki and Her daughter Laura, and to preserving the balance of Ki, a balance instituted by the ancient Agreement whereby the three groups resolved to live in harmony. To distinguish themselves from their Off-Sex "cousins," the Same-Sex men of Ki possess an anatomical difference: a powerful third testicle, called the third Egg, or the *Egg of the Eye*.

This testicle is directly connected to their brains—and some say to their very souls. It can convey thoughts telepathically. It can travel, under certain circumstances, on its own through space, reproducing itself and gathering vast folds of time and distance like a cosmic darning needle, knotting them into small manageable loops. By passing through these folds of space, intergalactic travel becomes almost instantly negotiable. But the problem is that once the Egg leaves its owner, he is left in a vulnerable state of suspended "sleep," making travel from one part of the Universe to another a dangerous adventure.

If this is your first trip to Ki, have no fear: *Albert, or The Book Of Man*, is a thrilling, cosmic voyage of a story that can be read and enjoyed independently. On the other hand, if you've visited Ki before, via *Mirage* and the second Kivian book, *Circles*, you will find *Albert* a natural extension of its history, introducing vivid new characters to a family of men that began with the ambitious hunter Greeland and his soulful mate Enkidu, who only reluctantly had the destiny of the planet thrust upon him. At the conclusion of *Circles*, after a war on Ki that has forced his Egg temporarily to Earth,

Enkidu found himself made the first king of Ki: a role he assumed only to preserve the balance of the planet. He was helped in this rise by the devious magician Woosh, leader of the enclave of the sinister Blue Monkeys.

On Earth, Enkidu's Egg had become lodged in the scrotum of Nick Lawrence, a married closeted man living in wealthy Beverly Hills, California. Because of the power of the Egg, Nick's homosexuality was forced into the open. Soon he encountered the passion of his life: a gay Russian mathematician named Reuvuer. After ingesting the powerful "seed" from Nick's Egg, Reuvuer discovered that he would do anything for Nick, even murder. But in a desperate attempt to break their bonds with Ki—and save their own lives—the gay couple was killed by Rich Quilter, a homophobic conservative politician. After their deaths, Enkidu, again whole and "awakened" on Ki, was able to do what was necessary to bring the planet back to its state of balance; and to use the power within himself to become its ruler. But first he had to kill Greeland, the mate promised to him as a boy, whose vicious plans started the war that threatened life on Ki. After Greeland's death, Enkidu took Greedu, an Off-Sex outcast, as his mate. By marrying Greedu, Enkidu finally created the harmony necessary for peace on Ki. But every day he was reminded that since Greedu was an Off-Sexer, they could not share seed from each other's Egg, an act necessary to extend the lives of Same-Sex men.

Albert is the story of the son of Greeland and Enkidu; it is the story of the love of fathers and sons. It is also the story of what we now see as the unfolding of "gay" consciousness into a deeper understanding of the Same-Sex role in the Universe, and in the complete Book Of Man. It is a story many of us are taking part in each day, as we search for our own Egg of the Eye.

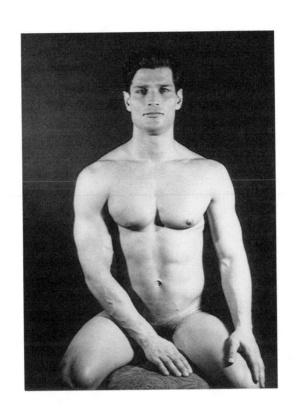

Part One

CHAPTER 1

The night that my father Enkidu died, he called me into his chamber in the towering castle edged by woods and endless plains that he and his beloved mate, the Off-Sexer Greedu, had erected. I was at that point thirty-two and unpromised, with no sexual experience to call my own. Such a thing was unheard of on the planet Ki. I had lost myself in endless hunting parties, learning to fight and wrestle, the reading that Enkidu had taught me, and gathering together the books that contained the story of our races: the wild Same-Sex brothers from whom I had sprung and the Off-Sex people of Ki, men and women, who for thousands of Ten Moons—our term for years—had been our enemies.

His chamber was dark. He was almost blind. He seemed to me as old as the caves and the mountains of our small planet. But always he had seemed that way, even going back to those years when I remembered him well, as a young man with Greeland, my other father, the crazy head-strong warrior whose face I had often seen myself when I looked into the mirror.

"Come closer," Enkidu whispered from his bed. "You look exactly as I remember you, Greeland."

"I am not Greeland," I reminded him. "I am Albert, your son."

"Albert!" He pulled me closer to him and kissed me lightly on the lips. His breath felt faint, barely escaping from his nostrils. "How could I forget? *I* called you here! How good of you to come to your old father. But for a moment, just as you walked through the door, I thought you were my first promised mate, Greeland, whom you hardly remember, I am sure."

"I remember him only too well," I said impatiently. "I cried bitterly after he was—"

"After I killed him?"

"Yes, sira-father," I said, using our word *sira* out of respect and affection. "You did what you had to do, then you took Greedu as your mate, a man I could never fully accept, as he was not one of us—"

"He was one of us, because he loved *me* and loved *you* as well."

"But he was an Off-Sexer."

"And you were born of an Off-Sex mother, whom you will never know. 15

Remember, that is only another mystery of our lives, Albert. It is amazing how Ki is still a constant mystery to me, my son. But soon I shall leave it."

"I know," I said, and then without warning, my knees gave way like water beneath me. I knelt down and starting crying at his side; I cared for him so much. He patted my head, running his old bony fingers through my hair. I felt as if my whole life were coming to an end. As if I were too young to be experiencing this terrible loss; yet I was hardly young anymore. The idea of being left so alone now—Greedu had died at least twelve Ten Moons before—sank into me.

"I must tell you the story of your name," Enkidu said to me. "I have never told it to you."

I got up and kissed his old hand, dry and wrinkled, and then sat down gently on the edge of his bed. "I know it is a secret. Greeland himself would never speak to me of it."

"Many Ten Moons ago, your father Greeland and I were made to leave Ki. Woosh, the crafty old magician of the Blue Monkeys, enabled us to go to another planet, called Earth, and there in the form of other men, persons very much like ourselves—"

"Same-Sexers?"

"Yes—people, I am afraid, very despised on that planet: in their form we embraced another life . . . eventually we even *took* a life."

"You murdered some one?"

"Yes."

"I did not think you were that sort of person," I said to my father.

"Greeland did it."

"Why?"

"It was part of Woosh's plan, and it saved Ki—for a while. But the most amazing thing was that I fell in love with the most beautiful creature, named Robert, and I could not bring him back here to Ki, because to do so," he halted, then said: "would mean to slaughter him."

"What was your name then, on Earth?" I asked.

"Allan."

"So I am *Albert*?"

"Yes, for I, Enkidu, loved both of them, both Allan *and* Robert. I loved them as if they were completely *separate* people, even though I lived in Allan's own body. I saw another world through his eyes, touched it with his skin. I pray that you can see that: that I loved both of them truly, just as I have loved both Greeland and Greedu." I could tell that he could hardly speak anymore. The diseases of old age, which our Same-Sex brothers kept away by ingesting seed, the special sperm from our Eggs, had infected him.

He leaned towards me, and said, just before closing his eyes, "My son, you must take a mate. I know you have not done so, out of loyalty to me: since I could not share seed with Greedu, you have not left me to go off with another. What a fine man *you* are. No one could ask for a finer son; but after I am gone, you *must* have a mate of your own. Not to do so is to court your own death—and also, you will condemn yourself to be alone on our beautiful dangerous planet. I know that when you are ruler of Ki—"

"I do not want to be ruler."

"You must be, dear sweet boy. For so many Ten Moons there has been peace here; your dark Same-Sex brothers have had the peace they needed. But without a ruler, with only these foolish Off-Sex chieftains to go back to their bickering and warfare, then all of this has been in vain; and my own life, lonely and painful as it has been, has been merely a waste of time."

"I am not meant to be ruler of Ki," I said. "I know I am a strong man— and sometimes my temper gets the worst of me—but I know inside that I am neither wise enough, nor settled enough, to be ruler."

Enkidu shook his head. "Greeland wanted to be ruler more than anything else in life, and I did not. Yet I bent myself to it. Of course I had Greedu at my side, and you—despite all the other young men who have wanted you— have taken no promised friend, and have no sons to prove it. The Sisters of Ki are disappointed in you, Albert."

"They can stay that way—if I took a mate, I am certain that these forests would start shaking with envy: every Same-Sex man would say, 'Why not me?' Besides, I would have had to leave you and go off on my own. I would have had to live somewhere else with a strange man."

He brought my head to his old white face and kissed me again. "Now, Albert, you *will* have to." He smiled. "My dear sweet child. How did I ever produce something as handsome as you? I am afraid I look like a monkey—"

"No, sira-father, you do not!"

"You are only being kind. I was never handsome like your other father Greeland. I still wonder how I ever had such a beautiful, tall, strong son. . . ."

With those words, he closed his eyes, and I left him. Later on in the night, Tolah, his chamber servant, came into my quarters in one of the farthest turrets of the castle and gave me the news. "I am afraid our Lord Sira-Enkidu is dead," he said. Great tears streamed down his face. "The Sisters of Ki will take him to the Temple for a funeral, and then he will be buried in the Cave of Mysteries, not far from Greeland and the body of his own Greedu, who was allowed to rest there—"

"Yes, I know," I said to the old servant. I had heard the story before. The

Same-Sex elders did not want Greedu's Off-Sex bones in their cave, but they gave in to Enkidu and allowed it. How small the whole planet seemed to me—too small for its own good. I walked out onto the parapets of my tower and saw torches winding through the distant paths, as far as I could see. Streams of torch-bearing mourners were trudging from the forests and the sullen, craggy mountains beyond them, as word of my father's death had moved faster than the wind. As the mourners got closer, their lights merged in a lustrous sea of fire marching on to Enkidu's castle. I ran down the stairs and hurried through the empty, echoing halls to his chamber. I had to see him before the people of Ki got to him, but my way was barred by Hortha, the elder priestess of Ki, who looked as ancient as a crocodile—and was twice as smart as one.

"Sorry, my son. Please do not enter. The Sisters are preparing Sira-Enkidu." She bowed her old, white head. "He will be dressed in his beautiful state robes and his face painted and rouged for this state occasion. We will take him to the Temple and there in front of the statue of Laura, his own chosen Goddess, we will have the service. I am afraid that he now belongs to all of Ki—not merely to you, my dear child."

I nodded my head. It was silly to argue. She was right. The old witch was always right! She used to drive my father crazy. But she was correct: he was no longer my father; he was now a painted god, next to Laura, his personal Goddess. He had proclaimed her the sacred Daughter of the planet and her own beguiling statue, with its distinct features, had been placed before the faceless, golden, ancient effigy of Ki: the original Great Goddess, who had ruled over all of us, Off-Sexer and Same-Sexer alike, since the time when Time had begun. Or at least, that was the *usual* line, as Enkidu joked with me.

I watched as eight solemn, sturdy Sisters bore him away on a gauze decked litter, sparkling with crystal beads and gold. He looked splendid in those gorgeous, state robes—the damn heavy ones he hated, but had to wear since he could no longer run around half-naked like his forest brothers did. His face was chalked a grisly sort of white, a smile had been painted on it and his old, sunken cheeks were as pink as a parrot's. To complete this image of the king now turned god, his hands were also chalked, and looking at him, I felt that I was now not in the presence of my father, but only a statue of him. As high as this occasion was—and already it was awash in ceremony—it made me feel miserably sad. I shrugged my shoulders, went back up to my turret, and desperately tried to sleep. My body felt as if it were an ancient, rotting pier, rolling about, ready to collapse into a stormy sea: it was so heavy with grief and fatigue. I repeatedly closed my eyes only to reopen them as the image of my dying father replayed in my sleepless brain.

Suddenly I became aware that somebody else was in my small room. *"Company?"* a grating voice asked, sounding straight from the Cave of Graves itself.

I opened my eyes and looked out into the dark. Then with much disbelief, I saw him: a strange, old man, who seemed more ape than human, in a blue robe surrounded by a thin blue light, was standing over my bed. "How did you get in here?"

"As long as Sira-Enkidu was alive, I could not approach his castle. We had an agreement." He let out a coarse, rude laugh. "It seems as if all of Ki has some kind of agreement, correct?" His laugh was truly blood chilling, the kind of nightmare shriek that had jagged nails impaling bits of living flesh in it. "The agreement was *I* would never try to bother *his* son—or have influence over you—and *he* would not tell anyone *any* of the secrets of the Blue Monkeys. But now that he is dead, our agreement is also!" He shrieked some more. I wanted to strangle him, anything to stop that revolting laugh.

"Woosh! My father spoke of you often, but never nicely. What do you want?" I demanded.

"Only to make a small introduction," the ape man said, laughing again. Ugly brown spittle dribbled from his leathery mouth. He caught it in the cracked palm of one of his shaggy old hands. Its claws were long, stiletto-like, and filthy. My stomach turned.

Suddenly, this *thing* that was bigger than I—and I am not a small man—jumped onto the bed and put its repulsive face next to mine. It tried to kiss me. I pushed it away, and then looked at it. Even in the darkness, I could tell that the face was also apish and leathery, but younger than Woosh's, with a low forehead and a small nose that tilted up, snout like. It had the strangest, dull amberish eyes, like small glass beads observed through dirty water. The sort of beads one might casually pick up on a river bank and wonder where they came from. I looked into them. The eyes became serious; they looked at me curiously in silence. He implored me, and I was struck by the intensity and sincerity of this repulsive face. I took his hand in mine for a moment, and held it, realizing this was the kind of gesture my father Enkdu, who was generous to all creatures, would have made. He nodded his homely head to me. Suddenly, I felt bad. I got up naked and lit the small oil lamp next to my bed, and looked at the two of them while they looked back—Woosh with that ungainly drunken smile that seemed plastered to his leering face and the other thing, looking downward, almost bashful, not really like Woosh—then I walked over to my chamber cupboard and found a narrow dressing wrap to tie around my waist.

19

"How civilized!" Woosh exclaimed. "To dress for my son! Permit me to introduce you, Albert, to Nafshee, my child." Then he added: "He is also the offspring of Tosh, one of my favorite Blue Monkeys."

"Who was his mother?"

"Bahh! *We* do not need a mother. He was cloned directly from Tosh and me. He came right out of my Egg! It is a little trick we Blue Monkeys can do—conceive a kid right in our own scrotums. If you Same-Sex men could do it, imagine how happy you'd be? None of that mating-for-life monkey doody!"

Nafshee backed away from me. Suddenly a human light seemed to turn on behind his yellow-flecked eyes. He touched me, at first tentatively, then grabbed me hard by the waist and tried to untie my dressing wrap.

"He wants to mate with you now!" Woosh said, laughing. "Give him time, Nafshee; his only living daddy just died."

But Nafshee would not be dissuaded. His thick, hairy fingers untied the wrap, then he violently wrapped himself all around me, running one hand through my hair while the other crawled its way into my rear opening. I slapped him down and he only smiled and flipped me onto the bed. The thing was strong; it took me a moment to recover. Just when his body was on top of mine and he was lifting my legs up to try to get himself into me, I used the full force of my shoulders and forearms and shoved him off the bed. He landed on the floor like a mess of dirty laundry.

"This is becoming interesting," Woosh said as Nafshee got up again and made one more attempt to take me. I threw him down again to the floor. "Frankly, I think my son should have you exactly when he wants, but that is not what we are doing here. Not at all."

"Then what in the name of Laura are you doing?"

I waited. There was quiet while Woosh and his son looked at me. Nafshee shook his head sadly.

"I like him," Nafshee growled softly. "He is mate for me."

"Shut up, you stupid monkey," Woosh said. "You think he is merely going to submit to you? Half the beautiful men of Ki want him and he has refused them. Right, Princess?"

I did not answer. Then I said: "So what *do* you want?"

"I want you to make Nafshee your promised friend, your mate."

"Never!" was all I could promise him. "My father told me all about you, Woosh. You are never to be trusted."

"All? He told you *all*? Did he tell you how I sent him and Greeland all the way to a planet called Earth, saving Greeland from lonely misery here on Ki? And—let me not forget—did he tell you that I saved Enkidu's Egg, after the

Sisters of Ki wanted to have it 'surgically' removed? Do you know what Enkidu's fate would have been after that *little* twist of the knife? And later, when Greeland turned on your father and reduced the whole planet to bloodshed, I again sent Enkidu away—allowing him to mate, later, with his own beloved Greedu and—"

"Yes, he told me all of that—and what a crafty bastard you are . . . that you are one monkey *never* to be trusted!"

"And you believed him, the man who murdered Greeland, your other father—making you one half an orphan—who then took an Off-Sexer as his mate?"

"Yes, I did." I looked over at Nafshee, who seemed bored and completely lost in this argument.

Woosh spit violently on the floor. "Then you are not as smart as Enkidu and you are not *fit* to be ruler of Ki. And whatever happens to you will be of your own doing, fool!"

I sat down naked on the bed. The two of them looked at me, and I could tell that Nafshee was still sizing me up. "So, tell me, Woosh, why should I make Nafshee my mate? It was bad enough that my father Enkidu intermarried with the Off-Sexers. Now, I should mate with a monkey?"

Woosh laughed. "Not just any monkey: my son. Nafshee is immensely strong. He could overcome you, rape you right now, *if* he wanted to. And probably kill you afterwards. All of this has only been a game, you see: he admires you terribly. He has been enthralled with you for years."

Nafshee's right hand bashfully went to his naked, hairy genitals, while his left hand clutched his chest. His eyes lowered to the floor. I could tell he was embarrassed by this ghoul's declaration of his feelings.

"I am afraid, Woosh, you still have not answered my question."

"Fair," Woosh agreed. "While you have been out having a good time this last decade of Ten Moons, your cousins the Off-Sexers have become increasingly stronger. Despite Enkidu's noble intentions to unite Ki into one peaceful whole, *they* have not been napping. There are plans for them to retake the planet. They will destroy your Same-Sex brothers, enslave you, and everything Enkidu worked for will be like little piles of muddy turds squeezed out on the banks of the Tanna: in other words, washed away by the storms of their hatred."

"This is merely another trick. Why should I believe you?"

"Because Enkidu, remember, knew that I was powerful. Just as I brought him to Earth twice, and then brought him back, I can see forward as well as backwards."

I started to grin when he said that: it sounded ridiculous—*if* he could see   21 forward, then why could he not see that I would never accept his hulking ape-son as my mate?

Woosh looked at me; then from another direction I heard his scratchy voice: "Let me do a little stunt for you, Albert."

I watched Woosh slowly twist his head, like a creaking rusty screw, in every direction of the compass. It made a grating noise as it revolved, clicking every three or four degrees.

He did this over and over again, each time making me more and more nervous. But while he did this, I, too, could see in every direction.

I saw through the walls of Enkidu's castle, walls now as transparent as the eyelids of a fish, to the fields belonging to Off-Sex warriors, who were presently engaged in putting on their war boots, armor, maces, helmets, and knives. Then I heard the screams and shrieks of warfare. I could smell rancid fires consuming villages and flesh. Thousands of bodies were dumped into our once peaceful rivers. I saw them floating like bloated rafts, as wild dogs waited on the shores to chew on them. But the worst sight was the small, terrified faces of children running from the corpses of their parents. These were the faces that had seen a tragedy, one Woosh wanted me to believe would be our future.

"Now do you believe me?" he asked.

My mouth went dry; my knees began to wobble. But I was able to grab my dressing wrap, and I began once more to cover myself with it. I would not let Woosh take control of me, no matter what. It was time to show these beasts to the door! "I think you should leave. I am not going to believe this fantasy."

"No, my dear," Woosh protested politely. "You should leave!" He grabbed my hand, cutting his dirty talons into my wrist, while his other hand snapped my dressing wrap aside. Then with both hands, he slammed my eyes closed. I tried to kick him hard, but only flailed about blindly, as Nafshee grabbed at my genitals forcefully with his leathery fingers; pain burned and crackled through my body. One of his callused thumbs pressed itself up into the sensitive skin of my scrotum, virtually touching the soft, trembling, delicate membrane of my third testicle, the Egg itself.

Because of the respect all had had for Enkidu, no one had ever handled me sexually. I had remained aloof from sex—both from its joys as well as its pains and disappointments. I was what others might describe as a *virgin*. I had heard that sex with men could be rough, but not *this* rough. I started crying from the pain; the humiliation. I should have been able to shove Woosh aside. He was an old man—or an old half-monkey. But I was in his power; I felt somehow drugged. Nafshee's thick fingers continued working on my

Egg—as if he were a demented cook—pushing and squeezing this sacred organ against the creased palms of his hands.

"Stop," I pleaded. "Please." Woosh took his filthy hands from my eyes, and now I could see the smile on his son's face: that dumb, strange, sickening smile. I had been prepared to fight both of them, but I realized I could not. There was no way that I could fight the sorcery of Woosh, leader of the Blue Monkeys. As strong as I was from hunting and trekking through Ki, I collapsed to the floor. I was sure that Nafshee would rape me now, that against my will he would enter me and then take me off to be his own. But instead I descended into total oblivion. Moments later my eyes were able to open, and I watched as the two of them managed to take me passively out of the castle, passing me naked but completely unseen except for a slight shifting of blue light through a sea of mourners crowding its gates: as if the stone battlements of Enkidu's residence had been made simply of the night air itself.

CHAPTER 2

I was now sitting haunched on unfamiliar ground, on a dead, infertile plain. I looked around me; not a mountain peak nor the leafy terrain of a forest could I identify. I reasoned that since I knew Ki so well, I must have been at least six days' journey from the castle—farther than I had ever gone. My head throbbed. It hurt so badly that for a moment I rested my eyes. I felt as if I had been drunk forever, although I rarely touched any fermented drink.

I opened my eyes and looked up again into the distance before me. A group of roughly twenty men approached. By their armor and helmets, I realized they were Off-Sexers.

"Lord! Lord! LORD!" one of them shouted. "What is THIS?" He strode up to me, leaving the others watching cautiously behind. He was huge, with massive shoulders and arms like tree trunks. I could see this through his jointed-leather armor. He removed a large helmet of patched hide; his hair, long, red, and flowing, fell in thick, dirty swirls to his shoulders. "I am Anvil," he announced. "We have waited a *lonnnng* time to see you, my friend. What good spirit has brought you to our humble camp, Sira-Albert?"

"I was brought against my will," I said groggily.

Anvil nodded his red head. ". . . yes, and naked, too! Come—" he offered a huge reddened hand to pull me up from the ground. "You *must* be our guest!" He laughed heartily with a deep voice that rang in the air, but I must say his laugh made me feel better than Woosh's. "Can you walk on your own with your bare, dainty feet, or do you need my men to carry you? We will be pleased to bear Enkidu's son with all the honor he deserves!"

"I can walk," I said, once I was back on my feet. But I did feel self-conscious being naked with these clothed Off-Sexers around me. He must have seen the embarrassment on my face; one of his men threw me a shirt. It was long, gray, and coarse; it covered me to my knees. I slipped into it and then began walking through the dark night, lit by four dim Moons, always favorable to the Off-Sexers. Anvil quickly put his arm about me.

"You are in luck, my woman Wifta is away—so only us men are here!" He pushed his beardy face close to mine and laughed heartily and his men— they were quickly joined by others; I could make out perhaps sixty of them now—laughed as well. "You Same-Sex scum like the company of big-scrotumed guys, right!" He laughed some more, and this time I felt sure that the laugh was on me.

We walked farther down the plain, until it started to roll with slight hills. Scrubby, dwarfed trees now appeared; then, lit by what seemed like the four Moons at their sharpest and most unclouded, I saw the dirty, mud-wattled walls of a keep, a garrisoned fortress. If there had been a wife around there, it was hard to believe it. No Off-Sex woman of any rank would stand for such a vile pig-run of a place. "My humble quarters," Anvil intoned, stooping to bow, as we walked through a filthy courtyard. "Please allow me to extend our hospitality." He opened a crude wooden door and let me in. Five of his men tried to follow, but he blocked their way with a scowl and a shake of his head, and then bolted the door in front of them.

The walls of his private chambers were pierced just below the roof with a single row of narrow eyeholes. Thin, mottled sheets of parchment had been stretched over these high openings, and through them drifts of moonlight settled in. The atmosphere was thick, gray, and awash inside with a fetid stale mist. Anvil immediately lit six oil lamps; essentially wicks set in gouged-out stones. They cast an eerie yellow light. "I must tell Wifey to clean!" He spat on the pounded-dirt floor and then ground his boot heel into it. I looked around: leather armor and weapons were piled up everywhere. On one side was a wooden table of massive planks neatly lashed together. Directly opposite this was a bed, made of more planks, sunk low and covered with a soft, enticing pallet of animal hides and fur coverlets. "You must be tired," Anvil observed. "I can offer you no bath at the moment, since our plumbing is in," he laughed, then belched out—"disrepair. But if you would like to lie yourself down, please feel free."

"I would like to go home. My father will be buried tomorrow. I am sure it is expected that I will be there."

"Yes," Anvil agreed slowly. "The death of the beloved Sira-Enkidu has reached every ear on Ki. Even our own waxy ones!" He began to take off his armor, slowly undoing the knots and fastenings that held each piece in place—first the shin pieces, then the short leather panels that girdled his hips. Then he unlashed his chest pieces, and I realized that unlike most Off-Sex men who wore several layers of clothing, he was completely naked, massive and glowing with sweaty, oily skin, underneath his armor. He stood before me, running his fingers through patches of wild, curly red hair on his chest, wearing only his boots. His huge male-piece was obviously swollen, but with what desire I was not sure. "Here," he said, pulling at my shirt with his hand:

"Why so formal? Let us get more comfortable!" He jerked the scratchy, vile shirt right off my back. "So, shall we take a well-deserved nap?"

He grabbed me, naked once more, by the hand and tossed me onto the fur bed, so that the hard wooden planks met my tired body. "I am afraid, sir, I am going to fuck you right here," he said, as spit drizzled down his chin.

"I thought sex with another man was looked down upon among your people."

"I am not *of* my people. I have *no* wife. I am a renegade. I would just as soon stick this pipe into you as I would into a girl, a cow, or a fat dog. Lift your legs, or I shall gladly beat you unconscious, Sira-Albert, and then have you."

"How about your men? Suppose they came in here? For them to find you with me—how would they feel?"

"Amusement . . . they are as much animals as I am. You see, I am Ertan's cousin, one that he hated—so he banished me to this terrible place. When Greeland's forces finally murdered Ertan during the war, I was happy. And all the time while your father Enkidu was working for peace, I have been building up my own forces on this, the *least* gracious part of our planet. The Off-Sexers are tired of you queer men having power on Ki. All of us are ready to attack again and own the planet. So for your sake, Albert, you will either join with me, or pay for your independence with your life."

"All of this has been waiting for the death of my father?" I asked.

He nodded his fiery red head.

Now I knew that everything Woosh had shown me had been correct. If Anvil had upwards of a hundred men here, there was no telling how many others were waiting in other places in his territory. I saw the whole thing again: Woosh twisting his head like a screw, and the future following it. But I doubted what Anvil told me about his men feeling only "amusement" at seeing him rape me. Off-Sex men had never found a public revelation of this type of behavior endearing—even if Anvil was the one doing the screwing.

"They will say you are secretly one of us," I whispered. "A secret Same-Sexer in Off-Sex clothes."

"They think that I am in here murdering you. I told them I wanted that right all to myself. That is why they are happy to wait outside—but not for long. I will either have you, Albert, or toss you out for them to kill, immediately."

"Then you *are* secretly one of us."

"Not on your life! Any man who says that, I will kick his balls off! Now get your legs up. This is strictly for my pleasure. I am going to stick my equipment up in you as far as it will go—and then some! And if any man is crazy enough to think that I am a Same-Sexer, I will stick it up him as well!"   27

"And if I do not let you?"

He reached with his big hand under one of the fur coverlets and produced a bone-handled knife big and sharp enough to rend a large stag in two. "Does this answer your question, Albert?"

I told him it did and lifted my legs over his knees, while he, still in his black boots, rammed his thick, garnet-headed male-pipe into me. Sweat poured from his face. He was pumping away, when suddenly his left hand, after squeezing any flesh of mine it could grab until I turned purple, found my scrotum. I became erect; I am afraid I could not help myself. "What have we got here?" Anvil asked, dripping and gasping. "A little response? I am not such a bad lay, am I?"

I looked into his eyes; then I realized that being so cut off even from his own people, Anvil must not have known anything about the Egg. Indeed, many Off-Sex men, aware of its power, wanted to possess it. They even desired its seed, but could never overcome their shame at being so intimate with one of us.

"The Egg . . ." I whispered. "You have found it."

"What?"

I directed his hand to my swollen third testicle. "The seed from this is magic. It prolongs life. It will make you see things . . . amazing things."

"You faggot!" He spit at me. "You think I am going to put my mouth on"—he paused, then said—"suck that? I do not care what the seed does. I should call my men in, and have them whack your head off right now!"

I smiled. "You have already fucked me, Anvil. So why not be done with it and take the seed as well? Do they know what you are doing in here?"

"Sure." Then his face dropped. He shook his head. "No. The truth is I told them I would only interrogate you, and kill you if I wanted to—*which* I may yet do!"

"Anvil, put your mouth on it. I will give you the seed. It will be the first time that anyone has had it. I am a virgin, I swear. I saved myself until my father Enkidu's death. The first man to take our seed possesses us: that is our law. I would not allow it before, but you have me in your power."

He cleared his throat, making a noise like a river mud hole being scooped out. "For real?"

"By the Goddess Laura Herself, I swear."

"I do not believe in your goddamn goddess, but I will accept your oath." He put his mouth on the tip of my male-pipe and then began sucking violently on my already hardened member, even while in one hand he clenched the bone handle of his knife. I could feel the rippling movement of seed in my third Egg. So many beautiful Same-Sexers had wanted me—and I had held

28

out—but who would believe that this would happen: that I would end up giving myself to this horrifying creature? Surely, Enkidu had given himself to an Off-Sexer, Greedu, although under vastly different circumstances. Perhaps, as upsetting as it was, I was only following in my own beloved father's footsteps.

Then, as the head of my pipe got thicker and hotter, it dawned on me what I had to do: a plan appeared. I realized I was watching it all now, watching Anvil's mouth and cheeks running up and down the length of me, sucking and squeezing the shaft. I had become detached, though extremely conscious at the same time of what was occurring. Now I saw everything: *I was in control and Anvil was not.* The blade was about to slip from his right hand, as the intensity of his actions increased. *Thus:* at the moment when I shot my seed into his stroking mouth, I could reach over, grab the knife, already slipping from his right hand, and kill him.

I knew that in a few more movements it would be over. My detachment amazed me: I could feel the churning seed, squeezing up the shaft of my pipe, urgent to fly out as I released it. Suddenly Anvil stopped. He looked up at me, with saliva dripping down his unshaven chin. "This is not as bad as I thought, you little shit! I think I like *this!*"

I did not say a word as he went back to work. I closed my eyes as the seed blasted out of the head of my pipe, exploding briefly to my view like a mushroom of light in the darkened room. I heard a scream that sounded like a trap door clanging and I opened my eyes and saw Nafshee's face in front of me. Then he opened his mouth filled with my white, glowing seed.

The faint blue light reappeared, bearing Woosh. In his hand, the old monkey grasped Anvil's throat, with the bone-handled knife stuck clear through it.

"You are mine now," Nafshee said. "Forever." He pulled my face to his and ran his tongue down my throat until I was sure I could feel it wetting my heart.

"Why have you done this to me?" I said, pushing myself away from the ape's strong son, a man whom I now hated has much as I had hated Anvil, for taking forcefully from me what had been mine solely, freely, to give.

Nafshee knelt at my feet. I heard Anvil's men outside, banging on the door. "I am your servant, Albert. I prostrate myself at your bare feet. I killed him only at the bidding of my father, only to possess you, I truly love you. . . ."

"Quiet!" the old monkey demanded. "You spineless shrimp! You did it to have power on Ki; that is the *only* important thing. Albert, you have a choice: we can take you safely from these men, and keep you with us—safe—

forever, with you and my son ruling Ki. Or we can leave you here and when Anvil's men ram this door open, they will tear you limb from limb."

I hesitated as the pounding doubled with fury. I could hear angry voices lashing above it. "Anvil! ANVIL! What are you doing with the Same-Sex prince! Question time is up! We will chop his heart into dog meat and throw his bowels to the buzzards!"

The door that Anvil had bolted was pried from its hinges. My face fell as I watched his men pour in from outside.

"Time's up, laddie," Woosh said, his eyes shot with glee. "You made your choice: I give you to your friends!" With that the old monkey extended his arms in a benevolent gesture; then with his blue light he disappeared. Six of Anvil's henchmen were barely half a length from me; their long knives drawn. They swang them in the air so that the whir of blades chopping wind reverberated against the dirty walls of Anvil's chamber. Then they stopped.

Each saw Anvil's face. Dead—his neck pierced through with his own blade. Blank silence fell: again all I could hear was my own heart—and a voice that came from my own beloved Enkidu: "Albert, there is one voice never to trust on this small planet—that belongs to Woosh, the leader of the Blue Monkeys!"

"*Killllll him!!!*" Anvil's men shouted at once and leaped at me but not before a hairy hand had grabbed me and I was buried in his arms and lips, only to disappear into the yellowish air right before the astonished eyes of Anvil's enraged army.

This must have been a dream. When I opened my eyes, I was in a different place. Nafshee was holding my hand, kneeling again at my feet. "I could not allow my father to have you sacrificed," he whispered as tears rolled down his leathery face. I looked out: I was now at the tops of the tallest trees I had ever seen. They were so tall that I could not even look down to their roots. But I could hear the voices of approaching dark men, who I knew were Enkidu's brothers as well as mine. They were going to the Temple of Ki. "He will be buried today—and rumor has it that his son, Sira-Albert, has disappeared."

"Yes, terrible! The Goddess Ki has already deserted us. Perhaps She is jealous of her daughter Laura, whom Enkidu declared to be the true Goddess of our planet."

"Oh, you silly one! Ki is not jealous. Ki is too big to be jealous. She is only biding Her time. But our Off-Sex cousins will take advantage of this as they always do—any time they can use our sorrows to their advantage they will. Unless Albert returns and takes a mate from one of his own tribe, the whole planet will be in jeopardy."

Then they were off, taking their voices with them.

"I *must* go to the Temple," I said. "I must show myself to the people of Ki."

"My father forbids it. He has given me strict orders that you will be our prisoner here. I went against his will bringing you up here. I am afraid, Albert, that he was prepared to watch you be torn apart by Anvil's men."

"And why not you?" I asked.

"Is it not obvious?" the large monkey asked bashfully. "I am in thrall to you."

I pulled him to my face—as much as I was appalled by him, I knew that to save my planet, I, myself, would have to make great sacrifices. "Then you will help me?"

"If I do, then Woosh would just as soon kill me, too. He is furious with you. He feels that you have rejected both of us."

"I do not!" Woosh said, suddenly coming into hearing range. "Let me give you something to eat, my beloved son Albert, for I feel that you are as much my son now as Nafshee, and certainly much more attractive to the eye." He gave a wink to both of us, which only made Nafshee shake and turn his gaze away. He pulled out some strange bread from the pocket of his blue robe and broke it into pieces and handed a small portion to me. I hesitated to eat it, though frankly I was starving. "Watch," the old man said. He began to eat some of it himself. I nodded my head and then pounced on my portion and ate the whole thing. "See, it did not kill you! You know, if you trust us, you will survive; and if you do not, then it all will be over with for everyone."

"I must go today to the Temple, for the funeral of my father."

"Sure," the old man said with a smile on his face that was at once both benevolent and chilling: a smile so positive of its own power. "So go! And old Hortha will crown you king; then you can pretend that you do not know the old Monkey Man and his son."

"I would not do that: you know that we Same-Sexers cannot lie."

"A lie in itself, my son."

"If I do not go to the Temple," I countered, "then I am sure Anvil's forces will choose another leader, one just as bloodthirsty as Anvil himself, and we will have the same results."

"Yes," the old man said, smiling that foul smile again. He looked directly at me, then his mouth opened and the smile dropped. The strange blue light that usually surrounded him like a vile mist turned ice cold. Thick animal hairs started to grow from his face.

31

"No!" Nafshee screamed, "Not that!" I stood transfixed as Woosh's face distorted itself, becoming monstrously baboonish: red-and-dung colored, all razor teeth, jutting jaw and flattened snout. Large, pointed hairy ears extended from the sides of his head. He threw off his blue robe, then fell naked onto his haunches and grabbed me. "Now!" he snarled. His thin, apish penis stood erect in front of him. He kicked at my groin, trying to part my legs, then thrust his long fingers into my face, blinding me once more. "Remember," he threatened. "My son has your seed. He now controls you."

"No," Nafshee warned, trying to pull Woosh off me. "I will not let you do this!" The two of them fought hard, biting and tearing at each other as I had never seen a father and son do. I was sure that Nafshee would lose, that this monster would overcome him. Then, almost vanquished, Nafshee reached for the old baboon's leathery scrotum and squeezed it until Woosh screamed, literally turning blue again: I watched as Woosh was retransformed into the Blue Monkey I had first seen in my chamber, reanimated with his sickening blue light. In this transformation I saw how Woosh did resemble his son, although Nafshee, at one point, did seem actually more *human* than Woosh.

"I must thank you," Woosh said to him, kissing Nafshee. "See, Albert, what could be in store for you in the future."

"You mean that little performance was for my sake?"

"No," Nafshee said bashfully. "But my father's rage is uncontrollable: for the most part, it terrifies me." He paused for a moment, and then knelt again at my feet. I watched Woosh's anger again reach the boiling point. "It is not true, Albert, that *I* have you under my control. But I must warn you that I have my father's anger—as well as his semen—inside of me. So do not toy with us, for to ignore me, my love, is as dangerous as it is to thwart him."

"Well said!" Woosh chuckled. "Unfortunately my Nafshee is not exactly a chip off the old block. But he has still got a *few* chips of mine in him!"

I realized all of this had been merely a warning, as I heard more voices come up into the branches from the ground far below.

"The word has come about that Albert has murdered Anvil," a deep, young voice said as more men wound their way through the forest paths.

"Who in the name of the Goddess is that?" another young voice asked.

"A renegade—cousin of the old Ertan!" an older man answered. I leaned over the branches trying to look, but all I could see was haze; a fine milky haze floated in swirling layers between me and these men.

"Ertan, that monster—we were so happy when Greeland's men killed him!" a new voice chimed in.

"The war was terrible," the first old man said. "Those of us who remember know how bad it was. You are too young, Tangoo and Britchart, to know about it."

"I only know," the one called Tangoo said, "that if Albert is not at the Temple, then we may have *another* war."

"Hush," the old man replied. "Rumors can kill as quickly as knives here!"

Woosh looked at me and smiled. "I will never let you go," he whispered, convincing me that now I was strictly in his power.

Suddenly I felt tired. Nafshee looked at me and smiled. "You must rest," he said. The platform where we were standing, which had low, wattled walls around it, also contained a quaint bed. Nafshee took me by the hand, and walked me over to it.

"I will leave you two boys to your pleasures," Woosh grinned. "There is great business I must do among the Blue Monkeys, before we have you two installed as twin rulers of Ki."

I looked up and could only wearily smile at Woosh's arrogance. A moment later, he disappeared, flapping in his blue robes from tree to tree. I could see him chatting to other Blue Monkeys on the upper branches. Although he was much bigger than they were, they accepted him and they chattered in the screeching Blue Monkey dialect that was foreign even to Same-Sexers. I was still naked and lay down on the bed. It was made soft with grasses and crudely covered but not uncomfortable pillows filled with small bird feathers.

"May I lie with you, Lord Albert?" Nafshee asked.

"No."

"Please?" he pleaded.

"Alright."

He lay down with me and soon had his hairy arm across my chest. He began to play with my penis and quickly found the third testicle. "I want more from this," he said. "You are as sweet as the syrup of blackberries."

"I will not give it freely unless you give me something."

He began licking the head of my male-pipe and I knew at that moment that he was in my power.

I was still almost naked, but at least I was now inside the walls of the Temple. The only thing I wore was a band of broad leaves around my waist, held there by a length of twine cast aside in the forest by Same-Sexers on their way to the funeral, that I had managed to find with Nafshee's help. Thank the Goddess for propitious littering! To be totally naked on such a state occasion was not something in which I wanted to indulge. As you can imagine, I did allow, willingly, Nafshee to have my seed. Some people would consider this a grave mistake. It was one thing to have my seed forced

33

from me, and certainly another to give it to this repulsive creature. But I did and as soon as I did, I knew he would give me anything: the look on his face told me this as soon as he tasted the sweet slickness of my semen. He brought me on his back to the forest floor and then easily transported me to the Temple grounds, which was at least half a day's journey on foot. We did this in a few moments. "Now you must leave," I said. I would not have him at my father's funeral—it was the bargain that we had made. But I told him to return for me the next day. He gave me one more look, like a whipped dog, and then disappeared.

Among the crowds in the Temple grounds, many recognized me and gasped. Two of Hortha's Sisters pushed their way towards me. One I recognized. She was a stout sturdy lady of a certain age, at least as old as Hortha who must have been around when Ki and her brother Kiwa first divided the planet. The god Kiwa, fathered by a huge tree, was the father of all Same-Sexers, who are descended directly from his twin sons, Sin, a fixed moon, and Ursha, a divine swimmer in the cosmos. "Thank Laura you are here!" Nohnie cried, rushing up to me. "Rumors have been dropping all day!"

"It is good to see you, too, Nohnie," I told her. "And who is your friend?" I turned to her companion, a striking, boyish young woman with closely cropped blond hair and a shyness I could detect instantly.

"This is Dyla, she is a novice Sister."

"How do you like it here?" I asked. Enkidu had told me that the way to make people feel at home is first to ask questions about them.

Dyla's soft sea-blue eyes glanced at the meticulously clean paving stones under our feet, then she said: "Better than being back home, sir."

"She is still used to deferring to men," Nohnie said. "She will not look you in the face!"

"I am not that bad," the young woman protested. She looked directly at me and smiled. "If you are at all adventurous or . . . interesting, well, you know how the Off-Sexers are: Marriage! Children! A boss for a husband! That is all."

"Then you have chosen your path wisely," I said.

"It was chosen for her!" the old priestess said to me. "Look at her! Have you ever seen a more convincing Sister of Ki?"

I told her no. "Now," Nohnie said. "We must get you cleaned up." I was to be presented to Hortha, who had been waiting for me.

I was led to a bathing chamber, where a beautiful bath was readied for me. The elder Sister and Dyla left me in privacy, and I quickly bathed myself and got all of the twigs and bird goo out of my hair that had settled in it from my time on Anvil's plains and up in the trees of the Blue Monkeys. After drying myself, I found a spotless white robe and put it on. A moment later, I was in front of Hortha in her spacious private chambers. She embraced me .

"Albert, dear, how lovely to see you. We had heard this awful story that you had been kidnapped and held by one of Ertan's old outlaw cousins, Anvil. Even *worse*, that you had been murdered by him."

"No, I was rescued," I told her. "And the truth is, I have killed him."

She looked at me seriously with her old, wrinkled eyes. "Is that really the truth?"

I bowed my head. "No. The truth is . . . Woosh did it."

"Woosh! I knew he *would* have to be at the bottom of this! But I am glad you did not murder anyone. To have Anvil's blood on your hands on the day that you are to be declared ruler of Ki is an awful thing: how can we hope for peace on Ki if you have already killed someone?"

"It seems we can hope for little peace," I said sadly.

"That is why you must take a mate, Albert. The time for this hesitation in choosing a promised friend is over. The only way for you to insure the security of the planet is to have a mate—and this time one from your own people! If you do that, I will be able to die in peace."

I took her thin, pale hands in mine. "Speak not of your dying. My father would never wish such a thing; you were a great support to him."

"I had to be. Look who his mate was—someone totally outside of his clan, an Off-Sexer. He might as well have married a monkey!"

I winced when she said this, and then followed her through crowds of solemn mourners, who parted as we approached. It seemed that most of the planet was now inside the Temple grounds as evening approached and the Moons of Ki came out like pearls to smile faintly in our sky. There were nine of them, a number sacred to the Same-Sexers: their appearance was totally out of sequence with the year. How this happened I had no idea, but somehow the heavens themselves were giving tribute to Enkidu.

We walked into the huge Temple, dominated at its end by the large golden statue of Laura, my father's own Goddess, who had taken over the position that the faceless statue of Ki had once held, although the Temple would always be known as the Temple of Ki and its vestals would always be known as Her Sisters. The huge gates of the Temple were closed with a great clang and I felt now the awesome power of the Temple that held our small, violent planet in its hands. I looked once more at the face on the statue of Laura, the face that my father said he had once seen in a dream. Laura, *our* Goddess, young and beautiful and sweet. I bowed before Her and then looked directly into my father's dead, painted face as he lay on a bier under Laura's statue.

Hortha then began the service with a short eulogy and told the story about   35 how she had first come to know Enkidu, after his promised friend, the impulsive hunter Greeland (a sad gasp came over the older Same-Sex men; the Off-Sexers, both men and women, uneasily cleared their throats), had mistakenly killed the son of Ertan and Candra, a son who in fact had been Enkidu's half brother. Then she skipped over ages of history, including my birth, until she came to Enkidu's crowning and his taking of Greedu as his consort. "We will have a moment of silence for the soul of Enkidu," Hortha said. "That he may be embraced by both Ki and Her daughter Laura, and that he will join the entire nature of Ki, the planet he loved so much, in his preparation for another Life."

We all bowed our heads in silence and as so often happens when a large number of people are quiet, you could hear every breath coming from the crowd, until the silence itself seemed to take on a sound: the murmuring, breathing sounds of Ki, its muddy rivers and wet forests, its haze-ringed mountains and caves, and its dry, dusty plains. I was sure that somehow my father's soul was over all of us, drifting and watching; I hoped that he would give me the blessings of his wisdom and endurance.

"Now," Hortha said loudly, "before we take Enkidu's body out to the Cave of Mysteries where his promised friend Greeland and his consort Greedu lie, we will ask his son, the next ruler of Ki, Albert, to speak."

As Hortha said those words "the next ruler of Ki," noise resumed. It was abrasive and hostile: I could tell that these people were no longer with me. Perhaps my Same-Sex brothers were, but the glue that had held Ki together, that had come from Enkidu and Greeland and even from Greedu, was wearing thin. I knew that this moment had to come, but I was trembling under my white robes. I knelt besides Enkidu's bier briefly and thought this was the most awful moment of my life. How was I ever to going to speak?

"Dear friends, on this sad occasion," I began—suddenly the noise died down, and I thought . . . perhaps this may not be so bad—"I promise you that like my father I will give this planet all of my heart and soul and—"

"YOUR HEAD!" A deep voice thundered from the gates as they were rammed open. An army of Off-Sex men, their weapons drawn, surged in. They were led by, of all people, the monster I had thought dead: Anvil.

"Take him into my custody," Anvil directed. "Murderer! First he tried to kill me, then he slaughtered six of my men in his escape from this deed."

I thought my eyes would fall out of my head, as well as Hortha's. "You are not dead?" I muttered.

"No," Anvil said. "Through the sweet care of our dear friend Woosh, I have been brought back to life."

Woosh now appeared through the iron gates of the Temple. "Yes," he said, slowly carrying his blue presence up the aisle, before the unbelieving silent crowd. "I was able to bring Anvil back to life, using the same power by which I was able to give life to my own dear son here, Nafshee." He extended his hand and suddenly, out of pure air, Nafshee appeared. Nafshee cringed when he saw me as if he were there against his will. Even I felt sorry for him. "So!" Woosh said, spitting the word into my face as he approached me. "It is *again* up to *you*. The choice is yours: either take my son to be your promised friend, or face death at the hands of Anvil!"

"Unbelievable!" Hortha said. "I do not believe a word of these lies, either yours or Anvil's. That you should come barging into the Temple, on the saddest day of our lives, at the funeral of Enkidu, is a sacrilege that both of you will pay for: let me assure you."

"We are not afraid of you, old woman," Anvil hissed.

"Quiet!" Woosh demanded of his friend. His old face changed as Hortha's piercing gaze looked daggers into him. Somehow, back in the primordial history of Ki, Woosh—and the Blue Monkeys themselves—knew that their destiny was linked to the Temple. I could see that Woosh was close to playing his final card. "We meant no disrespect or sacrilege, Lady Hortha, but meant only—" he bowed his head—"to bring the light of Truth into this gathering."

"Despite your blueness, you are Darkness itself," Hortha said in disgust. "And you prove something that I have always known: that by your very lies and tricks, Woosh, you and your kin are not descended from the god Kiwa. Never will your son be joined to Albert, as long as he and I are alive."

"Then I am prepared for your deaths, as well as my own," the old Monkey Man confessed. "Take the body back to our camp," he ordered Anvil. Anvil's men stormed up the aisle and grabbed the bier holding Enkidu's painted corpse. In a single breath they ran off with it, as silence in turn grabbed the whole Temple, including the assembled priestesses who were rarely at a loss for words. Anvil, Nafshee, and Woosh remained. "We will circle the Temple," Woosh announced. "Until you give us Albert."

Hortha bowed her head. "Do you know what that means?"

"Yes," Woosh answered. "As I said, I am prepared for my own death."

With those words, both Woosh and his son disappeared into the air around them. Then Anvil casually shrugged his shoulders at us, and walked out the huge door.

CHAPTER 3

The crowd had left and all the Temple lights were doused. In the darkness, Hortha, five of the elder Sisters of Ki, and I watched Anvil's armies watch us. We were up in the pinnacle watchtower of the Temple, over the tallest trees and at the height of the distant mountains that guarded a horizon as far as we could see. From the open parapets of the turret, we could watch their torches and bonfires spitting red and gold into the night. We could also hear their blood-lusting chants and the groans of captive dying men. Hortha went to the wall and looped her thumbs and forefingers into a eyepiece. I saw her squinting into the distance.

"What do you see, Lady Hortha?" said old Nohnie. "Your eyes are still the best of all for close seeing."

"They are bringing in captives. Same-Sex brothers from the enclaves. They are placing their heads on pikes. Some bodies are hanging, upside down, like so many slaughtered sheep."

I bent my head in shame. "This is horrible!" I cried. "It is better that I give myself up. The Same-Sexers are not ready for another war against the chieftains like my father Greeland fought."

"You cannot give yourself up," Hortha said sharply. "To do so would mean to give the entire planet up: that monster Anvil is aligned with Woosh. Woosh will geld you like a pig and everything your father fought for will be over: the women of Ki will once more be the hostages of their Off-Sex lords and the Same-Sex enclaves will live in constant fear and be treated as slaves. And this time, the entire balance of Ki will be destroyed. And"—she halted for a moment, and then resumed looking through her fingers. I asked her what was she seeing. "I can hear it as well, Sira-Albert."

"What?"

"Put your ear to my fingers."

I did this and could hear Woosh speaking privately to Nafshee, as if they were in the same room with us. "When you are joined to that fool Albert," Woosh said, grinning, "I will see to it that the two of you produce a son without a woman involved. Your son will be the Blue Monkey heir; then we will get rid of that fool. He is a child: he was spoiled by his silly father, Enkidu.

We do not need a child ruling Ki."

"Would you do that to him?" Nafshee asked.

"Yes, then *you* will be ruler, and your son, one of our kind, will follow you."

I looked through Hortha's fingers. Nafshee looked pained; hurt. But Woosh could read his own son's thoughts; he slapped him soundly. "I shall kill you!" Woosh screamed. "Nafshee, you will die if you balk at my words!" Anvil looked on, and then he and Woosh proceeded to direct the destruction around them.

Hortha closed her fingers. "That is enough for now," she said, and then clasped her fingers together in thought. "Ladies," she announced. "Allow me to have a moment alone with Albert."

Nohnie bowed her head, and then led the other Sisters out of the turret. When we were alone, with only a light wind whipping around us, Hortha spoke frankly to me, without sparing any of my feelings. "I am afraid, Albert, the old monkey is right: you have been a child. Your not taking a mate has left Ki in jeopardy. Even Enkidu, who spoiled you terribly, knew this."

"It was not my father's fault," I said. "He knew how difficult it was for me to forgive him for killing Greeland."

"Greeland was poisoning the planet."

"He was still my other father."

"And for this you did not take a mate?"

"How could I trust one of our own men when my father Enkidu had done that to his mate, Greeland?"

Suddenly Hortha kissed me on the cheek, embracing me. "I can see you are like dear Enkidu, you take the laws of our planet very seriously; much more so, my son, than Greeland did. But we are now in a quandary. It is too late for you to take a mate from here: if you do, then Woosh and Nafshee will destroy whomever you choose."

Noises bent my ears. I did not need Hortha's magical seeing and hearing fingers; the screams of victims were resounding from the distance of Anvil's camp. Shortly after, the Sisters, too, became alarmed, and we heard their feet hurrying up the stairs and then heard Nohnie's voice from outside the turret's door. "Lady Hortha! A delegation of men are banging on the gates! They say that if we give them Albert, our lives will be spared. What should we do, Lady Hortha? They shout for Albert!"

"One more moment," Hortha answered firmly. "Give us but one more moment."

My heart was banging louder than the disturbance at the gates. But I could see a plan being formed on Hortha's wrinkled face.

"You," she said softly, "will have to die."

My hear sank. "*Die?*"

"Yes," she whispered. "It will only take a moment. Painless."

"I will not die." I said. "I will fight until my breath is gone. Neither Enkidu nor Greeland whose seeds run through my blood would allow me to die up here. What are you saying, old lady?"

"We must have your mother; it is the only way to do these things."

I shook my head in disbelief. I would not let her send me over to Anvil's men, either to have them murder me or trade me over to Woosh and Nafshee: both outcomes appeared certain. Hortha opened the door, and quickly whispered something to Nohnie. Nohnie's face looked stricken with disbelief, but she bowed and then chased down the stairs again. I asked the old lady to explain what was going to happen, and she did. "I told them to go tell the men downstairs that when the light from the White Star first brightens our way, you will be given to them. I am afraid, my beloved Albert, that is your future. It is a steep price and you will pay it for playing 'hard-to-get' for so long; for being your father's spoilt favorite and taking no mate on Ki."

I began to weep, unashamedly. "I thought you loved me?"

"Yes, I do. That is why we are going to bring your mother, whom you have never met. You were conceived before Enkidu declared a change in the Agreement, when Same-Sexers still had their sons by unknown Off-Sex women. You never met your mother, but she will witness your . . . 'death.'"

"Why do you say 'death' that way?"

Hortha smiled. "That will be our secret. I cannot tell you any more. Perhaps you would like to get some rest."

I told her that would be impossible. There was no way I could let my body rest. I was too anxious, both for my own future and that of Ki. She grinned and I looked into her ancient eyes. They were gray, ringed with gold: they reminded me of an eclipse of the White Star. "You do not know the power of us Sisters," she said. "A power that even Woosh himself fears."

With those words, again she placed her thumbs and forefingers in a ring, and bade me to bow my head. I did so, and she placed her fingers on my forehead. I immediately felt all resistance in my body and mind disappear. My body softly slumped to the stone floor and my mind resigned itself to the most merciful sleep.

CHAPTER 4

I am not sure how long this sleeping trance lasted. But I soon became aware that I was not alone in it. Enkidu, covered in the paint of death, spoke to me.

"You will go on a long journey, my son. It has been arranged. Only in another place will you find the mate that you need."

"Somewhere else on Ki?"

"No. Beyond our planet Ki."

"I am afraid," I sobbed. Enkidu approached me and his pale hands gently brushed the tears from my eyes. He put his lips to mine. "I was afraid myself when I began that journey. But I will always be there with you, Albert. And I will show you the Tree."

"What *tree*?"

"The Tree on which blooms the answer to all of our questions. It is everlasting. Only across the River of Death—a river deeper and darker than our Tanna—will you find it. But I shall show it to you."

I smiled. "Then I should not be afraid of this death?"

"No. For I shall always be with you."

At that, I felt comforted, even in the sleep in which Hortha had placed me. And I realized that the Sisters were now stripping me of the robe I had worn at Enkidu's funeral. I was naked, with the huge dark sky of Ki over me, but still I felt a strange warmth and I knew it was because Enkidu's hands were still on my body. He was holding the Egg, as it pulsed in his fingers. I was smiling, but no other part of me was able to move: I became vaguely conscious; faces and distant voices emerged to me.

"We must paint him white, like Enkidu," Hortha commanded. "Prepare him for burial."

The Sisters began; cold whitewash was carefully brushed all over me. On my legs, arms, chest, and face. Then, white as a corpse, but my body feeling weightless, I was lifted down flights of stairs until I opened my eyes in another room, one in which I had never been before. I was laid out on a table, surrounded by beakers, jars and instruments. I was alone, save for Hortha. Light trapped in crystal flooded over me. A strange, nervous woman, as shy

43

as most of the Off-Sex women of Ki, approached, led by Nohnie. She was slightly above average in height, but thin, tired, and frightened looking. Her hair was piled up stylishly in the Off-Sex way, but she wore the ragged dress of a husbandless woman.

"This is M'raetha," Hortha announced, as my gaze went to the taller woman. "She has been waiting for this for a long time. She lives not far, alone, in a small house. Her husband was slaughtered in Greeland's war, leaving her by herself, without the strong arms of a man. But she bears no ill feelings towards you. She is your mother, Albert, who loved you until you were taken from her."

Tears rushed from my eyes. I knew I could speak; I was sure I would be allowed to; but nothing emerged from my mouth as much as I tried to form words. It was as if I had already passed through death, and was only waiting in one of its outer chambers. So I could merely look up at her, and recognized so much of my own face in hers. Her mouth formed a beautiful smile.

"I have thought about you often, Albert," M'raetha said and placed her hands on my shoulders. "You are as beautiful as I imagined you would be. When two of the Sisters came to our door to take you away, I cried, it seemed, forever. It was an awful pain: like death. But I had no idea that you would be so important: the son of Enkidu, the man who saved Ki. I know I am but a simple woman. My husband, Koodah, whom I truly loved, was chosen to die in that awful war. It was something that life ordered for him. When you are a man you have to do that. . . ."

I looked over at Hortha. I could see her eyes rolling away. "M'raetha, dear," she interrupted. "I am afraid this is no time for speeches."

"But it was Koodah's duty to die!"

"Yes, dear," Hortha said.

"Now that I know him, how can I harm Albert anymore?" The lady burst into tears. She hid her face in her hands, and her piled hair started to fall. Hortha whispered something to Nohnie, and Nohnie left. A moment later she returned, with Dyla.

"You will have to help the Lady M'raetha with this," Hortha informed the girl. "I am old, my hands tremble. Actually, I think it will be best, Dyla, for you to do this yourself. I want to tell you a secret—you have become my favorite novice, and one day when I die—"

"No!" Nohnie cried. "You will *never* die, dear Hortha."

"Nonsense, of course I will! I will and you will, just like everybody else will. And when that happens, Dyla will be there, as next in the line of succession."

44   "But I am so new to this!" the novice protested.

"Yes," the old Sister agreed, "but I can see in your face the talents you have. Here is the knife." Hortha picked up a thin, razor-sharp blade from a table. "It is obvious that M'raetha will not be able to do this, but I shall tell you what has to be done."

Hortha whispered into Dyla's ear, and the novice, after a nervous moment, agreed. Hortha once more placed her fingers on my forehead; again, the trance, but this time one in which I could see, but be without pain. Then Dyla took the knife and pointed it carefully at my scrotum. My mother watched, trembling and sobbing as the novice, with amazing, steady hands, slowly inserted the blade. She made a small, almost bloodless opening while Hortha watched her. I am not sure what else was being done "down there" to me, but I was aware that something had been tied off. Then Dyla executed a few more strokes with the blade, and—at that very moment—I knew that my life was in her young fingers.

Carefully, she extracted my third Egg. I could not resist: my body felt drugged; my mind blank and painless: all of this was done through Hortha's exceptional powers. But also adding to the calm—a ghostly calm that seemed to hover over the violence being done to me—was my dead father Enkidu whom I could feel, as with one spectral, powerful hand he restrained my chest, while with the other he cupped my scrotum, literally guiding the girl's knife as it cut into me, as if into the paper-thin cheek of a ripened plum.

The glowing third Egg rolled into Dyla's palm. I saw it: moist, pearly, perfect. Slightly elongated, it was a small, spherical thing glowing with the deep shimmering pink of the last setting rays of the White Star. Hortha placed the circle of her fingers on my forehead again: my eyes closed. She kissed me and I could feel for a moment her lips parting, as if she were saying a charm that I would never hear. Then I became aware of her old hand opening my mouth. "You must do this, M'raetha," she whispered. "You must. . . ."

"I cannot; I will faint!"

"For once," Hortha ordered M'raetha, "take courage into your own hand—take your son's Egg." The novice handed it to M'raetha. My mother, after hesitating for a second, pushed the Egg down my throat.

"You have given him life," Hortha said. "Now see him slide into death."

M'raetha closed her eyes. "The death of which you spoke?"

"Yes, dear Lady," Hortha answered calmly. "Not the death of your husband Koodah, but another one. Remember, for a short time, he will hear every word, but only as sounds: they have no meaning for him. He is going on a journey to another world. There, I believe, he will find the mate of his life."

I could feel the Egg sliding down my throat into my chest cavity. There it warmed my cold body, a body that had become merely a shell of myself. As this happened, the other Sisters redressed me in the finest robes of state, the robes my father Enkidu wore on the grandest occasions. And they brought me, once dressed, into the vast Temple of Ki, under the statue of Laura, where my father had lain a day earlier. As light from the White Star banded our horizon, the outer gates of the Temple compound were swung open. There Woosh, Nafshee, Anvil, and his armed men awaited. The Sisters showed them into the Temple, where Hortha, her eyes narrowed and grim, presented my body.

"Woosh, I hope you are satisfied," she said with a sneer. "Here is the promised mate you wanted for your son! Albert has killed himself rather than submit to you."

"It is a trick," Woosh spat. "A rotten trick! You killed him yourself, Hortha."

Hortha smiled. "His own mother was there." She brought M'raetha out from the shadows of Laura's statue. "She watched it. She would never lie."

M'raetha held her face in her hands and sobbed. "What the Elder Priestess said is true! I who gave him life watched him die by his own will!"

Nafshee crumpled to the floor, sobbing and crying, while Woosh only kicked his son brutally, heaping curses and scorn on him. Then Woosh announced: "It is only fitting that we bury both in the Cave of Mysteries, where Greeland and Greedu lie." He turned to Anvil's men and told them to seize me.

Anvil nodded to his men and motioned for them to approach the body. "Now," Anvil announced to the Sisters, "I presume *I* am ruler of Ki." His men picked up what they believed was my dead-white corpse. With a quick heave, they began quickly to trot out with me.

Hortha smiled. "Not so fast, my Lord!" The men suddenly froze, stopped in terror by her words.

Anvil reached to take his long war knife out of its scabbard; he was shaking with anger, but Woosh stayed his hand from any violence. He whispered something to the redheaded warrior, then both of them waited for Hortha again to speak.

"Albert will remain here. Tell your men *both* bodies will lie under the statue of the Goddess Laura in our Temple. And I, *Hortha*, will rule our planet, until the *next* child is born on Ki."

"WHAT?" Anvil shouted. "You old sow! I should cut off your head right now—and slurp moonberry wine from it!"

"Quiet!" Woosh commanded and then ordered the men to put the bier back—exactly where they had found it. This they did quickly, before the astonished eyes of all, including Anvil's, who in his arrogance had forgotten the power of the Temple and its effect on every inhabitant of Ki.

"What are you talking about?" Anvil whispered to the old monkey. "Why are you letting her push us around?"

Woosh ignored him. "Lady Hortha," he said humbly. "We bow to your *request* that you will be ruler of Ki until the next child is born of this planet."

Hortha nodded and thanked Woosh.

Woosh arose from his bow, then spoke loudly to Anvil: "And then when this child is born, you, Anvil, will be his regent, and rule in his stead until *he* takes a promised mate."

"AGREED!" Anvil bellowed, smiling. "Woosh, to this we agree!"

Woosh and Anvil smiled at each other and embraced, then watched as Anvil's men brought back the jeweled litter of the dead lord, Enkidu. Enkidu was placed next to me, while the Sisters of Ki watched in silence. Finally Hortha had the last word with the men. "We agree to your *request*, Lord Anvil, that you will be regent to this child. Now go in peace, and may peace reign this evening on our beloved Ki."

Woosh clasped Anvil's hand and then tried to drag Nafshee away from Albert's chalked white presence. "Allow me to stay a moment more with him, father," he beseeched Woosh.

Woosh spat at him and then walked out with Anvil. "He is stupid," Woosh cursed. "Ungrateful and a moron. I tried to lift him up from his monkey roots and what does he do?"

Anvil laughed. "Children! I am glad I have none. Screw them all!"

Hortha approached the homely Nafshee, who looked even more apelike and simple now, numbed and crumpled by his sorrow. "We will allow you a moment's solitude with the body of our poor, young dead lord. Then we must close the doors of the Temple."

All of the Sisters led by Hortha and Nohnie walked toward the Temple's huge, iron doors and waited as Nafshee knelt in front of Albert. He took Albert's cold hand in his and kissed it, getting white paint on his dark, leathery lips. "I will go, Albert, whereever you are to find you. If I have to go to the ends of Ki, to the ends of the Universe, to have you. Even Death will not allow you to escape my love."

But there was no reply to Nafshee's sorrow, or his promise. For Albert's Egg, which had been glowing inside the dark cavern of his chest and which had surrounded his heart with its unstoppable power, now slid further, through his stomach and down into his scrotum again, where it passed, invis-

47

ibly, through his penis, and then out into the vast, dark, vaulted chamber of the Temple of Ki itself. The Egg watched Nafshee trudge sorrowfully through the Temple doors as the Sisters closed them upon the bodies of Enkidu and Albert; then it began a journey darker and even more powerful than death.

Part Two

CHAPTER 5

"We must have a healing circle," insisted one of the sisters. "It is the only right thing to do, don't you think?"

The other women smiled and said words like "Absolutely! Cool! You got it!" What a beautiful afternoon it was, radiant and glowing, after so much darkness had come into their world: a world that seemed wracked now with constant turbulence . . . even war. It was a *war*, although no one had declared it, and as usual, these women who had tried so hard to make a world of their own felt especially tormented by it. Ten of them formed a circle in the sand, and the eldest of them announced, "Get *her* in the middle. Come on!"

She felt reticent, being a novice still to all of this. She shook her soft, blond hair and for a moment nervously ran her fingers through it. They were right: she had been present at a death and now it was important for her to be healed. But did she really want to be in the middle of the circle, to have all of her sisters praying and chanting over her?

The answer, she knew, was no; but they would have it no other way.

They took her soft hands gently and guided her. For a moment she closed her eyes, while the eldest began a prayer. "Oh, Goddess, allow our newest, dearest sister to heal. Take away her nightmares of death; bring her *new* Life. Bring it to *us* and to her. And we ask this in the name of you, Great Goddess, Healing Mother, who kindled Life in her—who took her away from her own family and gave her to us. Who will make her whole again—"

"No!" Sandy Feltner screamed. "I can't do this! Please stop talking about it!" She tore away from the circle and started dashing away from the women, running past Carol Parker, her partner, who tried to chase after her. "I have to be alone, don't you see—this only makes me feel worse!"

The water . . . Sandy needed to jump into the water. She was convinced of it. It sounded silly, really; too dramatic, in fact. But she knew this: only the water would make her feel clean and whole again.

It was a perfect afternoon in late September, at the end of the summer season in the year 2025. Most of the affluent summer boys had left

Provincetown. The locals could now enjoy it. The lesbian section of Herring Cove Beach sparkled, and the water seemed even warmer than it had been two long months ago, when on one of the worst "dog-day" nights of summer (a night thick with electricity, with a distant storm somewhere over Nantucket, that never quite broke, breathing down on them), an unendurable, breathless night that made the jolt of waking worse than any nightmare, Sandy had awakened.

Her head was burning up; she was bleeding. By the end of that night, she had (the only word her sisters heard) *miscarried*. That was what they told her when she woke up in a white room over Orleans Hospital's terrifying Emergency Room. The word got back to her sisters before she did: "Sandy had *miscarried*." MISCARRIED.

But nothing in the word *miscarried* contained the poison, the shame, the grief . . . of losing her son.

Carol watched Sandy bolt into the cold water, fully clothed in the gauzy pale cottons she wore so beautifully over her trim, tanned body. Sandy with her blond curly hair and delft blue eyes that always seemed to be smiling; asking silly questions. The only part of her that seemed Jewish was her nose, which had a small, delightful curve to it, which matched perfectly her cheek-bones. Carol watched Sandy's hair get wet. The curls floated lusciously for a moment: she looked like an angel . . . like a Botticelli Venus. (Well, actually, she looked like a wet cocker spaniel!) Carol could not hold back laughing. (Maybe it was just tension.) A big belly laugh came right out of her. Carol was tall and leggy. She had shoulders "like a man," her father had always said. Shoulders that liked to hold Sandy and nestle her beautiful face in them.

The strangeness of the scene did tickle her: there was Sandy, dashing out from her sisters into the water. Sandy, never quite catchable—there was never a question of holding her back. She always knew what she wanted. It was only a matter of getting it ready for her. Even the baby—longed for; waited for—*she* went after it. They'd only been together for a year, and Sandy had only been out for two, when one evening after Carol got back from her maintenance job at a local gay hotel, Sandy announced that she wanted to get pregnant. "I *need* it," she said. She had been married to Jeff for a longer time—and now she was living with Carol—but Sandy had decided that she *needed* it. *Now*. There was no question about Sandy's directness, her confidence, or her sureness which hid, though never really well, those long strings of fears tied tightly to her past. "How?" Carol asked. "I mean, with whom? You have somebody checked out, honey? Or do we just want to make it 'pot luck' at one of the in vitro centers?"

52

"Pot luck? No, I want it natural. With a *real* daddy. And I want him to be around—just not *too* much around. Is that alright?" She kissed Carol on her cheeks and then on her mouth. Then Sandy started to unbutton her blouse, slowly. She had beautiful small breasts and she loved the way Carol touched them; the way Carol licked her nipples, tasting the shy sweetness of them.

"Boy or girl?" Carol whispered, brushing Sandy's face with small, sweet, but intense kisses and softly filling her hands with Sandy's breasts.

"Whatever the Goddess wants."

"Even a boy?"

"Sure. You know I'm not a Dyke Sep type."

By now they were on the couch. Suddenly Carol came out of the erotic haze Sandy had invited her into. "He'll be the only male kid around."

"But not the only male," Sandy assured her, and she began kissing Carol again.

Sandy began at once, giving out new cards for herself with their home telecom number on them. On the back of each, discreetly, in longhand, she wrote, *Seeking donor. Want responsible co-parent relationship.* She thought about putting a notice on the P'town telecom board, but that was not necessary. Word got out very quickly around the men's and women's communities. For the last year or so men had just disappeared from her life; now she started to notice them again. She investigated healthy, attractive-looking guys at the supermarket, the beach, the library, the new bakery that produced wheat-free bagels and croissants every day, where the men sat over herbal teas and talked about politics; at the bookstore which sold up-to-date telecom sprints from other gay areas, print-ROMS, and even some old-fashioned books on paper; and at the mixed dances at the Provincetown Lesbi/Gay Community Government Center, which supposedly ran local things out on the tip of the Cape.

The dances were a holdover of what used to be called "p.c."; meaning, the women ran the show and the boys were nice to them. The guys who went to the dances were a different lot from many of the Provincetown queers: they were either in serious relationships, caught between serious relationships or looking for a serious one. Sandy took all this into account; she'd decided that she was not just going to stop some schmuck on the street because he had a fine pair of legs and could produce a great-looking kid.

The boys were crazy about the idea. Some had already heard about her. Some started to call her back and left their "resumes" with live pictures ("Sandy! Hi! This is *me*, see? I think I'm what you want—I mean, I'm an Aries, we love children, and I'm into nature walks and music, that kind of stuff. . . .") on Sandy and Carol's telecom machine. Some dropped over for a bit of Carol's own "herbal" tea spiked with flavored hashish extract, the beverage drug of choice in the 20s. The men were decent, polite, and cutely p.c. as mightly be expected of so many P'town guys. Even Carol started to shed some of her habitual suspicions about queer men. But none appealed to Sandy. There was something "ball-less" about them. When Carol smiled over the newest prospect, Sandy would say, "Carol, he's a wussy! Our kid is not going to be that way, no matter what gender *it* turns out to be, or even wants to be!"

Sandy was getting impatient. Months went by. Every time her fertile period came and the man needed to "ring her bell" did not show up, she felt desolate. No other woman in the dyke community had put the men through so much: Sandy was starting to get a rep; there were no more callbacks. Finally, Sandy narrowed it down to three guys. They were all involved in Provincetown Gay Government; they all had the necessary serious boyfriends and went to the dances; but they still left her feeling limp. Then she met Lee hanging outside the bakery café one night, smoking a joint of all things. They started talking to one another and although she did not smoke drugs there was something about him that in itself gave her a buzz. His voice was soft, yet had a convincing ring of its own to it, like he was looking for something real and would eventually find it. He was tall and darkly redheaded (not a washed-out, pale, freckly redhead; not just cute) with big expressive hands that had a work hardness to them and a face with beautiful lines in it. She told him directly what she was looking for. He smiled and wished her luck. "Well, good night," he said, smiling, as if he were ready to walk away—that was when she took out her pen and, without hesitation, asked for *his* com number to write on the back of one of her cards.

She called him the next day. She got him face-to-face on her telecom. She cleared her throat; for a moment her confidence evaporated. Then she said: "I think you're the winner."

Lee started laughing. "Who was in the running?" Sandy did not say a word. Suppose he refused her flat out? Then he smiled, bashfully; his voice softened. "Sandy. I'd love to do this—it's just," he hesitated, then admitted: "I'm not sure I can afford to raise a kid."

Sandy smiled. *The bell went off!* She told him money would be no problem. She and Carol would assume financial responsibility for the child; they wanted it that way. What Sandy wanted was someone who would put commitment into it; it couldn't just be an ego thing; a . . . p.c. thing. "I like your attitude," she said. "I feel you're sincere. That's what really counts." He came over that evening and they talked.

54   Thomas Lee Watson had lived in Provincetown for so long, "I feel like I

grew up here," he told her. He'd done odd jobs; had been a part of the community; had owned a small construction business that failed. Now he was doing freelance carpentry and driving a van for one of the guest houses. Sandy looked into his tanned face and smiled. Of all the men her parents would have liked to see her have a baby with . . . a carpenter? A van driver? Now it all seemed right; just perfect. Here was the kind of man her parents would never have dreamed about letting her marry, *impregnating* her—at least technologically.

The way he talked enchanted her. He seemed stable; even conservative; "old-fashioned" in the nicest way. But without a lot of left-over Twentieth Century garbage: the old self-hatred; the agony from the AIDS plague that so many men remembered. AIDS: they still talked about it. The viral serpent in the Garden of Eden, twisting queers into the most hideous shapes; inside and out. But Lee Watson seemed unaffected. He was cool, maybe even a bit too cool.

He was in his early thirties and single, which meant he did not have a lover to have conflicts with. It bothered Sandy that he had never been very good with his same-sex relationships, but he had women friends and she liked that. His body was in a nice, natural shape. He took good care of himself. Aside from blowing a joint every now and then, he was not into alcohol, meat, or some of the new techno drugs that you either shot up or used with a dermal patch. Sandy knew of men who had danced their brains out on them. But Lee was not one. She asked him about his health. "I've been checked out for everything, Sandy. I've had *it* done backwards, forwards, *and* in the middle!" He started laughing. She liked his sense of humor. He suddenly looked down, embarrassed. "I feel like a prize dog." She looked at him and smiled: he was.

Sandy had tried to get pregnant with Jeff for a long time, but there was something about his sperm that did not work with her "environment," as her Ob/Gyn, a woman who had taken care of her mother, had said. Finally Ruth Stein had sent them to a fertility expert who steered them to an in vitro center. But even then Sandy was adamant about "naturalness." She didn't want just anybody's "matter" inside of her. Many of the dykes in the cliques and collectives of lesbian Provincetown had resorted to the new recumbent sperm—you could literally assemble the Daddy contributions to your child, gene by gene. But Carol had said, "It's too *male* order even for me!" So Sandy really wanted the thing with Lee to work out; and she didn't want to go through a lot of tries doing it.

It was risky, this *thing* with a man: men being so unpredictable. But Sandy was determined to have a male friend for their child. "I want some-   55 body who'll pass on a guy's feelings," she told Carol. At first Carol argued. She had never been straight and did not believe that men had any feelings (or even ideas) that were different from women; at least not any worth saving. But eventually she began to believe it, too. Or believed it because she loved Sandy so much and knew how difficult she could be until she got her way.

Many of their friends were such separatists that they could not bear even to *bear* a male child, and if they did use natural sperm they did not want the donor hanging around later. But Sandy had actually come out fairly late—at twenty-eight—and she still harbored the idea that at some point kids needed a man in their lives. She had been married for five years to a Boston lawyer named Jeff Sumner, whom her parents had approved of; in fact, they had pushed her into the marriage. They were conservative, Jewish followers of Rich Quilter, the elderly Republican favorite son who had led his party's "Our Families First" crusade, gathering every "New Government/Old Values" (i.e. anti-gay, anti-feminist) element in America under one money-making tent. Although her parents had never been overt racists, they firmly believed that "illegitimacy" (a code word for the barely literate black, brown, and now, white, underclass) had destroyed America. Most of the time, as Sandy had looked out at the slums and crime-scarred streets of Boston, she could not argue with them.

Then, as in so many other coming out stories, something happened. A gnawing feeling began inside of her, began destroying her. It happened just as Jeff's career took off.

Sumner, who looked good in a sexless lawyer's suit, specialized in ultra-lucrative computer crimes. The stealing of "brain products": valuable concepts and "data-motions" that turned the wheels of the country's powerful infosystems. He defended clients who raked in millions and still had enough golden dollars left over to keep his firm very plush. They were a dual career couple. Sandy had her own public relations/marketing job; most of her clients were high profile, fast food accounts whose role in the food chain she'd never questioned, just as she had never questioned her parents, Sid and Lorna Feltner. From the outside her marriage had all the decorations of a good life. The Sumners lived in a sprawling condo close to the Charles River in a new, reclaimed neighborhood. Sandy dressed expensively. They ate out a lot. They belonged to a city club full of other corporate couples.

Then—it also seemed to happen as the problems with Jeff's sperm became known to her—she started having these strange feelings. Doors flew open that had once been locked, revealing that her marriage was a false front. It was like the windows of mall stores that only looked out on to other brick walls. She was unbearably lonely. At the city club she started to listen to what other couples were saying. The words started to come in distinctly: utterly clear. Everyone around her had only been going through the motions of life. And somehow—slowly—without even knowing it had been against her will, she had joined them.

Coldness crept in. She couldn't stand for Jeff to touch her. Every time he did, she felt that he was only rearranging her. As if she were a window mannequin he was only presenting to the world for his own ego: freshly fucked every day. Then he stopped: the coldness had become part of their marriage. At night he would click off his side of the telecom screen and fall asleep. She didn't care. He—his body—reminded her of just another telecom screen. Everything on the screen was pointless and flat. Especially the news, which she knew came canned, directly from offices exactly like her own. She started walking around Boston, aimlessly, sometimes doing it during the day for hours. She found excuses to get away from work. Nobody looked at her and she realized that like most women walking around by themselves, she had become good at making herself invisible. This made it easier for her to look at others.

She found herself looking at women.

At first she thought she was only wondering if any of them were going through what she was going through. The country (even the world) had settled into what the government intellectuals called the "New Conservatism." New Conservatism was not a party; it was more like a philosophical movement, as Existentialism had been during the old century. Basically it said that America's old, egalitarian secular democracy was a myth. America could (and would) feed on it publicly, the same way kids still pretended to believe in elves at Christmas; but it could not operate through it. The workings of the new technoculture were too complicated for the "common people," the grunt workers who still lived in the old shopping mall/tabloid culture. Only a small highly privileged class could manipulate and use technoculture. They would do this through the highest levels of literacy and information access, to which the grunts had no approach at all.

But the New Conservatives, in reality, were only the more educated upscale wing of the WCP, the often ridiculous White Christian Party, whose philosophy (in a nutshell: *the Peoples's Will is Christ's Will*) was now running the country. Most Eastern establishment types, like Sandy's comfortable parents, the Feltners, tried to joke off the WCP. "White-trash types with Amex cards," Lorna said scornfully; Sid dismissed them as "technopuppets," since they were the lower caste whose jobs were mostly to feed data into the info processing points, exactly as they dished out mass food at the chain slopperias that served them. ("No difference between their heads and their stomachs," Sid said. "They both process the same *dreck*.")

But the Feltners, like most establishment people, were also very scared of the WCP. There was something about its smiling, honey-sweet stupidity that belied the not-too-innocent movements of its power underneath. The WCP was a gorgon that only appeared to have a Santa Claus face. Its face was that of Brother Bob Dobson, the WCP's leader. Brother Bob was a telecom personality who brought in billions, mostly through the orchestrations of popular fears: crime; delinquency; the stigma-laden condition of illegitimacy; abortion; and the "tragedy of sexual deviancy," which never ran out of gas as a *family issue* and dollar-grabber. At the turn of the century, Brother Bob had tried to run for President, waging a grassroots, "Christian lifestyle" campaign. But after getting the pants beat off him, he learned that he could have more influence behind the scenes—preaching and "instructing"—than getting involved with the daily knee-to-the groin activities of professional politicians, which Dobson had found sickening. There was still a remnant then of an influential liberal press, which meant that Dobson had to shake hands with Jews, a few open gays, and members of the media who wrote distorted things about the Christian Right. For example, that it was attempting to take over the country and subvert the separation of Church and State.

This was exactly what Brother Bob wanted to do, and did do—all without ever running again for anything. Through constant "instruction," Dobson was able to turn his empire of White Christian schools, youth groups, universities, charities, and museums of "decent religious art" into the official public culture of America, replacing the old one that was based on a volatile mixture of sex and "anything-goes" commercialism. He appeared, in person and on the telecom, to be a plump, genial, smiling man of absolutely unlimited sincerity. His personality seemed totally transparent, as if all you saw of him on the telecom screen was what there was. It was a stupefying trick. Hardened media pros stood in awe of him. He was a perfect exponent of the art form of public "personhood" as it had been advanced by the more successful politico/cultural/"celeb" talking heads of the late Twentieth Century. In a world in which knowing anyone had become a dangerous, illusive activity, Brother Bob made you feel that knowing him was always safe. In truth, his devoted following was sure that Brother Bob Dobson had *never* had a private or subversive thought in his head.

Although J. Richland Quilter, as a pioneer New Conservative and the leader of "Our Families First," pretended to be *all inclusive*, he was smart enough never to kick Brother Bob and the White Christians, for whom he felt pure distaste, out of his political bed. Quilter often appeared at WCP rallies, smiling just as Brother Bob did and talking about the "new family values" that were in his (unoriginal) words "tying the good folks of our country back together, just like Christ Himself ties a good marriage together." When the occasion called for it, Quilter could *out-Brother-Bob* Brother Bob any day. Everything was now smoothly integrated. Brother Bob. *Brother Rich.* Marriage. The family. Divorce was strictly "out." Young, with-it people did not like to talk about divorce. It had become a credit-and-career risk. No kids was okay. But every couple desired more than anything to keep its Integrated Assets account intact and to keep themselves in the System.

One night, lying awake, Sandy had an intense feeling, as Jeff slept with his body and face turned away from her.

For the first time in ages she felt warm and happy. The bed was not as lonely, even with Jeff still in it. Someone else was there. Her arms reached into the dark air. She started kissing that person; holding on to another body. It was only in her mind, but the feelings that came with it—happiness; escape from the misery of her own loneliness—were there.

Then the body . . . it was so real; not just a dream . . . took on a shape. A woman—strong; dazzling; coltish—appeared like a swimmer, a climber, a horseman. She pulled Sandy into her strong arms and rode away with her, guiding Sandy like a beacon into the star-dusted night. Existence felt *alive* again and Sandy felt intensely loved: this woman, *whoever* she was, did not see her simply as an extension of *his* career.

An idea settled over her like a cloud of sweet water. The cloud glowed, but it had a word attached. A word that girls in her upper-middle-class-Jewish-stylish-Boston-suburban circle turned away from. Whereas someone of her mother Lorna's generation might have tittered and laughed nervously when it appeared, until a close friend's daughter was unexpectedly revealed to be one, Sandy's generation simply tried to avoid it.

The word was too close to them: It was *Lesbian.*

It took her a year to get out of her marriage. She had become an outcast at work during her divorce. But by then she'd already had an affair with Joni, a black dancer she had met at Courage, a crowded women's disco on a dangerous edge of Back Bay. What an aptly named club! It had taken every bit of hers to walk in. It was noisy and more sexual than she had ever felt; than she had ever thought women could be. Jeff was away on business. *What was she doing there?* Then Joni asked her to dance. Sandy felt shy; self-conscious about every move. She was happy that Joni was aggressive; she even began kissing Sandy during a slower movement. They left together and went to Joni's apartment, not far away. It was a funny, tiny, bohemian place without a single, pastel "designer" color in it. They saw each other for a few months after that. But the affair didn't last very long and Sandy had not expected it to.

But once she'd made up her mind that the word *lesbian* fit her, everything that went along with it seemed to fall into place. More and more of her friends were gay. She started to dress differently: not in the drag-queenie career clothes her mother helped her pick out, but in softer sheer cottons, and leather, and sexier, wilder clothes that her new sisters wore and that she started to buy on her own. But only after the divorce, which was horrible no matter how much she had come to hate her marriage—when she'd been living for the very first time really alone—did she decide to come out to her parents.

It was in their big house in Newton. She had been invited for dinner, but before she ate a thing, she told them. Lorna did not say a word, then cried out, "All the plans we had . . . even after you left Jeff, we had plans!" Her father was more practical: "Do you have someone?" Sandy announced that she did. It was actually the reason why she felt strong enough to tell them. She had met Carol at a dinner party in Cambridge. She told them about her, then said: "I'm going to move to the Cape. I can get a job there doing publicity for one of the hotels."

"You mean Provincetown?" Lorna asked. "You'll be cutting yourself off from us."

"It's not like I'm going to the Moon, Mommy. You two can visit."

"Sandy," Sid said, "Provincetown has a gay government. Your mother is trying to say that we may not feel welcome there."

"Of course you'll be welcome. I'm not joining a group of cannibals!"

"It's not that," Lorna explained. "The Cape is ringed with WCP people. Some can barely read. We feel anxious about you being cut off there. Sure, Provincetown's some kind of gay oasis, but it's surrounded by them."

"I'll be with people who love me, Mommy. Besides, you and Daddy are not exactly liberals."

Her mother turned her face from her. "We never said we were, honey. We just believe in people knowing their places. That's the way the world works. In the old century, they tried this 'everybody-is-equal' b.s.—and look where it got them? We had a full-scale class war, just a decade after the year 2000."

"I just meant to say, Mommy, that you and Daddy have always been New Conservatives, so what's the big deal about the WCP? They're a little lower than you, that's all."

"That's not true, Sandy," her father said, taking a sip of Scotch. "We're not all in the same boat. To begin with, we aren't even Christians. Bob Dobson has never exactly been a friend of the Jews, but we still have a few things in common—we support Rich Quilter and always will—but that's not the point. The point is we're still concerned about you."

"Daddy, there's nothing to worry about. You're just scared of losing me and you don't have to be."

"We aren't going to lose you," Lorna said. "*Ever.* I don't care what you *think* you are, honey, we love you. And if you ever need me, just call. We'll always take care of our baby. "

Her mother's words rang in her ears in the water. She felt suddenly cleansed as if the blood that had caked her thighs in Carol's pickup truck as her partner sped her over to the dingy hospital in Orleans (the only place, Carol was sure, that could save Sandy's life and the life of their baby in the emergency) was at last washed away. The feeling of purity was necessary.

She remembered the tears dribbling down her face and her head pounding with tension and pain and fear, as if it would shatter at any moment. And the blood blooming through the pale, yellow nightgown she wore; the blood clotting between her legs, until she hated the sight of her own lower body. "I'm going to lose it, Carol!" Then she screamed over and over again: "Mommy! Mommy! Mommy!"

Carol extended her right hand, trying to steer at eighty miles an hour at the same time. "You'll be okay. Sandy, I love you. Everything will be fine. . . ." They careened into the parking lot next to the Emergency entrance. Carol stopped the truck. "This is not going to be easy," she whispered to her.

"I'm so scared," Sandy said.

Carol hugged her and whispered, "Darling, this is *their* territory. The WCP have this hospital. They won't let one be built on our part of the Cape. Every time one of us has to come here, we know what they're thinking: we're unclean; we get what we deserve. You can see that look in their eyes. If I had the time, I'd take you right over to Boston, but I think this is the best we can do. Please don't be afraid. I love you, Sandy." Carol broke down and started to cry herself. Sandy looked at her and felt better. Even pregnant, if she had to, she could support Carol. Then Carol pulled herself together and said: "Can you get out of here and walk?"

Sandy ran her fingers through her hair. Carol was right: she had to show them what she was made out of. She walked straight into the Emergency Room on her own, with a gauntlet of eyes—unblinking and cold—on her. Orleans Hospital was the only full service center between Provincetown and Boston, since the New Government had locked so many people out of adequate medical care. In the Emergency Room, she felt a dozen hands immediately on her. She could not concentrate on anything. The room full of strange noises and people seemed to swim around her. She knew that her nightgown was stripped off, and she was pushed into a hospital gown, then made to lie down on a cold, paper-covered examining table in a small, unprivate cubicle.

Every few seconds another blurry face popped in, looked her over, and left. Finally she heard a man's very clipped, accented voice above the others. The voice sounded strangely English, then she realized it was Indian. "I'll see her in here. Who is she? Did her husband bring her in?" A middle-aged, East Indian doctor, his wrinkled face full of dark tan lines, looked at her. "Looks like a bad show here. How pregnant are you, dear?"

She told him that she was in her sixth month. Everything had been going well.

"And who is handling your condition?"

"I've been seeing a woman in Provincetown, Rachel Lawrence; she runs her own clinic."

"Yes, I've heard. A lot of herbal mumbo-jumbo! Back where I come from, in India, women like her have been outlawed. I don't understand why they allow them to practice in this advanced country."

Rachel Lawrence ran For This World, an alternative health center, where women from Sandy and Carol's Race Point collective went for their health needs. "Everything's going fine," Rachel had assured her. She was a strong, positive woman in her sixties. She had supervised hundreds of inseminations, from really primitive turkey-baster ones back in the Twentieth Century, to the new supertech jobs, where human hands touched nothing, including the doning male and the receiving woman. Suddenly Sandy wondered why they had not gone to Rachel. Then she realized her own fears prevented it. After she had woken Carol up—when Carol tried to call Rachel—Sandy had insisted, "This is *serious*!" They jumped into the truck and Carol immediately headed out of town.

"I gather this means you are a lesbian?" Sandy did not answer him; he went on: "I am Dr. Habib. I was hired by the Party to care for this area. Let me tell you right off the wicket that your being a lesbian will not affect your treatment at Orleans Hospital—not one iota. However, since we do not know who the donor was for this insemination, there is still a possibility of something, say, like the AIDS virus, being in that man's system."

Sandy felt furious. What a stupid statement—everyone knew AIDS was no longer a problem in Provincetown men. Habib was just bringing it up, like a red flag in front of her. For one thing, any jerk knew AIDS finally had been brought under control, ten years earlier, just as local gay governments got recognized. They'd found a vaccine that worked very much like the older one for rabies. Every same-sexualized man in America now took a dose once a year. It produced a round, purple rash on the shoulder that became an obvious identifying mark. (Naturally that left many straights ambivalent about taking it.) Point number two: every man that Sandy and Carol even considered was still involved with Self-Protection, the new name for what had once been called "Safe Sex." And lastly, Rachel had taken a first sperm sample from Lee, just for analysis in her lab. It was fine.

"AIDS?" Sandy shot back. "Why bring that up? He could have been straight for all you know."

He smiled at her. "Are you going to argue with me, young lady, or you going to let me help you?" Sandy looked at him; it was impossible to say how much she hated him. She wondered if Habib's wife still wore a veil—and if he thought all other women should. He began talking again: "Right now, we're going to give you something for your pain. I know how hysterical women get at birth problems. In my country we knock them out completely: that is the only modern way to deal with birth."

Despite her fear, she could not hold herself in any longer. "BIRTH? I'm not giving BIRTH yet. What are you talking about 'knock them out'? What are you going to do with me?"

Habib shook his head slowly. "Miss, you will be out of pain."

Suddenly Carol burst into the cubicle, followed by two big, blond-headed young men, who tried to grab her.

"Thank the Goddess you're here," Sandy cried and tried to take Carol's arm.

"You are not allowed in here, Miss," Habib said. "Unless you can prove you are either this lady's husband, which does not look possible, or one of her parents, I will not allow you into my emergency clinic."

"I don't care what you say. She's crying."

"Are you the *father* of this baby?"

"I live with her—isn't that enough? We registered in Provincetown. I have a right to be here—"

"Not in Orleans, you don't!" an older female nurse shot in. She rushed past Carol and took hold of Sandy's wrist, ostensibly to feel for a pulse. She wore a huge rhinestone cross on the breast of her uniform and a small pin under it that said, "Life Is Sacred! Stop Abortion NOW." "You lesbos are not what we call 'favored company' in Orleans. Dr. Habib, if this woman's not out of here, I will call for more security."

"I'm afraid, young lady, you must leave. You see, I have no real say in this. Mrs. Waters is the union organizer for the White Christian Party, which means that she has more power here than I have."

"Our Lord Jesus Christ has the only power," Mrs. Waters corrected him. "I am merely His servant. These women refuse to acknowledge the Savior, 63 and they are paying for this now." She turned her attention to Carol. "I want you to know, young woman, that our town was named for Saint Joan. She was a Christian saint—the Maid of Orleans."

Carol suddenly smiled: the whole thing was too damn crazy. There was her partner, Sandy, on a stretcher, with this nutty old lady going on to her about Joan of Arc, who—doubtlessly—would have been burned to death—again—right there at some shopping center in Orleans, if this nurse had had her way. "I'm afraid you're wrong, lady," Carol said. "Orleans was named for a famous queer duke. He was the brother of the King of France."

The nurse began to prepare Sandy's arm for an injection. Carol could see bruise marks where Waters had squeezed it. "I pray that Jesus forgives you, dear. Queer duke? Do you people believe everybody is like you? Well, most people are *normal*—remember that!"

"If you're 'normal,'" Carol said, slowly, "I think I'll just *stay* the way I am."

The nurse, now brandishing an ancient looking hypo needle, looked furiously at both women. "Then both of you had better get down on your knees and ask Jesus for His forgiveness!"

Habib tried to smile. "Perhaps you had better leave," he said to Carol. "If anything happens, I shall come out and inform you."

Sandy remembered the look on Carol's face as she left the Emergency Room. She looked whipped. It was a power game: it all depended upon which square you landed on in this strange checkerboard of America. In Provincetown, Key West, Manhattan; you could be totally gay. In Iowa, Tulsa—or some place like Orleans—you could be arrested for kissing another woman in public, even if she were your mother. The White Christians controlled the Senate and the House. The President appeared to be neutral, but mostly he was a figurehead. Rich Quilter had been President for ten years, after what had once been the Republican Party had rescinded time limitations on the office. Quilter? Who would ever believe this old relic from the Twentieth Century would finally capture the White House and stay put? But the truth was most people had stopped thinking about politics. The only thing they really cared about was staying alive.

Sandy remembered falling softly into unconsciousness, as Mrs. Waters mumbled, "It's going to be another little bastard born to a dyke. Born without a single hope of Jesus. It's a *shame*, Dr. Habib, *a sin and a shame*. I know that you are from another religion, but I know that your people hold the family just as sacred as we do. Ain't that the truth?"

64   "We do, Mrs. Waters," the doctor said smiling.

Sandy's hands managed to clutch the coarse cotton hospital gown. Her legs drew up protectively towards her belly. "What are you going to do with me?" she cried.

"Don't worry, Miss," Habib said. "We will knock you out just a little more and clean out this infection that has caused your pain and fever. No husband, I think, should allow a woman to be in such pain. I do not think your friend Carol has done a good job here. There is something to be said about the old-fashioned relationship of a man to a wife. In my country, these things are looked upon more seriously than in yours."

"The baby," Sandy sobbed. "The baby. . . ."

"Yes," Mrs. Waters said stiffly. "The Lord Himself will take care of your baby."

Sandy tried to stay awake. She wanted to jump off the table and leave. In her mind, she saw herself walking out of the Emergency Room into a flood of light, and then being held by Carol. She saw the future: the little boy that they would have, that they would raise together. With Lee coming in to teach him the things that boys needed to know; coming in to be his male friend. In her mind, she could still walk away and have her baby. She saw her sisters, the women of her collective, gathering around her, some of them already crying with happiness at the birth of her son.

But she could not walk away.

Suddenly she realized, in her last drift of consciousness, that something was coming up between her legs. A hand, cold and gloved. It was spraying something all the way up her. The spray felt cold and indecent. She felt it internally; it left her mouth numb. Nausea crawled through her, leaving a taste in her mouth like rotting seaweed. The table itself began to revolve. She felt as if she were out . . . really far out . . . on a small shaky boat and the boat was encased in a dream.

"The Lord Jesus does *not* want this child to be born," Mrs. Waters affirmed. "He works His miracles in the strangest ways, Dr. Habib. I believe He is going to work one through you!"

"What are you saying, Mrs. Waters? That *I* should abort this child?"

"That is a vile word, Doctor. Disgusting. But we do not serve Life by serving idolatry."

"I don't understand you, Mrs. Waters. As the representative of the White Christian Party at this hospital, are *you* telling me to abort this child?"

"I am telling you"—she looked at him; her face taut with determination—"to deliver us from Evil."

Sandy heard it all. Out in the small, shaky boat, on the Sea of Unconsciousness. A storm was approaching. Black thick clouds. The

65

Goddess Herself had seen it coming and She had sent Carol to protect her and love her. She and Carol hugged each other while the waves grew more menacing. Monstrous faces from the deep looked up at them from the sides of their craft. The faces were cold, smug. They looked like the nurse and the doctor and the orderlies at Orleans Hospital. She saw these faces with their cynical, smug smiles lining up on the two long sides of the boat to mock her and hurt her. In her nausea and fear, she knew that a hand with an instrument in it had invaded the most private place she had. The hand was now pulling something out of her womb.

She had been blank. Blank and numb when the "painkillers" wore off. She was now in a private room. Several strange nurses were with her. She did not know them, but they too wore their uniforms with the large rhinestone crosses and the motto "Life Is Sacred! Stop Abortion NOW" under them.

"I guess you understand we could not save your little boy," Habib said when he entered.

"Where is he?" Sandy asked. "Where is Carol?"

"Your friend has been waiting outside. She knows about the problem with your pregnancy. We will let you see her, but Mrs. Waters will not give you permission to see the child. He will be given a Christian burial. She promised me that."

He left the room, and then Carol came in. Sandy felt ripped apart. They hugged each other and did not say another word for a long time. Then Carol told her that as soon as possible she would get her out of Orleans, even if she had to kidnap her to get her out of there.

The other women were waiting for her, but the water felt so good she did not want to leave. She did not mind that she was not wearing a bathing suit and the gauzy cottons she wore were now soaked with sea water. They only felt thicker and softer to her. Suddenly she started crying right there in the water. She realized she missed her mother and the baby she was not allowed to have, the boy who would have been Lee's friend as well as hers. She knew that she wanted to drown; she started to swim out farther into the bay. She knew she had to do this fast, before Carol came in after her. She was not a strong swimmer, but she knew that with a little luck, the depression that she could not shake would be over with.

Then thirty—maybe forty yards out—something grabbed her. She felt it taking over her thighs. It felt thicker than her own flesh. Harder. It pulled her under the surface; for a moment she was terrified. If she were going to kill herself, she did not want outside help. She opened her eyes and saw it.

There was something glowing down there in the dark green water of Herring Cove Bay; thick; strangely slick; but formless. It carried a current of its own that swam around her lower body, caressing her thighs, making her feel almost giddy. Happy. It entered her, pushing her into a tightly clenched ball, with her eyes closed in ecstasy. There was space now around her, black and omniscient, and within it were a million twinkling bits of light. And one of them—amazingly—she was convinced, was inside of her.

Nothing like this had ever happened to her, except that moment in bed when she was next to Jeff and realized she was embracing another woman whose time with her had not yet come. But she knew, in the water, that something would happen to her. Significant. *Serious.* She wanted to live. Still submerged, she opened her eyes in the dark, jet-green water. Tiny lights swam around her. "Thank you," she said, the words escaping as bubbles. A hand grasped her. It was Carol, who pulled her up to the surface.

"Oh, Goddess, you worried the hell out of me."

"It's okay, Carol." Sandy grabbed her. "I love you so much."

Both of them were now crying and holding each other, somewhat back towards the beach, in a calm tide. Then at least ten other sisters came into the water fully clothed. They circled the two women, and then they all waded back to the shore.

"Unbelievable!" Rachel Lawrence announced. "You're pregnant."

"I know," Sandy said, glowing, holding onto Carol's lean, strong hand.

"Who's the father?"

"I'm not sure; I don't know how it happened."

"We have no idea," Carol said. "But Sandy became aware of it after swimming at Herring Cove. Is it possible that one of Lee's sperms could have . . . just been dormant in her?"

"Anything's possible," Rachel said, wearing her white lab coat and trying to look clinical. "But the one thing we have to realize is that if this is a problematic pregnancy, you cannot have it in Provincetown. We know what those assholes in Orleans did to you. I'm sure they stole your baby."

"But I'd only carried him for six months."

"That's no problem. Babies live after six months. It happens all the time. The truth is your pregnancy was completely normal; I'm not sure what caused the fever and bleeding—but you panicked and that's the worse thing you can do around people like the WCP. They could have saved him, even in a hole as primitive as Orleans." Rachel let out a sigh. "He did not die inside of you—I know that. And they didn't abort him, either—although I don't hold it past them. I bet they stole him and put him into neonatal. Now he's living with some White Christian couple who'll force feed him their version of Jesus for the rest of his life. That's happened before in Orleans, but the local cops never investigate. See, they're a part of the Party, too."

"Goddess," said Sandy. "If only I had known this before we set out in the truck—I thought we were going to have a storm and I was going to lose the baby, and—

"You had the storm, alright," Rachel said. "And it was right there in Orleans Hospital."

"What should we do?" Carol asked. They were in a quandary: Sandy had to have this baby and Carol knew her partner would do anything to keep it.

"Darling!" Lorna Feltner cried. "You're home." She hugged her daughter so hard that Sandy had to pull herself away. The house looked all pastel as usual, full of precious, little knick-knacks and expensive old department store pieces that had been in the family for years. Her mother was perfectly dressed, her nails and hair impeccable as ever. Sandy felt, as her father would say, like a schlep. She had let herself go and she was not going to wear the kind of robot-tailored dresses that Lorna loved. Sandy would not give up her soft cottons or her leather jackets and leggings. They went into the solarium where Lorna had her wild orchids and miniature fruit trees. "This one is new," Lorna said. "It's a peach from China and it'll only grow a foot high!"

Sandy sat down on a pink settee. She was starting to feel like a miniature fruit tree herself. "I'm pregnant," she told Lorna.

Her mother was taken back. Like most New Conservatives, she did not believe in births out of wedlock, but she was glad to have her daughter home. "Who is the father?" she whispered.

Sandy hesitated. "A man named Lee."

"So you've gone back to men?"

"No. I was inseminated by him. I'm still with Carol. I love her, but I want to come here and have the baby. I need you. I know you and Daddy love me. You once promised, Mommy, to take care of me."

Lorna started crying. Her mascara, which never ran, began to bleed. She settled down on the settee next to Sandy. "Of course we will, baby. We just never thought we'd have a grandchild. Does this Lee want to move in, too?"

"No," Sandy said firmly. "But I want Carol to."

Her mother's eyes closed. "That's impossible. I couldn't have it—I mean all of our friends believe the way we do."

"There are parents who have lesbian children. They change."

"Sure, honey, and they lose their jobs and their homes and their friends. Things are not easy anymore. Brother Bob is on the telecom every week saying how homosexuality is the only thing left of the old decadent Twentieth Century that we have to get rid of for a perfect world. That's baloney! We don't believe it, but we can't just fly in the face of the whole society. The White Christians are going to establish a colony on the Moon—do you know what that means? They've taken over the *whole* damn Moon!"

"Carol's got to be here, Mommy." Sandy did not know whether to cry or to laugh at her mother's remark about the Moon. But she had become convinced of one thing, after leaving home for Jeff and then living with Carol: her mother was not a dumb woman. She was still attractive and she had held her marriage together beautifully. Despite her weakness for drag-queen clothes and Jewish ladies groups, she was always aware of what lay behind every comment and whisper and joke.

Lorna got up. "Your Dad's going to be back soon. He's taken another consultancy job. The New Conservatives are working through City Hall to redo the slum areas that took over inner Cambridge. Your father's amazing. So many guys like him have been forced into retirement, and he's still at it. The problem is that if you and Carol live here, the neighbors will know, and so will City Hall. Brother Bob has an effective network here in Massachusetts, despite the fact that years back it was such a Catholic state."

Sandy looked at her. "If I go back to Provincetown, I may lose this baby. He's your grandchild."

Lorna smiled. "How do you know he's a *he*?"

"I do."

Lorna shook her head. "Sometimes we know. Listen, do you think Carol can look like a man? She is kind of boyish."

"Sure."

"Maybe we can hire her as a gardener. If anyone asks, we'll just say 'he's a student living in the back and your husband's away in the Far East for a while.' People out here in Newton aren't that nosy—"

"They aren't!" Sandy said ebulliently. She hugged her mother and felt again as happy as she had that moment in the water, when she knew something wonderful had happened.

Lorna looked at her. "I'm putting your daddy on the line for this, Sandy. We're all on the line. I want you to know that. We'll have to be careful, that's all."

CHAPTER 6

I was born in a swirl of blood and screams. From the moment I opened my eyes, I was conscious. I knew who I was: a small, pulsing body already filled with memories. My mother Sandy said that her two doctors at the superhospital in Newton had never heard such a scream. Long; high—then sinking into this amazing lower pitch. The whole O.R. staff listened; some of the nurses believed they'd heard an almost inaudible string of recognizable foreign words in it. It was like a "visitation." They were unnerved.

Then I was silent. Things were done to me: parts snipped, machine-sucked; swabbed. My eyes surveyed the room. I was handed first to a boy (Carol) and then to my smiling grandmother. Then to another woman named Rachel, who was there, as a kind of doctor, while the other two doctors looked on, shaking their heads.

I was large. Later I was told how perfectly formed I was, with muscles already. I could sit up. Within a day I was brought back to my grandparents. They doted on me, especially my grandfather, who one day while washing me felt something strange circling in my scrotum. He turned away in shock; I'm quite sure he didn't mention it again for years.

A week later, my mothers drove me by truck to Provincetown; one was still dressed as a man. Later Sandy told me that Carol had stayed in secret in a small furnished garden apartment, behind the large house in Newton. She would sneak into the house at night, so that neighbors would not suspect her in bed with the Feltners' pregnant daughter. In the busy Race Point house, I was a male among many women. They came to look at me and care for me; I was treated with love and tenderness. "I thought that you were a miracle. Now I know you are," Sandy cooed when I was only a few weeks old. I knew what she was saying, although I could say nothing back. The most I can say was that from the very beginning I was not like other people.

Sometime later on the beach as evening dropped (maybe a bare two months after my birth, although reckoning time is difficult when you're very small), *I* had a visitation. A man dressed in blue came out of the sky. My mothers were speaking to each other only a few feet away, when he appeared, speaking softly to me in a human voice. "So, you have come back this way? That makes sense. You were sent away from Ki *by* women, so of course you end up in the womb of one. And now there has not been one *single* birth on Ki—so those foolish women thought that I would not know about *your* birth. Idiots! I was able to follow your third Egg; it glows in my eyes through a million layers of space. Trust me, the Lady Hortha is not the *only* one with powers of her own. Now, my friend, I shall go back and tell Hortha that—*on* Ki—I know of this birth! And I will tell her that Anvil is now to be the regent of Ki, until you—*Albert*—are old enough to come back with a mate."

I understood hardly a word he was saying. The words slipped through me, until he came to one: *Albert.* Then I knew that it was my name. That night, Sandy and Carol came into my room to kiss me goodnight. With them was Lee, who I knew was acting as my father. The three of them leaned over my crib; I felt Lee's breath over my face and I smiled. "He knows who you are," Sandy said and she embraced Lee. "There is something amazing about this little guy. It's like he's a part of us, and yet he's not. I feel so blessed that I gave birth to him. He's a real miracle!"

"Sandy thinks she's the Virgin Mary," Carol said, smiling.

"She was another Jewish girl!" Sandy said.

"I just can't believe this story you concocted about becoming pregnant by swimming in the Bay."

"Something happened while swimming there, Carol. I don't know what it was. This spirit just took over me—invaded me. Maybe it *was* the Goddess Herself. How can we say not?"

"I think it was just my tough sperm," Lee said. He smiled broadly. He had grown a short trimmed beard. It made him look very handsome. I saw that he was tall and well formed, with large beautiful shoulders, arms and hands. "My sperm must have gotten into another ovary. How it happened, I don't know. But this kid must be the twin of the one who. . . ."

"Was aborted by those monsters?" Sandy asked. "Those perverters of religion?" She started crying.

"Maybe you'd better go," Carol whispered. "She always gets upset when we mention that."

Lee apologized. He felt concerned and strangely crushed, trying to figure it all out. "I guess I mentioned the wrong thing, Sandy. I'm sorry."

"It's not your fault," Sandy said, pulling herself back together. "I'll always grieve for that child. But I'm glad we got this one. We don't even know what to call him yet. On the birth certificate, I had them write 'Not Yet Named.' Then I was in a hurry to leave Newton before we could write anything in."

Lee looked perplexed; then Carol said, "How about 'Lee'?"

"No," Lee objected. "I don't want him to be a junior."

"We could name him after my father," Sandy suggested. "But 'Sid' never made it for me."

"Maybe we should just wait," Carol said. "He's been unnamed so far. Let's think on it for a day or so."

The three of them left my room. I stood up in my crib and I could see from my window the low evening sky and a thin ribbon of sapphire-blue water beyond. The water reminded me of my origins; my conception. While I was standing, holding on to the crib bars, Sandy came back in. She leaned over and put her face to mine. I could tell that she had been crying. I kissed her cheek. She picked me up; I held on to her hands with my tiny fingers. "*I am Albert*," I said.

She looked at me in disbelief.

"*Albert.*"

"I must be hearing things. Can you repeat that?"

"Albert," I repeated.

She cocked her head. "*Einstein* or *Schweitzer*?"

I looked at her curiously. She put me back in the crib, and I did not say another word. It seemed silly to talk to her if she was going to answer me with strange words, but I had to tell her who I was. She left and I looked out the window again. I knew I would not be spending much more time in a crib; that was for certain. A few days later I was christened, in the name of the Goddess, "Albert Lee Feltner Parker." Or, if I wanted it, "Feltpark." I decided there, at the christening, that *I* wanted to be called Albert *Lee*.

I began to grow fast. Very, *very* fast. At three months I was too big to be in a crib anymore. I was already speaking and not simply in baby talk. I had what people called an astonishing memory; I could identify things that I'd never seen and knew the words for them in English, a language that I understood innately. At one year I could distinguish letters; soon I could read. Sums came to me immediately. The other Race Point women were convinced that I was "magical": that I had resulted from the magic inherent in my conception, something that Sandy never quite accepted simply as "Goddess magic." She was sure that I was larger; exceptional; of world value. Still, sometimes, when she was with Carol, she would try to joke me off: "I guess every Jewish mom feels that her son is, well, like Jesus!"

Both mothers were sure I was a genius; that they didn't argue about. But Lorna Feltner took it all in stride; she was proud of me but was sure that, deep down, I was like any other smart Jewish kid. Lee argued that I took after him. He was a good father, spending hours with me whenever he could; soon his life revolved around me. As a rapidly growing child, I became aware of the vast love around me, from my two mothers, from the other women of Race Point, from Lee—and from the Feltners who drove out through staunch White Christian territory to the "gay reserve" to see me whenever they could.

Then one day, when I was almost two years old and the two of us were in the bathtub, Lee found the thing that my grandfather had found after my birth. He was using a washcloth and foaming bubble bath all over me. We were at his house, where we liked to take baths together. We usually ended up goofing and giggling at the duckies and plastic people Lee floated in the tub. Suddenly he became alarmed. Was it a growth or a tumor in my scrotum? He put his large hand on my testicles and started gently examining them.

Infant boys get erections all the time, especially if they've not been slapped when they do it. I was a very large small boy, growing faster than anyone had ever seen. I started pumping my small, hard penis against his soapy hand, as the third Egg moved inside my sac on its own. Lee's hand responded unconsciously to this movement, while his fingers, curiously, stroked the Egg. I put my face next to Lee's, then my small mouth found his. His eyes closed. "God," he moaned. "What sort of kid are you?"

For the first time, I understood every word. I answered him directly. "Maybe it's time you know that I'm not your little boy."

His mouth fell open. "Wait one damn second. *Where* did you learn to talk like this? Albert, you're barely two years old!"

"But I'm not a two-year-old."

"Then what are you?"

He looked at me and then shook his head. I put my arms around him and kneaded myself against his chest. His hands cradled me tenderly, but I kept pushing my boner into them and his fingers began to play with my Egg again. His large chest began to shake. Suddenly he looked at me. "This can't be happening," he said. My small hands reached down there, to the thing he called his pee-pee and to the large balls under it. "You aren't even two years old," he whispered. "I didn't come out till I was *twenty-two*!" I could tell he was getting excited, even against his will. His thing got larger. I put my small soapy fingers on it, sliding it up and down.

He started breathing faster and suddenly hugged me to him. "We've got to stop this."

74

My hands began to play with his hard nipples. I thought they were a lot of fun. "What does 'come out' mean?" I asked, giggling. "Like come out of the water?"

"*He's two years old!*" He threw his hands up. "Holy shit, my kid's a sexual Einstein!" I put my hands around his neck and kissed him. Really kissed him. "Albert, you've got to stop. 'Come out' means the first time you have sex with a man—and really know it!"

"Is that what we're doing?"

"No, we are not having sex! I'm Daddy. I am not into this kind of scene, you understand?"

He got up out of the bathtub, trying very hard to contain himself. I could see that "down there" he had become much larger. It seemed magical to me; big and beautiful. I couldn't wait till my mine was as large as his, and I had hair on my chest and belly, under my arms, and in my crotch. He washed the soap off me, while I looked into his serious, deep eyes. "Albert, don't you see I'm your father?"

"You're not," I told him.

He shook his head. "Then who the hell are you?"

"Just *Albert*. I am Albert—that's all that I can tell you."

Lee became my real friend after this. The truth was that I had bonded with him; the part of me that was still attached to Ki would not allow any other kind of thing to happen. On Ki, after one year, we were returned to our fathers. And here I was still living with two women! I accepted this for a while. I did love my mothers very much. But I could not feel close to them the way I felt close to Lee.

He watched me grow so fast that my mothers could not believe it; but he did. I got used to talking a sort of baby talk around them, but not around him. But by the time I was four—when I was as big as most twelve year olds—I refused to live with my mothers anymore. I could now speak as well as an adult, and I told Carol and Sandy that we had to have a talk.

Carol smiled. "Okay," she said. I think she expected that I was going to ask for a bicycle. "I want to leave you," I said, calmly. "And live with Lee."

There was silence: I felt like I had dropped a bomb. I explained to them that I could only live with another man. *Lee.* Carol looked at me with blunt anger. I felt awful, but what else could I do? I promised we would visit them whenever we could—"I told you we didn't need a father!" Carol interrupted me, talking directly to Sandy. I felt, like most children do, completely ignored. Then Carol looked at me: "Albert, tell us: has Lee said ever anything that made you *not* want to live with us? *Anything?*"

"No," I said. "I just have to live with a man. Where I come from the men mate for life."

"Well, that *can't* be Provincetown," Sandy said smiling.

"No, it's not," I answered.

Carol looked straight at me. "Is this all coming from some kind of fantasy life? I mean, Lee has not been filling you with these ideas, has he?" I told her no. I gave her my word. "Alright," she said, then asked: "Son, can you tell us anything about yourself? You are a mystery to us."

"Only that I am Albert. That is who I am, and I've known it before I was born."

"You are strange," Carol said. "Even in gay Provincetown, with the White Christians breathing down our necks—you're still *really* strange, Albert!"

"He's not just strange," Sandy broke in. "Look at his birth. Sometimes, we have to accept miracles and expect not to understand them."

"Sandy, he's *our* little boy," Carol said impatiently.

"But I've got to live with Lee."

"Okay," Sandy agreed. "But forget this 'mating' with him. You're only four years old." She stopped for a moment, then said, "My parents are going to have a fit. Suppose something happens to you, darling? Do you have any idea how much Granny Feltner will worry?"

"I've got to live with him," I repeated. "But I love you both very much." I kissed them and told them that I also loved Granny and Grandpa.

Sandy sighed. "I expected that a man would take you away; I just didn't think it would happen so fast!" Carol looked befuddled, betrayed, and still very angry. She shook her head. "This was not what we wanted from a child," she said. Then Lee came by and gathered my things in several sacks and duffel bags. From then on, I slept in his bed. We secretly made love, as he caressed my third Egg.

One night while we were doing this, I was brought back to Ki. I had grown so quickly that I was as big as a normal teenager, although in Earth chronology I was still only six years old. Lee kissed and stroked the Egg, making it spin faster and faster until it took me back with it. We were facing each other. I closed my eyes and when I opened them, only the whites were showing. My eyes were now up behind their lids: observing life on Ki.

I had slipped back into the Temple and there I saw Enkidu, dead, resting under the statue of the Goddess Laura. Next to him was my own body, bathed in the sleep of death, taking in just enough air for an insect to survive. It was dark and quiet. Even on Ki I was the Earth boy, though moving with a comet's speed towards manhood.

76   "You must leave where you are, son," Enkidu commanded.

"You are dead, sira."

"I speak to you through your own Egg, son. I love you, Albert, and even death will not separate us. You must go to a place called California, to seek the remains of Nick Lawrence and his mate, Reuvuer. There you will find your own mate. And when you find him, you will be able to come back to Ki and claim its throne."

"I have to leave Provincetown? But I'm only a boy."

"No. You are a man. You will see. When you wake from this dream, you will be no longer a child."

"I will have to leave my mothers—not see them again?"

My father nodded his head.

"And Lee?"

"You must allow him to come with you, and be your protector. But *not* your mate. He was once your father; he cannot mate with you."

I opened my eyes. Our small bedroom was just as it had been. Nothing had been disturbed; a container of hand cream was just where it was, knocked over on the bedside table. Lee was asleep, but now my body was as big as his. I felt cold for a second; the largeness of me had not yet warmed the bed. I pulled closer to him; he bolted up with a start.

"Who are you? Where's Albert?"

I tried very hard to smile. "I *am* Albert."

"You're a . . . man."

"Yes."

It was the first hour of dawn. We could hear the gulls calling and a few distant trucks beginning deliveries. After loading up sleeping bags, some clothes, and a few books and items Lee thought were indispensable (including some of my baby pictures), we began driving across the country. I was terribly nervous. My new body both amazed and frightened me. I had a beard, actually only a day's growth, but it was dark and bristly. I had a dusting of curly dark hair on my chest, which was now almost as deep and wide as Lee's. Before we left, I took a shower alone. I touched myself all over: my legs were a man's legs, strong and muscular, my arms a man's arms. I had a dark, circumcised, penis, fairly thick, with a large fleshy head on it. Under it were two heavy, male testicles, and behind them, slightly larger and revolving slowly—just as the Earth did that morning—was the third Egg.

I knew what it was: I had known all along, from my very first instinct of myself. Spreading away from my "man"'s equipment was a thick forest of black pubic hair. It glittered like spun black glass. When I looked into the mirror after the shower, I realized I did not look one bit like Sandy, who was blond—and certainly I did not look at all like Lee, even with his dark, reddish glow. I looked Semitic, vaguely Middle Eastern; but why I should look that way escaped me. Lee came into the bathroom of his small cottage. I had just dried off and he was dressed. He put his arms around my warm, naked body. He told me he was ready to go. He had not questioned me for a moment when I told him that we had to leave.

CHAPTER 7

The trip across the country took four days of actual travel. We did it in Lee's old red, beat-up, Ford PT— an ancient "Personal Transport" that dated from 2008 just before American cars became self running and you could sleep or watch laser-scans transmitted from your home telecom network while driving. We could not do any of that—Lee was always on the lookout, especially going through heavy White Christian territories, which took up most of the midsection of the United States. Outside of Boston we stopped at a dreary, huge McTotal and Lee called Sandy. He did not want me to appear on her telecom screen, so I ducked out of the phone stop. He was sure that she would never buy the fact that not only had we become lovers, but that I was . . . well, now I had a beard, a grown man's dick, and I still was only six years old. Basically, he was afraid she'd freak out if she found us gone. Although I lived with Lee, I was still her "little" boy; she had never changed in her unqualified love for me. He called; there was no one home. They must have gone out to breakfast with some of the other women. He left a message on their message center. "Hi, ladies, the kid and I are going to be away for a while. Albert's fine, but he's bored—if you ask me, he's growing too fast for his own good!" He clicked the Off button.

From where I stood, I could listen. "Suppose she doesn't believe it?"

"We'll call again in a few days."

In Lee's PT, I munched on a breakfast McProtein burger. It was made with a meat substitute and seaweed and tasted like chicken if you had never tasted real chicken. "I'm scared about Carol," I said between mouthfuls. "I don't think she ever got used to the idea of me being with you."

"Yeh, she took it hard. She probably thinks *I've* been molesting you."

There were no prying White Christian eyes around, so I kissed him. "Nobody said you molested me . . . you're my *dad*," I said.

"Sure. Ain't this is the weirdest daddy-son relationship in history? I get the kid that grows like hell from outer space—but what the hell do they get?"

"We'll call them again, just before San Francisco. We'll tell them that's where we want to live."

"Yeh, and all of dyke P'town will come after me with a butcher knife!"

In Chicago, where there was a large gay reserve in what used to be the Old Town area, we went immediately to a gay government center and Lee arranged an ID for me. The story was that I'd lost my ID in a fire and we were mated and needed matching micro-info. It was the only thing that would get us out of trouble if Carol or Sandy, not knowing what had happened, tried anything. I mean, how could they tell that I had gone from being six to approximately twenty-six? The man at the gay government center, which was in a large, clean building with an arts wing, a sports section, and a facility for health maintenance, was very cool. He was middle-aged and kind of lumpy, but with beautiful, dreamy blue eyes. "My name is Gene. I'll have to get you through this. Since you're both from the Eastern Sector there's a lot of paperwork involved. The New Conservatives who think they run City Hall don't want us to give out any more couple IDs. They just passed this bullshit to keep them from circulating. So I'm going to bypass all of that and give them to you."

Lee thanked him while he ran all of our info through a formatter that processed a simple holographic ID card for me and amended Lee's to show that he was mated with me. He was about to hand us both our IDs, when he paused. "Wait a second. I need to look at your arms."

I had no idea what he was talking about, but Lee pushed up his left shirt sleeve. "Okay," the man said. "Your ID stated this was fresh. How about Albert?"

Lee looked embarrassed. "He's just joined the club." He turned redder than I had seen him in years.

"What?"

"He was straight—I mean, not really straight, but—"

"Oh, just came out? Well, we'll fix that." Gene led me into the health maintenance area, where I took off my shirt for a white-uniformed tech. He pushed a metal instrument against my left shoulder; I painlessly felt something shoot into it. "You're protected," Gene said. "Just be careful the next few days. You may feel a little tired; nausea. If you get really sick—sometimes people do after their first inoculation, we'll have to quarantine you for a month. I know it sounds tough, but it's better than dying!"

I felt cornered now, walking back with Gene to the records area where Lee waited. He smiled when he saw me. "You're all set," Gene announced. "Now do I get to kiss both grooms?"

Lee nodded his head and Gene gave both of us a friendly kiss on the cheek. When we walked out, I said to Lee, "Why didn't you tell me about the shots?"

"Holy shit, Albert, give me a break—I forgot about it. Most six year olds don't get them. Besides, everything we've done has been protected anyway." I looked worried. "You'll be okay," he hugged me as we walked out the center. "They just tell you that to shake you up. No one's been quarantined for years; mostly they say that to keep the White Christians happy. Bureaucrats are bureaucrats, even the gay ones!"

We stayed three nights in Chicago at a gay habitation house—sort of like a guest house but larger, where you had your own small apartment. We were scheduled to go back to the health maintenance department to have my AIDS inoculation "read" at the end of three days. I was nervous about it. The idea that my life depended upon a vaccine bothered me. But Lee took it in stride. I was amazed how cool he seemed to be about everything; he was just happy to be with me.

Lee had never been to Chicago before and he was excited by it. Unlike New York which had never been converted to White Christian principles, Chicago was filled with the WCP but they did not seem as strident as they were on Cape Cod and Boston. Lee told me that in the old century Chicago had been very Eastern European Catholic and fairly independent. The Chicago Catholics, unlike the Boston ones—that is, except for a few morons—never fell for the WC line. We could go, for instance, into any store or restaurant and no one stared at us or made us feel unwelcome—something that Lee said happened in Boston or even out on the Cape a lot.

It was fall and I realized there were kids going back to school, something I'd never do. A certain part of me wanted to talk to them in the language of kids, like "Where ya goin'? How ya like school?" That sort of stuff. But the truth was that I'd never been to school, and in many ways I did feel like a kid in an adult's body. Sometimes I had almost startling memories of Ki, and I knew that there, also, I'd been a "kid" in an adult's body. But I don't think Lee saw me that way. I think he was just, well, overwhelmed with me. It was oddly wonderful. But the worst thing was that every night, while I made love with Lee—and I could see on his face that he was crazy about me—I had to face the inevitable that when we got to California, I would have to leave him. Once, right after sex, he told me that he couldn't believe *anything* that had happened—it was all "too weird"—but he would follow me anyplace. "I'm nuts about you," he admitted. "I just can't understand how you went from being six to . . . whatever age you are."

I thought that it was best that I explained as much about myself as I could: that I had come from this small planet named Ki, where Same-Sex men mated for life and had this thing—Lee called it my "third nut"—that transmitted thoughts and could even transmit us. This made us different from the 81 kind of men on Earth they would call "normal," the same tribe of men that the White Christians believed were special to their own god, Jesus, who—on Ki, I was certain—would have been a Same-Sexer Himself if everything I'd heard about Him were true.

"So, tell me, how did you come here . . . and end up inside of Sandy Feltner?" he asked, while he nuzzled my neck and face.

I had to do something that was not going to be easy for me: lie. I could not tell Lee the complete truth that I had come to Earth to find a mate—and that he would *not* be that mate. Lee was my companion, not my mate. The thought sickened me: I really loved him; he had been first my father and now my lover. But my own father Enkidu had directed what would happen, just as he had directed my life so often before, but never cruelly, back on Ki. "There are forces on Ki that are after me. The planet's in turmoil. They want to kill me and take over—"

"So you're . . . ?" he paused, then said: "Like the Prince there, or something?"

I nodded my head. That seemed the strangest thing to admit, especially to a "normal" American man who just happened to be in bed with me. "They either want to kill me or mate with me—"

"Sounds like a good choice!"

"It's not funny; they're awful. So the women who run Ki, they're called the Sisters of Ki—"

"You mean women run it? Sounds like Provincetown. . . ."

"I guess it does," I admitted. "Anyway, as crazy as this sounds, they arranged for me to get away. But to do so, I ended up in—" the story started to sound too nuts even for me—"Sandy's womb."

"Gosh! And the whole time she thought she was the lesbian Virgin Mary!" Lee sat up and pulled me to him, locking me in his arms. I found him very attractive, with his glossy dark red hair and long beautiful legs. His cock was hard. My hands found it. My heart started beating very quickly and just as quickly a memory passed through me: a redheaded man on Ki. Who? Then I remembered he was an Off-Sexer, but I could not remember exactly who he was. Lee's lips found the front of my neck, and he ran his large soft tongue along my Adam's apple. "So you're going to find a mate here on Earth?" he whispered.

I turned my head slightly away from him. My third Egg started spinning faster. I felt uneasy, yet excited. "Yes."

"I want it to be me."

I pulled his handsome face to mine and put my lips on his. Our tongues merged; then all I could say was, "Thanks."

"You're fine," Gene said. "The inoculation's taken perfectly. Of course this is no reason to go hog wild." I looked at him curiously. "Self-Protection is still the order of the day," he went on. "You never can tell what sort of strange stuff is running around here in some guy's sperm." Lee looked at me and smiled. I smiled back. Gene laughed, "Not that anybody ever turns down a little taste of cum every now and then—I miss the hell out of it, myself— but just remember: Self-Protection. Even if you don't do it every time, it's still what we want you to keep in mind. I'm afraid you've also got to sign this."

He handed me a form that said I had "voluntarily" allowed myself to be inoculated, had had the inoculation "read," and I would practice Self-Protection for the rest of my life. I signed.

"The White Christians make us get these signed. That way if you do screw up and get sick, they feel *they* have the right to decide what to do with you."

"What is that?"

"Maybe you shouldn't know," Lee said. "It's not very nice."

"Depends upon your circumstances," Gene said. "With gays, they just throw you back onto the local reserves. You'll get about ninety days of health maintenance treatment, and if nothing gets better, they could—"

Lee looked shaken. I had never seen him look like that. He blurted out: "They euthanize you!"

"Euthanize?" I asked him to explain.

"It happened," Lee said, "to Tom Bannister, a nice young guy I knew in P'town. We thought AIDS was conquered. Then he caught it in Peru, screw-ing around in a rain forest. He'd saved up some money. He'd always wanted to travel to really far-off places, where they don't read or write, and gays didn't have to go through the hell we've got here. But AIDS had already found that place and stayed. When he came back and got sick, our local council took care of him. But he had to be reported to the WCP. They put a 'resources' cap on him, and when he got worse, they eliminated him."

Gene put his arm on Lee's shoulder. "I'm sorry. It's one of the prices we have to pay for our lives now." He looked at me, then smiled. "Just be careful, Albert."

Lee did not mention Tom Bannister to me ever again. I wondered if he were buried somewhere secret on Cape Cod, maybe . . . in a cave. We left Chicago and for next the two days, Lee asked me questions. He told me he wanted to drive slowly "and get used" to me. Sometimes he put his arm around me or kept his hand on my knee, but he was always wary of problems 83 with federal cops as we went through obvious White Christian areas. You could tell these quickly. Mostly by the big neon crosses on the highway; but sometimes you saw smaller, crudely lettered signs that proclaimed things like, "Kikes, Queers, Niggers Keep Out." The signs chilled my blood. One of the worst was billboard size. On it was a cartoonish tableau of very skinny men being hanged and then sliced up. On it, in blood-red letters was, "GAYS WELCOME."

On the big national, super highlanes the cops could flash easily into your PT, since the lanes were radar controlled. This meant most highlane travelers no longer drove their transports, it was done automatically so they were pretty much in the hands of a transport control that spotted, guided, and put each vehicle under surveillance. To avoid the highlanes we drove on out-of-the-way single lanes. This way I got to see a lot of the country rolling ahead and then behind me. Much of it was devastated because of the abortive class war that had flared up in the early twenty hundreds. We passed through small towns that had never been rebuilt and drove out on one old road that came to a complete dead end. It just stopped in the middle of nothing, so we had to go back about sixty miles to find another route west.

The strangest things were the empty malls and burnt-out shopping centers. They were in rural, dead-end places. We drove up to one in the middle of the night and parked out of sight in the back—the two of us scrunched together in the backseat. It was eerie; quiet as the Moon; with its huge empty parking lot out front, cracked and overgrown with weeds. Early the next morning we discovered, as we drove off, the stomach-turning carcasses of dead animals piled up at one end of the lot: a raccoon, two dogs, a feral cat, and the repulsive, half-eaten skeleton of some creature that looked like a horse. Lee tried to guess how the animals ended up there. From poison left on an abandoned farm? Starvation? The empty malls haunted me. In the middle of all this technology, more than we could even imagine on Ki, we'd find these "primitive" places, like abandoned temples in a desert.

Finally, not that far outside of San Francisco—near this big lake Lee told me was called Tahoe—in the early evening when we were the only travelers on a small county road, a cop vehicle came out of nowhere. It looked like it'd just been waiting on the side of the road and spotted us. A recorded voice told us to pull over, then a burly officer in blue with White Christian insignia on his chest got out. His name tag said his name was Miller. His dissolver, a light high-impact plastic gun that shot plastic bullets, was still in his holster. He looked like he could draw it at any moment. "Thomas Lee Watson?"

Lee shook his head and took out his ID card. "What's this about, Officer? We weren't speeding, I know that. This old buggy really can't speed anyway."

"Speeding, Mr. Watson, ain't yer problem. *Kidnappin'*. I just ran yer license plate bar through my scanner, and it seems that a Miss Carol Parker, a concerned young woman in Massachusetts, wants you to be questioned for kidnappin' her six-year-old son, who goes by the name"—he halted for a moment, then took out a small printout—"Albert Lee."

"That's me," I said.

"What?"

"That's my name," I said. I took out my ID card and showed it to him.

Miller looked at my ID and then ran it through a miniscanner attached to his belt. He suddenly turned very red; his mouth tensed. "It says you two are mated."

"We are," Lee said.

"So what are you doin' with this woman's son?"

"He's my son," Lee said.

The cop got angry. "He's yer son, he's six years old, he's this guy—what the hell do you think I am? What did you two do with the real Albert Lee, kill him?"

"No, sir," Lee said, slowly. "This is Albert Lee, I once adopted him and later we mated. But as you can see, he is definitely *not* six years old. He's a young adult man. Miss Parker's a little crazy. I don't know what her problem is, but. . . ."

"I don't know what *yer* problem is, Mister!" the cop spat out. "I want both of you out of yer car. Slowly." Miller took out his dissolver and pointed it at us. "Do this careful, now. Do *nothing* that will make me want to use my weapon. Now," he glanced at our IDs again, "Mr. Watson . . . Mr. Lee, I want you both to lean against the side of your vehicle, facing away from me, and then I'm gonna call for reinforcements. We're gonna take you two in and you're gonna spend a little time as guests of the state of Nevada, which I might as well inform you, ain't happy with yer type of people. You're supposed to stay over there in goddamn San Francisco, not in our Jesus-blessed state." He suddenly crossed himself with the hand not holding his dissolver and then used that hand to take out a small pocket-card phone. He punched one button and we could hear two other law enforcement agents talking and then he told them where he was. He then pressed the pocket phone to his miniscanner and punched another button on his phone, sending our ID info someplace else.

I thought I was going to fall through the asphalt: I'd never get to San Francisco this way. We faced one side of Lee's Ford as Miller frisked us with his free hand. He started blathering on about AIDS and Jesus, and how

Jesus's own medicine was the way to cure AIDS, "not that vaccine you sick-os put into your veins once a year." I closed my eyes. This was becoming like the most awful dream I'd ever had; then Miller added: "And hear this, if we find out either of you's got AIDS, we ain't gonna give you ninety-days' free care on our taxpayers' bills!"

Lee turned carefully to him. "Officer, uh sir, I don't mean to interrupt you while you're quotin' Scripture, but I thought that bein' mated with IDs meant that we would have safe passage through this part of our dear country. It is against the law just to put us away because we're gay. We can explain this situation with Miss Parker—"

"You talkin' *old* rules, feller. The New Conservatives in Congress have given White Christian areas all rights to privacy *and* freedom of religious preference. That was passed this year. That means *our* religion must be respected in *our* localities. That's *our* private rights. You have no special rights here. Now we can jail you guys for being gay or being anything else, *if* you go against Christian law. This matin' business went on for a while, but that all's done and over with in this part of Nevada."

Lee suddenly became amazingly calm. I was not sure where his control came from, but it impressed me. "So I guess you're saying we're going to need a lawyer, sir?"

"Pronto!"

Lee lowered his head. "I understand now, Officer."

I looked over at Lee, then saw him turn his face as far as he could towards Miller. Then, from outside of my range of vision, I heard a faint *tinng* sound, like a shower of tiny glass beads against a sidewalk. I looked over at Lee; his eyes looked like they were going to bug out of his head. "Get in the car," he said to me.

"What do you mean—?"

"GET IN THE DAMN CAR!"

I turned around. Miller was dead on the side of the road. A hole was burned straight through the side of his brain. His eyes were still open, and his hand was still holding his dissolver. We heard a loud voice coming through his pocket phone.

"You okay, Miller?"

Lee and I looked at each other, then he grabbed the phone card from the dead man's belt. Talking through the side of his mouth, he put on the deepest voice he could: "Ever' things fine, guys. Turns out these two fellers are in the right. No problem here at *all*."

"Okay, we got your scan-out. You got any problems, you just let us know."

"You were wonderful," I said as Lee sped farther up the road that suddenly went from asphalt to dry, gullied-out dirt.

"Wonderful?"

"How'd you kill him? I was amazed—and you were so in control. God, Lee," I said, shaking, now out of control myself, "I really love you!"

"What are you talking about? Me? *Kill him?* I just wanted to cool things out, that's why I talked to him like that. One thing I've learned with WC cops is that you don't get them riled up. I mean, what could they do to us? I did *not* kidnap you. You're certainly *not* a kid, no matter what Carol tries to do to us. I'm sure Sandy's not behind this, she always liked me."

"Lee," I said, putting my hand on his thigh while he kept his hands riveted to the steering wheel, "you really think they were going to believe us? How about AIDS? They'd nail us for that!"

"I didn't kill him, Albert. I don't know what happened. I couldn't kill him just by talking to him!"

I looked ahead. There was another burned out shopping area, this time only a strip mall that looked as if it had been abandoned fairly recently. The road to it was washed out; only dried mud and gravel. "You think we bought any time with that trick with the cops?"

"I don't know," Lee answered. "I don't know what killed him. I don't even own a weapon." The Ford's brakes squeaked on the rough road as he slowed down. "Albert, we're going to have to get rid of this fucking car, and find new IDs, and only the Goddess Herself knows what else!"

CHAPTER 8

Lee drove the Ford around to the back of the mall, to what had been a short loading zone for the stores. The back looked cleaned up. No dead animals, no litter. "Why don't we try something?" I said. I told him to park, and we traded places. Once in the driver's seat, I realized I could drive without any problems. I don't know how I learned how to do it, but it must have been the same way I learned how to speak and read English. I drove the Ford about a half mile from the mall. There, as if I knew where it had been all along, I spotted a shallow washout. We dragged Miller's cold body out from the backseat, took his uniform off, and then covered him with weeds and brush. Farther down, in another washout, we hid the Ford and covered it with more brush. A bit further, we stuffed his uniform and dissolver into a dried mud hole. Then we walked back to the mall. "We're going to have to hold out here for the night," Lee said, "and then just hope that things remain sane until tomorrow."

"What'll we do then?"

He shook his head. "How far away is that planet you were telling me about?"

The back exit of one of the stores was conveniently open. This should have been a tip-off in itself, but we were tired and the promise of a dry, protected floor to stretch our sleeping bags out on, even without any food, was too good to miss. Luckily, I had a few chocolate bars and some stale corn chips that I had managed to accumulate along the way. The front was boarded up; it was as dark as a grave inside. The store had been a QuikMart, one of those shops that sold everything; the remains of sagging, filthy shelves, old fixtures, and counters bore witness to it. Stumbling about with the help of Lee's pocket minilight, we felt our way from the back, through a small, dirty storeroom, and then to the front service area. This was jumbled with litter, dirty clothes, torn mattresses, wads of toilet paper, and other stuff left from past squatters. Lee flashed his light up above: a peeling metal sign said, "Need Snacks? Relax!"

Lee sighed. "Yeh, that's what we need to do—relax!"

Then two heads popped up from behind the counter. "Hold it. Right there!"

They got out from behind the counter and flashed a larger beam on us. I could see that one of them—a dark, wiry, gristly looking guy with greasy, spiky hair that looked like it had been coifed by a machete—had his dissolver aimed right at us. "What the fuck are you two doin' here?"

Lee, again the model of calm, spoke up: "We lost our way and we needed . . . uh . . . a place to spend the night and we . . uh . . . . "

"You uh-what?" the guy with the dissolver demanded; his eyes narrowed.

"Had some problems with the police," Lee volunteered.

The other one, who was a bit heavier and blond, or bleached out by the sun and perhaps some drugstore product, started to smirk. "Tsk tsk tsk. Bad little boys, are we?" He had a foreign accent that somehow I realized was English.

"We killed a cop," Lee let out. "Or one was killed, right next to us. Highlane patrol." Suddenly Lee smirked. "Nasty type; he didn't like us at all!"

The blond one cracked up. "Sam, they're a couple of queers!" He went over and shook Lee's hand. Lee's face brightened automatically; he looked as if somehow he recognized the blond man, and yet he really didn't. "My name's Jake and this is Sam. You could say we're queers, too. It's just that *we* do women, instead of men!"

I smiled. Lee started to laugh, or at least try to; then as I looked over at Jake, I saw that each of his hands contained six fingers. I tried not to stare at them: who was I to call attention to "abnormalities"? But Jake must have seen that I had noticed them. He looked straight at me, and then raised both of his hands, palms outward. "A little something extra I've got!" he said grinning.

"It never hurts to have *one* extra," I said and broke into a grin. That must have broken the ice; a moment later we were all sitting down on the mattresses, our sleeping bags, and some fairly clean blankets that Jake and Sam had brought out. We had some beer that they offered, and I brought out my stale chips. Then Sam brought out a small cigarette filled with a drug that made me feel slightly dizzy when I tried to smoke it. "Guess you ain't never had Mary Jane," he drawled. "Try a little more of it. Lee, you want some?"

Lee said sure, and took a long, very deep drag on it.

"Lee, you are a professional!" Jake observed.

"Back in P'town, the guys have been smoking it for generations. Some men don't. They feel it gives us a bad name with the straights—I mean the White Christians—who believe all drugs except liquor and government-dis-

90

pensed anti-depressants are the work of the Devil."

"Yes," Jake agreed. "As the long as the government does it, it's the veritable work of Jesus." He pronounced Jesus's name with a very long "a," like *Jay-zus*. It made me laugh.

"Why are these people so hot on Jesus?" I asked, as Lee handed me back the cigarette.

"What planet you from, friend?" Sam asked. "They're hot on Jesus because he's the best friend of Brother Bob, who runs the whole goddamn show now, along with that old fart Quilter. Sometimes I think Quilter's not even alive. He's just mummified and they put a voice chip in his head to make him talk. 'The Fam-ilee is the bulwark of America.' That kind of bull. . . ."

"He's not very political," Lee said, trying to cut into the conversation before I actually told them that I *was* from another planet.

"That's okay," Sam said. "Neither was I, before I got fucked by the cops and the White Christians who decided that I was against God because I had sex with a sweet, young, fifteen-year-old gal in North Carolina I was crazy about and her parents decided to have me strung up for it. They went up to their local WC deacon and started yellin' 'Kid-rape! Drug crimes!'—and I wasn't even smokin' this shit then—'*Pornography*,' they found me readin' stuff they had worked to get out of the local public library. It was a mess. Then in Chapel Hill I met Jake here, who had come over to teach English—"

"To convert the natives," Jake said sweetly. "Teach the young buggers civilization; intolerable ideas like that."

"Anyway, we decided it was better bein' on the outs than on the ins. I guess Jake felt bein' English with twelve fingers made the outlaw life sort of nat'ral for him, right, Jake?" Jake nodded. "So here we are, on the run now, and you know what—I like it! But you say you guys killed a cop? That's *mean* trouble, boys."

I tried smoking a little more of the drug—which Jake informed me had been smoked for "millennia," and was called "weed"—and then I said, "The truth is Lee did not kill him. Neither did I."

"Then who did?" Sam asked. "It sure weren't us."

Lee looked at me quizzically. I shrugged my shoulders. "Maybe," I said, "it was someone who just happened to be following us."

"Wait a sec," Sam said. He got up with his dissolver and wove his way through the dark to the back exit. Then he went out and was gone for a while. Lee and I looked at each other, while Jake only smiled and lit up two more of the drug sticks. He passed one to us. I turned it down, but Lee smoked it; the other one Jake polished off by himself. Sam returned. "I found your friend," he announced.

"How the hell did you do that?" Lee asked.

"When you been messin' around for years, you get radar for these things. The buzzards were already chewin' him. One. And two, you gents didn't exac'ly bury him deep, tho' I liked that you stripped him. Harder to trace that way. I found a better hole for the naked shit, so you owe me one. You sure he's a cop?"

"Yes," I said. "We'll take you to his uniform tomorrow. It was my idea to strip him—"

"Excellent," Jake admitted. "And you got rid of his dissolver, too, I guess. Nice coupla' lads!"

"You have any idea who did it?" Lee asked. "I mean, we don't even have a dissolver, and it was a perfect shot that got him. Clean right through."

"Sure was. Looked like a cigarette burn through his noggin. But whoever it was," Sam said positively, "ain't around now." I asked him how he knew. "I fired some mean shots out there in the dark where you left him. Nothin' fired back. Whoever it was is either invisible, or long gone. Sometimes— believe it or not—I think it's just spirits. They want to help you, and they find you."

I smiled. "You guys seem like that," I said. "Thanks for helping us."

"Speaking of helping, you lads ready to fall out?" Jake asked. "You're welcome to sleep here. This place is as safe as the old Bank of England, or at least what used to be the Bank while there was still an England!"

Lee and I agreed to sleep there, and we spread out our sleeping bags, took off our clothes, and got into them. I wanted to squeeze into the same bag as Lee, but I could tell he felt self-conscious about it in front of these two strange gents who watched us and kept smiling at us and then at each other. I was dog tired. The small amount of the Mary Jane, or "weed" or whatever it was called, made me feel strangely sad and euphoric at the same time; as if I were missing something, yet getting closer to it. I rolled over on my stomach and nestled my head into my bare forearms. Then, as soon as I closed my eyes, I had this vision: I was back on Ki, talking again to my father. "Sometimes you must trust strangers," Enkidu said, "but watch out for signs."

"What signs, Father?"

"Signs of real love. Or signs of veiled hate."

"You mean both love and hate masquerading?" I asked.

"Yes. *Both.*"

"I will be careful," I said.

"Good. You will find the man who will be your mate without looking. He will know you as soon as you know him. And he will give you something, unbidden. He will hand it to you, and then you will know him."

Now I shuddered. I was sure he could see fear in my face.

"Fear not; all of your fathers are with you. They go back forever."

"Where?"

At first I could not hear him, then he said: "*The Tree.*"

"The Three?"

"Yeh, just the three of us," a groggy voice said. I woke up and realized that a man was on top of me: it was Sam. He was naked and shoving his hard dick into my ass, attempting to rape me. He had one hand over my mouth, and with the other, he had his dissolver pointed at the back of my head. He smiled. "We saw you got the devil's kiss on you. That was all we needed to see."

I managed to get his hand away from my mouth: I remembered what Enkidu had said about being given something, then I realized he could *not* have been talking about this—this *was* veiled hate; I was sure of it. "What kiss? What are you talking about?"

"The AIDS shot, man. We're up for a little man-pussy, Albert. Me and Jake, we're gonna get our dicks into you, you cute little shit." I looked over at Lee; he was totally conked out on the drug in the cigarettes. What could he do for me now? I knew I had to do something—I was not going to let them rape me, just use me this way.

"You guys are supposed to be straight," I said.

"Yeh," Sam said, smiling in the dark. "We don't suck dick, but we fuck ass."

With all of my strength I got Sam off my backside. He started wrestling with me, getting me into holds I easily got out of. I had been a good wrestler on Ki and all of it came back to me—even here in another time and body. Suddenly he slapped me with the rough heel of his palm. My head rang from the pain. He started giggling, like the whole thing was fun. He shoved his dissolver away, and began choking me with both hands. The dissolver spun around on the concrete floor until it was almost out of sight. He was bigger than I, but I managed to pull his hands from my throat, then I tripped him over twice. "Strong little bastard," he said, out of breath but still grinning. "I like a guy who puts up a fight, as long as it ain't too much of one."

"I can do more than that," I lied: "*I* was the one who killed that highlane cop. Lee doesn't know it—but *I* did it, and I can do it to you, anytime I want."

"I don't believe it," Jake said, who, quite stoned himself, was watching us with his clothes still on. "I contend the crazy little fuck's lying."

"Do you want to take that chance? I can follow you, make myself invisible." I looked straight at them. "Believe me, I can."

"Suppose you can, what of it?" Jake drawled. "Then I guess you can *invisibilize* your way into San Francisco? That's where you want to go, right? Let's see you do that. Sam *is* straight, but I'll take anything I can get, and at the moment, my young friend, I want you."

"I'll kill you if you try to fuck me."

"Naw, you'll like it, lad." Jake shucked his clothes off, and I could see that his stubby cock, which looked like it was covered by a leathery pigskin foreskin, was hard. I jumped up and tried to force Lee to wake up, but I couldn't budge him. Then Sam grabbed me and this time slammed me down to the hard floor. He pinned my hands behind my back, and pushed my face into the concrete. Then Jake jumped on me and using only spit to lubricate himself, entered me, riding me like I was something in a rodeo.

"You're going to like this, lad," he kept saying. His voice repeated like a clanging bell. He ran his hands down my chest, and started squeezing my cock and balls. Suddenly, out of pure fear, I got hard. "I told you you'd like it, boy. Wait till Sam gets his into you!"

He started pounding away at my ass; I could feel his heat rising up inside of me. His fingers—all twelve of them—started groping me, like a crazed centipede crawling under my chest and stomach, then further down. Sam laughed like a Martian.

"Jay-zus CHRIST!" Jake exclaimed. Suddenly, he stopped and pulled out of me. Sam's mouth dropped. "I think the shit's telling the truth. He's got three balls, *for real,* like my fingers! This is no crap to fuck around with. Three balls—you ever heard about three-balled dudes? They're scary, like witches."

"You're full of shit," Sam said. "And you probably got some of his on your dick. If you don't want him, I do."

He had his cock in his hand. It was big and hard, and he had this gooney "What'cha-think-I-should-do-with-this?" look. Sam pushed Jake aside and then jumped on top of me. He had picked his dissolver back up and was waving it at me like he was play-threatening, but there was no play in it. The threat was real. He stuck its barrel into my mouth. I went limp with fear; I realized I didn't have the strength left to resist. I felt sick, like I was going to throw up. I could taste the beer and chips in me coming back up as Sam laughed again and removed the barrel. He started fucking me like a jackhammer. I felt dead; I was sure I'd stopped breathing. But it was Sam who stopped; his body frozen, even with his piece still stuck in me. Like a lumpy bag full of sand, he fell off of me. Had he come already? I didn't think so.

Then his body rolled across the concrete, as blood oozed all over the dirty floor of the QuikMart.

A dissolver pellet had whistled straight through his head.

Lee was awake now. "What's going on?"

"You BASTARD!" Jake screamed. "What the hell have you done? We were just having a spot of fun. That's all." A long, awful scream came out of him, then he started sobbing uncontrollably. "I wanted to leave you alone. That third ball—I've heard of it. Chaps who have the third ball can do mean things; I guess Sam knows that now."

I wanted to wash myself. I felt filthy. I knew there was a bathroom in the back for employees. I went over to it. Water still trickled from the faucet, and I sat down on the crapper and then washed myself as much as I could. When I came back, Lee was holding Jake, who was still sobbing. Sam still had the dissolver in his hand; I took it away. I could tell he had not fired it. Frankly, I had no idea what had happened. I put my clothes back on, and took the dissolver into the back lot of the mall. I fired it several times into the darkness and then saw the discharge of one, like a small shred of sparks, glow back at me in the dark. I walked towards it. I figured that if twice some one had tried to protect me, they weren't going to shoot me.

Back by a small hill, next to a lone tree, was this man who looked like an ape but was wearing loose, human clothes. I started shaking all over when I saw him. "Nafshee? What are you doing here?"

"I come for you."

"Nafshee, I can't go back with you. I will *not* be your mate. You killed two men. Do you realize the danger you have put me in?"

"I would kill the Earth for you," he answered, and pulled me to him and made me kiss his lips. "Anvil is the regent of Ki. He waits for your return. Now he ruins the whole planet—with the help of my father Woosh. But I am helpless in my love for you."

"Then you must go back," I said. "I order you to. I will never mate with you. I would die first. I know it—even as Albert Lee, I know it."

He fell to his knees and held me by the legs. He tried to take my pants down as he caressed and kissed my legs. I brushed him away, while his face streamed with tears. "If I go away, Albert, you will be unprotected."

"Lee will help me," I said. "And so will Jake. Now Jake knows that I am his superior."

"Then I will do as you say, and only hope that my love will keep you until you return. But Lord Albert, I swear: I will kill any mate of yours once you return."

I looked at him. I felt sorry for Nafshee, but I could not mate with an ape:

it would be a mistake, endangering the balance of life on Ki. I sank to my knees and lowered my face to his. "Nafshee, to kill my mate will do you no good. I will share myself with you, if only out of love for my mate. I will even allow you sex with me, but you will *never* father a son with me and I will *never* mate with you."

"Share—do you promise, Lord Albert?"

"Yes."

He smiled through a glaze of tears in his eyes. "Then the Goddess has answered my prayers. I will be content without your son. I will hold you to your promise, Lord Albert." He took my hand and drizzled kisses on it. "I will leave you and wait for your return."

He was gone. The presence I had been speaking with was out of my sight. But the dissolver he had used to kill Miller and Sam was left at my feet. I picked it up. Now we had two weapons, although I loathed handling either of them. What a strange story, I thought, that Nafshee had done so much for me, risking his own life, I was sure, by leaving Ki. His heavy, dumb, animal intensity moved me to silence. I went back into the dark, empty QuikMart and saw Lee speaking with Jake.

"I told him the story—your story, Albert."

"Wow! Blows me away," the Englishman said. "Makes me want to get the fuck away from you two."

"Can you get us into San Francisco?" I asked.

"Yes, I can do that. We have a PT in a garage about a mile away from here. The garage man hides it for us. He's one of us—another queer."

"Don't tell me he only does women, too," Lee said.

"No, he's your type. He was born around here, and he won't leave. The underground people in this part of Nevada know each other. Maybe all underground people know each other: it's part of our lives. What do you think we should do with poor Sam?"

"Bury him tomorrow," I said.

Jake looked at me. "So you weren't lying. But how did you kill Sam while he was screwing you?"

"I didn't do it."

"Who did?" Lee asked.

"Another Kivian. He's been following me."

Lee smiled. "So you *are* the Lord of Ki?"

"'Fraid so," I said bashfully.

"Who was following you?" Lee asked. "Not some jealous boyfriend from
outer space?"

I swallowed hard. This was closer to the truth than I wanted to come. "No," I said. "Just a very sad spirit who's now back on my planet. Where he belongs."

We buried Sam very early the next morning, not far from the back of the deserted strip mall. Jake said some words over him about God taking care of him in an old style of English that I could barely understand. Then we walked over to the garage where Jake, whose last name he told us was Armstrong, had his transport. Lowry, the bearish, heavyset garage man, was very sweet. He greeted Jake warmly and asked where Sam was. Jake told him that Sam had been killed. "White Christians?" Lowry asked. Jake nodded solemnly. The car had been fitted out with new bar strips on the plates that could get us onto the main highlanes. If we wanted, radar could drive us straight through to San Francisco, but Lee did not trust that. Jake gave Lowry a stack of "Mary Jane" cigarettes and he thanked him, and then the three of us drove off to Northern California.

CHAPTER 9

In San Francisco, we again got new IDs. This one said that my name was Lee Marks and Lee's new name was Mark Allman. Lee picked the names out himself (I had wanted the name Lee Albert, but Lee thought it was too obvious, too easy to trace back to my real name, or at least what was supposed to be my real name); he liked the idea that I would bear his name no matter what. He glowed with his new name, first because it reminded him of a rock singer from the mid-old century whose sounds were still circulating and also because he thought Mark Allman sounded like "Mark All-Man." The names became instant fantasies for both of us, and Lee began to take on his "Mark Allman" persona: bigger, butcher, and bolder than the old Lee Watson who seemed more of a pussycat to me. Despite having these names on our "gay IDs," we still called each other Lee and Albert, and when anyone read my name off my ID I had to look around for a second, expecting Lee Marks to come through the door.

Of course he was I, just as I was Albert Lee and simply Albert, son of Enkidu and Greeland, someplace else. San Francisco was truly amazing. It was almost completely gay, or "queer," which I learned was an old-century term for people outside the New Conservative-WCP agenda. As Jake drove us in over a long bridge, I thought my heart was going to skip a beat: the city was wrapped in hills and clouds and high glass turrets; it was pure fairy tale. "Just like Oz, ain't it?" Jake drawled in his funny English accent. Lee turned to me and said that Jake reminded him of Vivien Leigh in "Gone With The Wind." (*"Who?"* I asked. "An old English movie star who played Southern ladies," Lee answered. I tried to figure out what that sounded like as we drove in.)

At the habitation, or dormo, where we stayed in an area called Folsom, an old geezer who managed the floor said that in his youth, back in the old century, the queers were sometimes called "hippies" and sometimes "beatniks." That seemed like a funny word, like they went around beating on people. I asked him about that and he said it was because their *attitude* was beat up. "They weren't so uptight—hard—like now. Now we have a couple of gay reserve areas, but mostly people act like they've got barbed wire around their necks: they're always in some kind of pain."

Now that Jake had driven us into the city, he disappeared. We saw him once and while, sometimes at a bar we all went to on New Castro street, the principal gay avenue after the old one had been burned to the ground during the old civil problems. New Castro was not near the old Castro, but in the area that had once been called the Mission. This had become the center of the gay reserve government of San Francisco. The bar was called Figass, which everybody laughed at since it upset the occasional WCs who got lost and wandered in. I was in there once and a man called the place "Fig-*ahse*" and was told, "No, man, it's just Fig-ass." I had no idea why it was called Figass, but homo bars in New Castro had very up front sexual names, like Knob Head, Sweet Balls, and Cocksucker Heaven, or just C.H., which was a loud popular one. Anyway, we met Jake in Figass occasionally, usually with a queer woman with him, one of those women who dressed and acted like gay men or tough boys. "Ain't she a dish?" Jake asked, and one of his dates replied, "No, Jake, I'm a dick."

The truth we learned was that Jake was right on the edge, dealing drugs again, sometimes running them right through WC territory, down into Southern California, and then back up again. One whole continuous region—including much of what once had been Los Angeles and San Diego and then down into the Mexican border towns—had been renamed *Los Lingos*. Los Lingos was a Spanglish fiefdom, where the Mexican and American cultures mingled and melted and real borders meant nothing. It had become, to the embarrassment of the WCP, all business-as-usual: anything could go on, and only the very stupid—or very powerful—asked questions. The WCP had little effect there. The Mexicans were still too Catholic and anti-American to swallow the whole WCP line, which got devoutly anti-Catholic in many red-neck areas: this meant that Jake could deal his "items" as he called them fairly freely. But I still wondered when he was going to run out of luck. "You should come down to Los Lingos," he said one night to us. Why? I asked. "Money's easy to come by, gents. San Francisco's easy about everything except the almighty American dollar, if you haven't noticed."

I had.

"And guys like you are no sweat there. I ain't saying the Mexes like you; they still have *poccito macho*. But hating queers is pure gringo, so they give us left-handed types of various persuasions a wider seat."

I think that was all we needed to hear. The next day we set out with Jake for Los Lingos. Lee and I were both broke, down to our last two hundred dollars, which was sure to last us only a few more days. Lee never really trusted Jake, but he was sure that I could get him out of anything. I think he had already forgotten that *I* had gotten him into *everything*. I could tell that he was in love with me: I knew it. Although I had not really had that much experience, certainly Earth experience, with love, there's a feeling you have when someone is nuts about you—it's that every expenditure of energy for you on their part takes nothing, and Lee was like that. I loved him, too, dearly, ravenously, and we were still having near-earthquake sex every night—he had long swept past the idea that I had once been his son and he'd seen me in diapers and had bathed me and put me to bed—and now we had this bond between us that seemed stone solid. Still I knew that I could not mate with him and that my mate was waiting somewhere else. But how far away, I had no idea.

"What we're going to do in Los Lingos," Jake explained at the controls of his new transport, a really impressive Jaguar in a dark, rich, money-green color that just came out of thin air, or, as Jake said, he'd "borrowed" it for this trip, "is pick up some items about forty miles south of San Diego, in a place called Lingo Santos. Its a snazzy place full of successful White Christian types, the kind who think they're on a first name basis with *Jay-zus*—they winter there—and then there are the South Americans who come to do business with them . . . if you get my drift." He looked over at me. He could see the uncertainty in my eyes. He waved one of his six-fingered hands. "Look, it's safe, lads. That's why we're driving this Jag. The Lingo Santos people are used to transport like this. It they weren't, we wouldn't be driving it."

"So you're saying it's stolen?" Lee asked.

"Naw, luv, 'borrowed,' with new bar plates. It's been registered in my name over in New Castro. The Mexicans you see believe that dicksuckers are more trustworthy than gringo White Christians. It's like we're not really white people."

"But you're not a dicksucker," Lee pointed out.

"Honorary, my love. Any true Englishman is an honorary dicksucker. Ask any goddamn, red-blooded American snatch-chaser. Now, when we get down there, I want you guys to act the part, too. So I also 'borrowed' some new clothes for you as well."

Getting down the main highlane from San Francisco was a cinch. To avoid any problems, Jake did it on radar the whole way, until we came to the cutoff for Lingo Santos. This meant that the Highlane Patrol knew the Jag was on the road and who was driving it as long as they were directing it from their control tower. At the exit, Jake switched to manual. We found a "natural rest area" a few miles down right on the beach, and there we changed into the clothes Jake fished out of the back. They were really splendid outfits, a white, silk-and-linen two-piece suit for me, with leather shoulder details and a zippered sleeveless tee underneath; for Lee a white linen "planters suit," very old century and classy as hell, the sort of outfit a man who had no problems with money would wear.

We got back into the car and a few miles down the road, Jake announced: "We're driving into this place." It was a vast, country club type compound with circular drives leading up to a guard house gate. A dark Hispanic man in full armored uniform, carrying a dissolver with a retractable telescope viewer in a side holster, came out. "Hello, distinguished guests. How can we be of service to you at Lingo Santos?"

"I'm Mr. Beauchamps," Jake said. "We have reservations at the Main House Inn under my name."

"One moment, sir." He took out a small screen and clicked it until he got to reservations. I heard several clicks in response to his clicks. "Definitely, sir. Please be on your way and remember we are always at your service here at Lingo Santos."

"Well, that was easy as a good crap after prune juice," Lee said.

"Sure was," Jake agreed. "All you need in this world is a good car and the right words. This was all set up by my friends over here. Wait till you see this place, as the Jews say, you will *plotz.*"

Whatever *plotz* meant, Jake was right. Never in any world had I seen anything like Lingo Santos, a series of tall white buildings surrounded by polished dark marble stairs, white terraces and pink granite swimming pools, all attended by herds of employees who did everything for you. We got out of the Jag; a valet handed Jake a ticket and then got in to park it. Our bags were taken from us as we entered the lobby under a soaring ten-story atrium. The lobby overflowed with vast tubs of tropical flowers, cages of noisy, brilliantly-colored jungle birds, and more subdued flocks of uncaged wealthy tourists, in expensive "cruise" outfits.

Jake stopped at the desk and a dark young man in some version of a "native" officer's uniform told us to come this way. "Your first time at Lingo Santos?"

I did not say a word, but just looked around trying not to be awestruck. "Naw, mate," Jake said. "Been here before. Beauchamps' my name. And yours?"

"Miguel. If there's anything I can do for you—anything at all—ask for me."

Our suite was in another, smaller building, overlooking a huge, tropical inlet, edged with palms, tennis courts, and more swimming pools. Jake tipped Miguel. Our bags were already in the suite, which had two bedrooms and a sleeping alcove. There was a balcony that overlooked everything, and in the distance yachts and sport boats were moored at a swank marina. After coming back in from the balcony, I noticed a series of small grilled screens throughout the suite. "Back on the balcony, mates," Jake said. "The little screens can see everything. That's why I like staying here. The security is tops. The cops never come in here. If we tried to do any of this business back in the town, you'd have crooked Los Lingos cops all over you. A lot of the types staying here are shadier than I am, let me tell you. A good tip though—don't ever say anything back in the suite you *wouldn't* want your ol' Mum to hear ."

"How about sex?" Lee asked.

"Doesn't faze 'em. They don't care about gay sex, just about gay money." Jake smiled. "You have some very high level White Christian individuals who stay here, too. Even Brother Bob, I've been told, stays here whenever he can."

It was getting dark and very romantic out on the balcony. I took Lee's hand in mine. "So why are we here?" I asked.

"Mr. Beauchamps is going to be staying in his room a lot. Frankly I'm much too known in the town. So tomorrow, you two chaps are going to a location in Lingo Santos proper to pick up some items for me. And then the next day, very early on, I'll have a couple of more items for you. Simple as that. Now, isn't this a nice place to cool out for a few days?"

It seemed too nice. "How are we going to do this?" I asked.

"Simple as good rum, luv. You'll take the Jag, go into town and look like you're shopping for native bargains. Over breakfast I'll tell you exactly what to do and how to do it."

"So what's the risk?" Lee asked.

"Nothing, luvs. Just that at the end, you'll make ten thousand new dollars. That should keep you two happy in San Francisco for a while. Now, I wonder what Miguel charges for 'anything at all'? Usually the going rate for that is about thirty *en dees.*"

"En dees?" I asked.

"Luv, don't you two know anything? New bucks. You can use them anywhere from San Francisco down into Peru. Wave a few of them here at anyone and they get very excited. Then, when you get back up North, you can trade 'em in for regular American currency." He handed me a packet containing twenty ten-dollar bills of them. One side was engraved in English, the other in Spanish. They were very new and their corner holograms showing dollar amounts sparkled. Jake smiled. "Now, that should do you two for a little while."

There were two baths in the suite and Lee and I cleaned up in one and

Jake took the other. I had never been so lavishly cared for—and certainly never with such a presentment that someone was or could be watching at any moment. It was unsettling. The little grills were even in the bathroom, even over the toilet. Jake told us that if that offended us, just cover the grill with a towel. The staff was used to it, and would not take offense—at least in the john. By the telecom center was a list of the resort's extensions and a suggestion that we punch a button that put an "Introduction to Lingo Santos Resort" on the telecom screen. We did. A very well made-up lady told us that the grills were called "security eyes"; we were warned that it was against the law to cover them up in any place except the bathroom. "They are here for your protection in case of fire, theft, or accident. Please feel secure in knowing that you are protected at all times by your gracious staff." I punched the button again and the same message was presented in Spanish, French, Polish, German, Chinese, Arabic, and Japanese.

The resort had seven restaurants and we went out to dinner in an "authentic French bistro" with prices that seemed almost fictional to me. I thought the food seemed plastic and tasteless, not at all what I thought French food would be like. Jake had a lot of wine and then "Mr. Beauchamps" just signed for it at the end of the meal. Jake could barely talk by now. He was tired he said, and excused himself and went back to the suite. Lee and I decided to take a walk through the resort. Although the place attracted, as Jake pointed out, a plethora of earnest White Christians, it also had a glitzy gambling casino and several loud bars worked by scantily clad hostesses. We walked through the casino, which at the moment seemed to be full of Arabs and Japanese holding on to the slot and blackjack machines for dear life. Then we walked back into the main lobby. An extremely earnest young man grabbed us. "Are you here for late chapel?"

I had no idea what he was talking about, but we could not get away from him, and frankly, he had a kind of sweetness to him after the bald cynicism of Lingo Santos. We followed him down the hallways to a room marked Chapel. He opened the door. Several hundred people were sitting on hard folding chairs, watching a huge telecom monitor. "I want you to know," the plump man with a smooth smiling face promised, "that I am with you, like the Lord Jesus, *wherever* you go. If you go into the Land of Sin I am with you. If you go into the Land of Death, I am there, too. Brother Bob Dobson is always here for you, taking care of you in your every need. Friends, husbands, wives—we know they can scoot out on us, right?" The whole room nodded its head. I looked over at Lee, and he pretended to keep the same glazed face that we saw all over the room. "Can we get out of here?" I whispered to him. He shook his head. "Just stay a second," he whispered without looking at me. "BUT NOT I," Brother Bob proclaimed. "I will always be here with you. Even Rich Quilter, a friend of the Lord, knows that I will always be here for you."

"That's true," another voice from the monitor said. The camera brought in another face, that looked very much like Brother Bob's, except that it was quite wrinkled and its eyes had no sparkle in them. Even the amount of makeup on the face could not hide the dullness in those eyes. "Brother Bob, you are an inspiration to all of our nation. Your steadfastness on behalf of White Christian principles is unwavering."

"Thank you, Mr. President. Now, will you join us, Brother Quilter, in our White Christian Pledge of Allegiance?"

The whole room got up. The image on the monitor was a huge American flag, rippling in the breeze. It was brought in and out of focus and was replaced with pictures of Brother Bob's face and then the President's. I thought I was going to be sick. I wanted to stay seated, but Lee grabbed my hand and forced me to stand as well. It all seemed so strange—here we were in this resort where everything could be bought, including the staff—and they were saying this speech that began, "I pledge allegiance to the principles of America and Christianity, to the sanctity of the family, to the honor and separation of the sexes, to the true goodness inside of all Americans, and to the love of Jesus in our hearts."

After the Pledge, the monitor was turned off. A young woman in a prim white dress that covered her neck said, "Please go back to your rooms and to your families. And be sure to have a *good* time while you're here!"

The young man who had led us in took our hands and asked us if we loved Jesus. Lee nodded his head, and I did not say a thing. The room emptied out. I could see the same people going back into the lobby area and then on to some of the bars and into the casino. We managed to get away from the young man who told us his name was Jesse—he'd be there for us if we needed him "for spiritual guidance"—and we found a small bar off to itself. It had a nice view of the inlet and marina and it was dark with some privacy. "What'll you two guys have?" a bartender said. I could tell just the way he smiled at us, without that glazed, "earnest" look, that he took everything here with the right attitude. He had very dark, almost black hair, but pale, hardly tanned, clear skin. He looked wonderfully fresh and appealing; I could tell that his face freckled easily. We ordered two tequila melons and told him we'd just been to Chapel. He grinned. "You don't seem the type." I told him flat out we were not. There was no one else in the bar, so he had a drink with us. Then he refused to ring up our drinks. "The White Christians are really

105

funny here. They get it on with Brother Bob in the Chapel room and then they get it on with anyone they can outside. The *real* rich who come here, especially the foreigners, think they're a gas; but the White Christians need a little change themselves from so much *goodness*, so they come here on vacation. They can even get the place as a package deal, so we book blocks of rooms for them." He asked us our names and where we were from. Lee told him our names—the new ones—then suddenly I spilt out my real one. "I'm called Albert," I said.

He smiled at me. "Nice name. I'm called Vince, but I'm really Vincent: as in Vincent 'Van Gogh' Lanier. My mother was nuts about Van Gogh—she loved outsiders and underdogs; maybe because she was French Canadian. But she ended up working in a restaurant down on the Gulf coast in Louisiana, where she raised me. I didn't know much about my dad. He's Hispanic—Mexican—but I think there were Germans somewhere in his background." He smiled at us and poured us some more of the tequila melons. "Strange story," he said, slowly shaking his head. "It kind of makes me know what it feels like to be a stranger anyplace."

When he said that I realized something: that his eyes, amazingly green even in the dark light of the bar, were looking directly at me as he leaned across the bar. And I also realized that I wanted him so badly . . . that my hands had started to shake. I'd never felt like that about another person. I knocked over the tequila melon he'd just poured for me. The drink got to his white shirt. It was sopping. Suddenly I looked over at Lee. He was gone.

"Where'd your friend go?"

I told him I didn't know; but I did. Lee had never seen me attracted to anyone. "Maybe I should go," I said.

"Wait a second," Vincent said; I decided that I was going to call him Vincent, not Vince. His hand went out towards mine. "God," he said. "It feels like you're trembling, too"—his hand was also shaking. "Let me hold your hand," he asked. We looked at each other. The longest, most intense, tiny moment passed. I relaxed, but neither of us moved away. Then he pulled my face towards him and with the dark bar between us, before I could *not* believe what was going on, he kissed me. "Usually, I don't talk to people about myself," he whispered. "I still feel ashamed that my parents weren't married."

I smiled. I had no idea if that was really bad. "Neither were mine," I said. Which was true: they weren't married on either planet. He still had my hand, when suddenly people came into the bar. He let go and leaned over. "I want to find someone to close up for me," he said. "Maybe change my shirt; would you walk with me outside? There's a place by the marina where I can get a sport boat."

I told him alright. My heart was really beating. None of this made any sense. Here I was putting myself in danger on every level: but I simply couldn't help what was happening to me. He grabbed another bartender from a small service bar across the hall and told him he had to leave. I met him a moment later in front of the back bar where we'd met. I asked him if wanted to change shirts and he said no. We left the resort and walked down to the inlet, alone and in the dark. He took his shirt off and then pulled me to him. We walked down to the marina holding each other without any fear. "You're the first person I've met in a long time that I'm not scared of," he said. "It's funny how that can happen anyplace. Even here, where most of the crowd thinks it's such hot crap!"

We found a sport boat tied up in an area called "Reserved for Security." He explained that one of his friends was a guard, and he knew the combination to get into the boat. We got into the boat and he punched some buttons on the lock. This unlocked the motor and he drove it out, farther off from Lingo Santos resort until we were completely by ourselves on another cove in the inlet. There was a silvery, three-quarter moon and zillions of stars out. "It's really beautiful here," he said. "Why don't we take our clothes off and swim?"

We did, jumping off the boat naked, me kissing him until I thought my mouth would dissolve into his. My brain went blank as he held my cock in his hand, and then went down into the water and started sucking it. He came back up, smiling. "I thought," he said, gluing his face to mine, "I've seen everything, but you are really full of surprises." I asked him what he meant. "You know. . . ." I did; I knew exactly. "*Three* balls," he said. "No wonder you attract me so much."

We got back onto the boat and started making love in a way that made me feel as if I'd never done it before, which was true that I had not, except with Lee. Suddenly he stopped. His beautiful hands became nervous again, as if he were cold. He had a thin gold chain around his bare neck; on it was a small pendant that glowed softly. He managed to unclasped it. "I want you to have this," he said. I took it in my hand and asked him what it was. "I picked it up in a village market in Mexico. A funny old man, dressed in a kind of drag—with a skirt—like a queer magician, was selling old blankets and trinkets. He told me it's an ancient, pre-Aztec symbol. The Church had tried to blot it out for years. They don't like 'hombre love,' he told me, then he whispered: 'For your *bueno amigo.*'"

I took it over to the dials of the sport boat control. On the pendant were two snakes entwined around each other, outlining the shape of an upturned 107 triangle. At the bottom of the triangle were the two snakes' heads, each holding the tail of the other in its mouth. In the center of the triangle were three small balls, outlined in fine lines as if they were spinning continuously. He came up behind me and put his still wet arms around me. "You must know something," I said.

"I do. It's like I've known you before, but I'm not sure how."

"Thank you for giving me this," I said. A moment later, we were on the deck of the boat, making hot flagrant love again, and this time, when he took my cock into his mouth, I poured out the full force of the seed from my third Egg. I could feel it rumbling all the way up from the depths of the Egg into him. I knew that this force came all the way from space: from Ki. In the moonlight, I could see it illuminate his whole body as he ingested it and it, in its powerful, uncontrollable way, ingested him. I'd never given it to Lee; I had never shared seed with him. But now it was Vincent's and he was mine and in doing so I was thrust back to Ki: drifting slowly once more through the time/space bubble itself. There my father Enkidu awoke from the dead to tell me what I knew inside: that I had found *him* without looking and he had given me something without asking. "*Now you must bring him back.* But beware, my son. Every form of night is around you, except death, the Real darkness: which is filled with Light."

"I've come from a very long way," I told Vincent as I held him in my arms. "I want to bring you back with me."

"You have to," he answered. "Now I *know*: you have to do that."

We drove the boat back to the marina. I felt stunned into silence. One of those moments when you feel that you know every answer, even to the questions you haven't got around to asking yourself. At the marina, Vincent locked the boat up again using the lock code and we walked back on the dock until we got to the wharf. I knew that I had to leave Lee: it was tearing me up inside. But the immediate question was how could I do it, and how could I bring Vincent back with me to face the terrors of the planet Ki?

He asked me where I was going and I told him that I would have to go back to Lee—I would have to tell him what had happened. Vincent looked displeased. "I guess I will have to fight for you," he said, trying to smile. I tried to smile, too, but felt at the moment too frightened to do it. I left him at the end of the marina wharf, after I had found out where he stayed in the resort's employee compound. I gave him our suite number and walked towards it.

After I had walked only a few yards with the crescent moon still bright above me, I saw two figures ahead of me. They were dressed in black from head to toe, which was unusual at Lingo Santos where everyone seemed to be dressed in white. What an odd, terrifying omen they seemed. They were moving slowly towards me. My first feeling was to run away as fast as I could, even though I would have to pass them to get to our suite in the resort. I had to steel myself and face them. My heart pounded terribly; I began to stare uncontrollably at them. Finally, when I got close enough to see their features I realized that one of them was an old woman, her face wrinkled and careworn. It had once been a beautiful face, but now it was a face full of character, like a once-splendid palace that had seen wars and defeats. She looked at me and smiled. Her eyes were full of tears. With her was a younger woman, who by her face I could see was her daughter. Although she herself was no longer young, she had a quality of the most immense innocence; it showed through her like the movement of water through crystal. I looked at her for a while as the three of us stood transfixed in the night, and it became obvious that I had known her younger face all of my life.

She was the Goddess Laura.

CHAPTER 10

"You look *very* familiar," the older woman said. "How is it possible that we know you?"

"My name is Albert," I replied, and turned to the younger woman. "Are you Laura?"

"Yes, how did you know?"

"Your father was killed before you were born, right?"

"My name is Jennifer Cohen Lawrence," her mother said. "But how would you know these things?"

"Maybe he does know us," Laura said. "He seems so familiar. I can see a resemblance between him and myself. It's there. I know it."

Suddenly Jennifer spoke up: "I didn't want to come here, but my daughter made me do it. I said, 'Why should we go to this silly resort?' and now suddenly you pop up. It's not possible that you knew my husband, you're too young; yet I feel that—"

"You're my brother, aren't you?" Laura asked.

I smiled. "Only in the strangest way. My father had been your father . . . but in another life."

"That's not possible," Jennifer said. "You're so young." She started walking. "This is all too strange for me!"

"Mother," Laura said. "Nothing is so strange. Let's sit."

We sat down on a bench on a boardwalk overlooking the marina. The night seemed suddenly almost new again, and I felt refreshed—not tired at all. "You have to believe in a life beyond death," I said. Laura smiled at me, but her mother looked away, staring into the water. "I know that sounds crazy, that suddenly we should meet here; but we've all been drawn to each other. My father spoke to me about the two of you, about you, Jennifer, and Laura, his own daughter—from a different life."

Jennifer turned to me. "Where is he now?"

"He's dead. He died only a few years ago."

"Where?" the old woman asked.

"Miles and miles away. Millions, really."

Suddenly Jennifer looked at me directly. "I believed this would happen. 111

That's why I never married again. I believed that Nick would come back to me in some form."

Laura bolted up from the bench. "Imagine! The brother that I never knew—and he's so young!" She grabbed me and held me to her. "I don't want to lose you. Where are you staying? How can we find you?"

I told her I wasn't sure: I was staying in a suite in the resort, but there was no telling where I would be in a week. Jennifer took out a small pen from her purse and scribbled something on a slip of paper. "Take this," she said. "It's where we live in an old section of Los Lingos called Venice. It's very run down, but charming. You can always find us there."

I took the paper and put it into my pocket. Then they both approached me and kissed me and then left me, simply disappearing into the misty distance of the lights of the resort.

Using my passcard, I got into the suite. Jake's room was closed, although there was evidence of drinking and some clothes tossed all over the sitting room. I snuck into the other bedroom, and quietly stripped, brushed my teeth in the bath, and got into bed. I could tell that Lee was only pretending to be asleep. "You're not asleep?" "No." "I guess you want to know what's happened to me?" "No." "I can just tell you that nothing like this has ever happened to me before."

Before he could say no again, he reached out and found the chain around my neck. "What's this?"

"A pendant. Two snakes traveling around three balls."

"Sounds like the story of my life. You're going off with that bartender, aren't you?"

I told him I didn't know, but I'm sure he could see the lie going right through me. Even though he was not from Ki, he could spot what a liar I was: it was true; we could not lie.

Suddenly he grabbed me and kissed me, opening my mouth with his. "I knew this was going to happen: there's nothing I can do about it. My job was simply to bring you here."

He stopped kissing me, and held me in his large, redhaired arms and fell asleep. It happened very fast, as if everything had simply settled in his mind. A short while later, I nodded out, just fell into complete darkness, that lucky immersion into oblivion that is only restful. Nothing came. No visions. No trip back to Ki. And I did not wake up again until I heard footsteps coming from Jake's room into the sitting room. Then I heard a voice that I knew was Miguel's say, "Gracias, Jake. It has been a pleasure. Next time you need *any-*

thing, just ask."

"'Night, Miguel," Jake said, sleepily, and the door to the suite was shut.

At ten o' clock on the balcony, Jake greeted us. "'Morning, lads!" We had both managed to crawl out of bed and throw on some thick terry guest robes. Jake was already showered and presentable, drinking coffee outside. It was a beautiful morning with the sun sparkling on the water in the cove ahead of us. Lee did not look so sparkling, and I have to admit that the evening had finally gotten to me. In a normal world, I could have used another four hours sleep! But that was not going to happen. We sat down and thoughtfully Jake poured us some coffee.

"This is the plan," Jake whispered cheerily. "All you have to do, my little sweethearts, is get into the nice Jag and head into Lingo Santos proper, about five miles from here: you can't miss it. There's a posh hotel in the center of town. It's a totally Anglo establishment, called the Victoria and it's got a very foofy bar called Hampton Court. One of those places where traveling English queens hang out. At night the *clee-ontel* is très queer, but during the day it's usually old ladies and their tired husbands on holiday. Anyway, there will be a very well-dressed man who goes by the name of Austin waiting for you. Austin is Latin and very Pan-American. He goes back and forth a lot between the States and the S.A. countries. He is very professional; rest assured. He will have a tourist shopping bag at his table. It's from one of those shops the rich WCP people down here love. He's expecting you and will nod when you come in. In fact, you're going to be carrying an identical bag. So you'll joke and have something in common. He'll ask you to join him and he will even know your names. You will talk a bit and drink a very English Bloody Mary, without any ice, and then you will leave with his bag instead of yours. Simple as that."

"So where's this bag?" Lee asked.

Jake smiled mysteriously. "You'll get it just before you leave. I guess you two should get cleaned up." He started drumming his six-fingered hands together. "I must say, you both look like you've been whoring through Hell."

"Only one of us," Lee frowned.

"Family squabble?"

"No," I said. "No squabble. But I noticed your amazing hands weren't exactly staying to themselves last night."

"What can I say? The level of service here is commendable." He paused, and then added, matter-of-factly, "Now, gents, after you do the first pickup, there's a second."

"You never mentioned a second pickup on the first day," Lee scowled.

113

"In for a penny, in for a pound, luvs. Why not get as much work done as we can while we're here? It will shorten the load tomorrow, anyway. The second pickup will be in a slightly less posh setting: there's a flower shop called 'Keith's' three blocks from the Victoria. You'll go in there and see Keith. Just tell him you're there to pick up Mr. Beauchamps's flowers. Keith does these wonderful arrangements, and he always packs them beautifully. So there will be two lovely baskets for you. Don't be surprised if they weigh a little more than you think. But I want to warn you: only one of you should go into the shop. The other should stay in the car with Austin's bag. A little trick in this trade: *never leave your shopping bags unattended.* Ever. And your car, too. Remember that."

I let Lee shower first, and got on the phone on the terrace and called Vincent's room. I knew that everything we said would be intercepted, but I felt better being outside talking to him. "Glad to hear from you," he said warmly. Obviously he knew that someone could hear us as well. I told him that I would see him that evening. "No matter what." He told me that if he wasn't down at the bar, he would be at the marina, waiting.

After Lee got out of the bath, I got in. After using the toilet for some necessary 'morning functions,' I got into the shower, without taking off the pendant Vincent had given me. I did not want to let go of it for a second. I felt such tremendous tenderness towards him that I felt for a moment literally weak. I could not account for this feeling, but I knew that I had never felt it on Ki. As I lathered up with the luxurious sandalwood guest soap, I had a fantasy of being back on my planet with him—I being only Albert again, and Vincent being the mate that I had come to Earth for—that I had never found as long as Enkidu was alive. I started getting hard just thinking about him, about the two of us roaming the forests of Ki, naked and free, and I had to hold myself back from touching myself since I knew that I wanted to save myself for Vincent that night.

After we had dressed, both of us looking like respectable Nord Americano tourists, Jake gave us the shopping bag. It was a heavy white plastic carry-sack, splashed with names like Gucci, Chanel, Saks, and various perfume and designer names. Jake had already filled it with a few bottles of colored water, just in case we were stopped anywhere. "Take this with you, but be a bit careful with it," Jake warned, handing Lee a small dissolver. "It's a little mini. You shouldn't need it. But better safe than sorry, right lads?" Lee stuck it inside his planter jacket, where it made no bulge at all.

Nothing about the little town of Lingo Santos seemed to be what it really was, except "tourist tacky." Lee told me that it was all "genuine bullshit.

Either 'Old Me-hee-co' or 'Old California'," he said, bitterly, "with nothing of either." There were streets of overpriced little shops run by bored Anglo women in expensive outfits, followed by blocks of cheap plazas, side malls, and fast-food-pizza haciendas.

Under all of this I spotted the furtive shadow of the Mexicans, threadbare gringos, and Hispanic natives who either labored in town or were waiting for something to land their way. Ragged and desperate, they made me feel that it would be easy to wander off from one of the little squares, follow any number of winding back streets, and never come back alive. A constant ripple of eyes was on us as we walked through the plazas, before going into the old hotel for our one o' clock appointment.

Hampton Court was already geared up for lunch: older ladies in straw complexion-saving hats with men in summer suits or casual wear; not one empty table. Eyes quickly turned to us and a brief quiet hit the wave of polite luncheon talk. We spotted Austin. He smiled and rose from his seat. We went over to him, and shook hands. "How is our friend Jake?" he asked as we sat down. "Fine," Lee said.

"Busy as ever? Lucky guy. He keeps those fingers of his in every pie!" He drummed his fingers. I nervously laughed. A young waiter with the most beautiful dark eyes and Latin face appeared and took our orders for two Bloody Marys. "Enjoying our weather? Not like San Francisco!" Austin asked, then looked up at the waiter. "What specials today?" The waiter told him the soup was a vegetable bisque and lunch featured a chicken-bacon-and-watercress sandwich. He smiled and ordered both. Jake was right: this place was about as gringo as you could get. "My friends, what would you like?"

I told him we were only there for drinks, but Lee decided to order the sandwich. I looked daggers at him; I wanted to get this over with. The waiter left; Austin looked at me. "Jakie's a smart man. He really knows how to work here, but some day even Jake will run out of fingers!" The food arrived quickly, but the conversation ran dry. It became tense even appearing to be genial. Lee was distant from me, and I from him. I ordered a gin-and-tonic, which also came without ice, and watched Lee slowly eat. Every bite chewed into my nerves. Finally, they were both through and I was jumping to leave. Austin lifted up the shopping bag and waved. "Don't forget!" We smiled and Lee took it.

On the way out—this time not a single face looked up from its bisque—I grabbed the bag from Lee. I remembered Jake's warning about the shopping bags. I made sure that ours was in the front seat, right under my legs. We began to drive towards "Keith's." Now I knew people were watching us. 115

Constant eyes followed the car. When we stopped at an intersection, a face smeared itself on my passenger side window, followed by a greasy hand. A gang of street kids trailed the Jag through the narrow streets—I had no idea what to do. Some of them slapped on the rear fenders while they looked directly at us. In front of "Keith's," everything quieted again when two border cops came out of the shop and watched us park. Lee's hands shook. Then the police walked away, turning a corner until they disappeared. "Here goes nothing," I said. Lee closed his eyes, then said: "I guess we know why Jake didn't want to do this himself."

"You must be here for Mr. Beauchamps's flowers!" a willowy blond Englishman said. "Pedro, Señor Beauchamps's *flores*!"

A heavyset Mexican kid hauled in two baskets from a back room. Keith started fingering around in them, adjusting some carnations and a spray of snapdragons that appeared at the top of each basket. I cleared my throat and casually asked Keith about the police. "Don't worry, they're old friends. Here, I think you'll find everything in order. Give Mr. Beauchamps our regards and tell him his business is fine with us!"

I left with the baskets. They were heavy—about fifteen pounds each. Heavy flowers. But the same two cops were back, now hanging around next to Lee parked in the Jaguar. This time *I* got nervous. They looked me over for an instant, then walked back into the flower shop. "What do you think they wanted?" I asked Lee as I got in. He shook his head. I put the flowers in the backseat of the Jag and Lee hit the ignition. I could tell he was rattled by the cops, but was trying hard not to show it. "You don't know who to trust *less* around here," he said, looking at me.

The truth exploded right out of me: "Lee, I *can't* mate with you!" I said. "The forces of Ki will not allow it . . . I love you, but I just can't!"

Then he replied: "*Love me?* What does that mean, that you're setting me up to bump me off?"

I felt shitty and nervous. "No, let's just get the hell out of here."

We were half way back to the resort on an empty bend in the road, when the car was fired on. I had no idea who or what did it—a dissolver was not something you used against auto glass; the plastic ammunition in them just ended up dissolving down the glass. So for all I knew these could have been old-fashioned bullets like hick banditos carried. Or friends of Austin's, Keith's, or those cops. Two bullets hit some glass and metal on the driver's side, but the speed of the Jag kept them from doing much damage. Lee ducked, then gunned it until I was sure he was going to take off and fly to get us back into traffic. "So!" he shouted, "you and little *Jakie* are going to get rid of me?"

First I thought I was going to crap on the seat from fear, and now Lee was the one acting like an asshole. "No! Why would I harm you?"

We made it back to the resort a few minutes later, and drove through the guardhouse. The guard noticed the damage from the bullets and just shook his head a bit. *Routine.* He told Lee they could repair it quickly if he wanted. Lee shook his head, clenched his teeth, and drove on. "I knew I was going to have to die because of you, Albert. This whole thing's been nuts: first you're my son—then you're my lover!" He got out of the Jag, grabbed the two florist baskets, and threw the keys to the valet. I took the shopping bag. I wanted to tell Lee that I would never let anyone—or anything—harm him. But how could I promise that . . . he hurried ahead of me and a stony wall of silence fell between us. By the time we used the passcard to get into the suite, I knew that I couldn't lie to him that way. All I could hope was that Enkidu himself—who had forbidden my mating with him—would preserve him from danger.

You could feel the silence in the suite. The door to Jake's room was closed.

"We're back!" I called.

No answer. Lee had both of his hands full. "Stay here," I said, and pulled the dissolver out of his jacket. I went over to Jake's door and kicked it open. A six-fingered hand greeted me. From the floor.

He was staring face up at the ceiling, his eyes wide open. A hole through the side of his head, but little blood to speak of. An expert dissolver shot could do that: sealing off small blood vessels with heat. His room had been ransacked; the spy screen knocked out; drawers all over the place; the mattress on the floor. I looked around: there would be no money now. Jake thought he'd be safe in the room, that's why he had sent us out. I sank down and looked at him. In his other hand he clutched something. I straightened out his fingers. A room service menu. I dropped the dissolver into the shopping bag and ran back into the living room. Lee still had the baskets in each hand. "Get out!" I said, grabbing him and leading him through the short hallway of the suite to the door.

"What about this stuff?"

I remembered what Jake had said about the bag. "Leave the flowers here! We'll take the bag. Jake's dead. Somebody's already been here."

A knock on the door. "Room service!"

The door opened. Miguel, dissolver in hand, pushed in; behind him, someone who looked eerily familiar. *Jesse.* The young White Christian who'd made such a fuss over us the night before. He smiled. "Don't you boys know the wages of sin is death? We believe you've got some souvenirs here that we are very interested in."

I started to back away, towards the balcony. I did not want to be cornered in the hallway. My mind flashed to the small dissolver burning a "hole" in the shopping bag. I had to get to it. "Why'd you have to kill Jake?" I asked. "He would have given you the crap. He was that kind of person."

"We give excellent service here," Miguel said. "But you have to tip."

Lee looked at them. "If you guys want this shit, it's yours. Christ, I thought Security can see everything in here."

"Afraid so," Jesse said. "That's why we have friends in Security."

Miguel laughed. "We *are* Security!" He pointed the weapon directly at Lee. I knew that I had to reach that dissolver in the bag—and I wasn't even sure how to fire it. "Now, drop all your nice souvenirs on the floor," he ordered.

"Sure," Lee said. "Just take the crap!" He lifted the baskets above his head and then threw both of them hard at Miguel. One of them hit him directly in the face. That gave me enough time to get the dissolver out of the bag— but not enough time to use it.

Some one else fired at them, nailing them both in the back of the head. It all happened so fast that my first thought was that I'd been hit. *I was going to die.* My knees turned watery; I was sure my blood was all over the fine carpet. Then I realized it wasn't my blood . . . or Lee's—and I saw Vincent's face.

He dashed towards me. "You okay?" he asked; I nodded my head numbly. "I'm glad I could get into Security," he said. "I thought I should keep an eye on you. What the hell's going on here?"

I shook my head and led Vincent into the other bedroom, past Lee, who seemed as dazed as I was and just as amazed that we were alive. In the bedroom, Vincent saw what they'd done to Jake. His eyes ran through the room; "I'm glad I got here for you," he said, pulling my cheek to his lips. I told him quickly about Miguel and Jesse. Vincent had an old-fashioned pistol, the kind that used real bullets, and he stuck it back inside the short jacket of his uniform. Lee walked in. "We're getting out of here," Vincent said to us both. "Any second the real Security will be here, and this game will be over with. Just leave this shit where it is. Whatever's in it will nail Miguel and his Jesus friend."

The three of us left the suite. "Now ya'll just smile and act casual," he said, straightening out the tie of his uniform. "And walk slowly." We walked down the hallway, and then out of the wing where our suite had been.

Outside, I put on a pair of sunglasses and saw a group of uniformed Security guards hurrying towards us. "*Very* casual," Vincent whispered. He smiled at the guards, and they ignored him, and rushed past us towards the suite. "Now," he said, "We're going to walk a little faster towards the boat."

I'm not sure how I made it down the boardwalk to the marina, with swarms of swank foreign tourists and vacationing White Christians around us. From fear I must have been whiter than any White Christian. It was only after we got into the sport boat that Vincent had taken me out in the night before that I realized that I still had the shopping bag glued to my hand, which was probably why no one had questioned me. There was something so silly about it that it seemed perfectly normal. It made me blend in with the other tourists, and as we left the cove and then got into a waterway that led to the coastline, I remembered Jake's wise admonition: *Never leave your shopping bags unattended.*

CHAPTER 11

Los Lingos. Not far from Venice, we ditched the boat. In the shopping bag, besides the dissolver, we found enough drugs of various sorts, some of them very advanced creations that were suddenly becoming popular with the most *progressive* people, to keep us in money for a while. The question was how to turn the stuff into cash, and where to hang out until that happened. I took Jennifer Lawrence's address and telecom number out of my wallet. She told me that she had been waiting for my call.

"Can she deal with the three of us?" Vincent asked.

"You won't have to 'deal' with me much longer," Lee said. "I'm going to get lost."

"Wait a second," I said. "What gives you the *right* to just get lost?"

"What are you talking about, *right*?" Lee asked. "Who the hell are you? I used to. . . ."

"I know you used to powder my ass," I said, while Vincent looked on, totally bewildered. "But where I come from, I'm used to having people do what I tell them, after all, I was prince. . . ."

Vincent looked up in the air and started howling. "Get *her*!" he screamed. "You're all nuts. This is the craziest shit. . . ."

"Afraid not," Lee said. "What he said is right. He was a prince." He then told Vincent my story, or at least as much as Lee knew while we got on MT, mass transport, to Venice. The MT was part monorail and part underground. It went through some of the old burned-out sections of Los Lingos and some newer ones. At one time, Vincent told us, the whole Los Lingos area, when it had been named Los Angeles, had been clogged with traffic and you could barely breathe the air. The traffic also created major crime problems, like carjacking and freeway murders. After the large, very efficient MT system had been put together, crime went down. The MT made it easier to control people, since you had to use your ID card to get onto it and a record was kept of all your movements. Now the air was better. But some people complained that the MT system avoided many of the worse sections of the Los Lingos megalopolis, sections referred to by the old century term "ghettos," where car bandits still roamed freely.

We must have looked a little worse for wear when Laura answered the door. "My mother's taking a nap," she said. She invited us into the sitting room of their home, a large bungalow perched on a hill. I had this feeling that I had been to the house before, although that was impossible; it was romantic and florid; each room had its own character. The dining room was reached through two wooden doors that had been carved with a scene of tall, rain-forest trees and flights of birds and running range animals. "My mother took up sculpture for a while. She wanted these doors to be the entrance to her own personal world."

"A world of forests?" I asked.

"Yes. This is the sitting room. It's in the back. You can see the beach from here. Years ago there were houses between us and the water, but a lot of them were burned down. Some of them just sank into the sand and no one ever raised them back up again." We looked out the large windows at the rolling hilly fields of sea oats and dune grasses between Jennifer's house and the water. Then I noticed two portraits etched in glowing stained glass set at the top of the windows. "That was my father, Nick. Mama had his picture done in glass a few years after he died; the other man is his friend Reuvuer, a Russian that he was . . . well, I guess you could say they were attached to each other."

"I'm so glad you could make it." I looked up to see Jennifer approach in a black silk, Japanese-style robe. I introduced her to Lee and Vincent. "Another complicated relationship," she said. "I can tell that right away." I asked her how she knew. "Years ago I was the silliest woman who ever lived. My parents spoiled me and tried to shelter me all the time. Then after I had Laura, and my parents died and I lost most of the money I'd inherited, I realized that it is not so much that people are stupid as much as they don't give themselves credit for knowing. The truth is we can see much more than we believe. That is why I can tell that the three of you are engaged in a difficult situation."

I told her that it was true, what she had said, about seeing. We all sat down. Laura served us some iced tea. "It has primrose in it," Laura said. "Very healing and calming." I drank mine quickly and she poured some more for me.

Jennifer looked at me and smiled. "So what brought you to California?" She asked this question as if it were the most natural thing in the world and did not open up my whole strange history.

I realized I had to tell her. "I was born in Provincetown, Massachusetts."

"That's a gay reserve," Jennifer noted.

"Yeh," Lee said. "And he's only six years old."

Vincent's eyes rolled. "Not more of this weird story."

"Yes," I said. "More of this weird story. Just before Lee and I left Provincetown, I had this—well, I can only call it visit—from Enkidu."

"Gilgamesh's friend?" Jennifer asked incredulously.

"No, Enkidu was my father. That was his name. And in a different life, he was Nick Lawrence, your husband."

"You mean by a 'different life' he had been divorced once, or he had a name change."

"No, Mother. He means in a different *life*! Right, Albert?"

"Yes," I said. "That is exactly what I meant. And I mean in a different place, too. A place called *Ki*."

Jennifer leaned forward. "Where is that?"

"Maybe we shouldn't ask," Laura said. Vincent looked at her questioningly and she added: "Maybe none of us should ask."

Jennifer looked at me. "This man Enkidu, he's also dead?" I told her yes. "What did he say to you?"

"He said, 'I love you, Albert'—even death would not separate us. He told me to go to a place called 'California,' close to the remains of someone named 'Nick Lawrence'—and his mate, 'Reuvuer.' He said that there I would find 'the mate' that *I* sought. And when I found him—he told me—I would be able to 'return to Ki and reclaim my place there.'"

Lee looked at me. I could see the anger in his face; it tore me apart. "So you knew this would happen all along. That you'd meet Vincent—I guess that was the end for me, wasn't it?"

"Wait a second," Jennifer said. "You mean you'd never heard of Nick Lawrence and Reuvuer before? Ever?"

I told her no.

"Mother, he could not have just made up the names. Nick, a couple of people knew about him. But not Reuvuer." She got up and stared at the window, at the stained glass pictures of the two men. "You knew my father in a different life; I can't believe it! What was he like?"

"He was very nice. I loved him very much."

"And this place called Ki; how do I get there?"

"Oh, you've been there. You're worshipped there. At least, your image is. You're called the Goddess Laura."

She smiled. Her face looked exactly like the statue in the Temple. "Imagine being a goddess? It seems like all the gods are dead in this world, unless you're a White Christian! *They* act as if Jesus was a movie star."

Lee looked sullen and embarrassed. "I guess we have to tell them about the third ball."

"The what?" Jennifer asked.

"A third testicle," Vincent said. "It's this part of his anatomy. It makes him different from other people, other guys certainly. It got me hooked on him."

"I'm not sure I want to see that," Jennifer said. "Maybe it's time we should show you the guest room. I'm not sure how well three will sleep in it, but you should get some rest, because tomorrow we're going up to Still Waters."

"Where is that?" I asked.

"It's the place near Guerneville, where Nick and Reuvuer are buried."

The three of us climbed up into the guest room which was raised above the rest of the house. Like the sitting room, it had windows watching out into the sandy distance, with the ocean brooding ahead. The sun was setting and the room was filled with amber light. It had two beds in it, one a double and the other a smaller twin. I felt that I had not slept for weeks and took my clothes off as Vincent and Lee watched me. They stripped and followed me, with me between the two of them on the double bed. Their arms soon folded around me and they kissed me, softly, at the same time. I could feel the play of light, the sun setting, and the whole room breathing, trembling in anticipation as I knew that we were all soon erect, touching each other, kissing and holding each other, and I could not control my feelings for Lee who had been my father on Earth or for Vincent, my mate. The three of us soon became like one amazing organism, or like the three testicles within my male pouch, within me.

The three of us had, indeed, transcended our human forms and had become a part of the Egg itself, transmitting information among us in a silent, unconscious way—information alive, yet passive—simply waiting there to be exposed to the living world, as they took turns sucking, holding, and kissing me. I realized I was becoming "empty," as if this transition from one existence and character to another had left me with virtually nothing inside of me, except a vast recognition of the bends within time-space itself.

"You *must* give it to him," Vincent whispered into my ear, while Lee sucked greedily at my cock.

"But I have never before given to him what I gave to you."

Vincent fondled the pendant that hung from my neck, and then kissed it. His eyes looked like viridian-glowing amber in the golden light. He urged me to be generous: in doing so Lee would be allowed to live—and to leave me. Vincent thrust his tongue into my mouth; I was sure that I could taste my

124

own sperm, like thickened, pulsing rain water, there. But it was not; it was only that my mate had become myself: in the circular, flowing, transcendental way of Ki.

Lee sucked deeper and harder. Seed shot out of me. I could feel him twist and jolt as it chemically coursed through his body. The seed from the Egg of the Eye: hot; volatile; forever a mystery. Now I did feel emptied . . . and strangely ready for anything. "I love you," I said to Vincent. "With all my heart and soul. You've allowed Lee to live; I know this now."

I closed my eyes and was thrown through space, black and dense, until my innate consciousness/identity, expanding once more after the journey, filled the air of Ki. I saw Ki's devastation at the hands of Woosh and Anvil. The Sisters looked blank faced but patient: they had experienced evil and hostility before, and were awaiting my return. I saw my own body and that of Enkidu lying rigidly in the Temple, but I could say nothing either to my father or to myself. Hortha spoke, alone to me: "I know that you are here, Albert, and I know what Enkidu wants you to do. But do you realize *all* that you risk?"

I told her no, although the words did not come out of me. The answer was a trembling in space, a wrinkle in the true plasma of time. Only this made the old woman aware of my presence.

"Yes, you do not know, my son: but you risk the future of all Ki in the limbs of the Tree."

"The Tree?" I asked. "What Tree?"

But there was no answer. All I could see from the ramparts of Hortha's turret were immense fires fanned by the winds of war and power. And I could see the faces of Woosh and Anvil, also waiting, but smiling.

I was now coming back: preparing to return to Earth. Vincent and Lee remained attached to my body; Lee still holding my cock in his mouth; Vincent now grasping me, fucking me. They were overwhelmed by the power I had inside of me, but I was not there yet—not in Venice; not on Earth. I had not yet gone through the vast rebirthing contractions of space. I was still only a thing within my own Egg: a mass of spinning cells reverting to prehistory. I had to re-evolve: the motions of eons—eras—began to assert themselves within me.

First as a soft creature in primal salt water; then an amphibian attempting to walk on land. Next a mammal, primitive, pig-like, working its way, fetally, to ape. Finally, I arrived as Man: complete; evolved; divine: awaking slowly into human consciousness. All of this took place within my Egg, the precious "Egg of the Eye," whose seed Lee had tasted and in doing so, finally, was able to watch me passing through evolution.

Here was I—*Albert*—awake.

"*God*," Lee said. "It's been worth it. Nothing I've ever known has been close to this." I smiled, then kissed him. Vincent, after orgasm, was asleep at my side. "I saw you become a man."

I nodded my head. "Twice."

"This time was even more amazing."

Tears flowed from my eyes; he asked me why I was sad. "Because you have to leave."

"I know," he said. "But you gave me one fabulous present! What will happen now?"

"You must go back to Provincetown. To Sandy and Carol—and present them with their son."

He began to get dressed. "I have no idea what you're talking about," he said puzzled. "But I'm prepared to leave you. My love for you will never die, Albert. I realize now I'm a complete person. I have loved you completely, and you have given me the knowledge of my own humanness. Only you could do that for me. Most people achieve that only after death, so I'll always thank you for it."

I got up and handed him the shopping bag that had cost Jake his life. "If you go into Los Lingos," I said, "you will be able to get rid of this and make enough money to get back to Massachusetts. You will have my protection, and the protection of Enkidu and all the other Same-Sex men of Ki. I am their prince, and they will know me."

He left. I could hear the door shut quietly behind him. I went back to sleep with Vincent. Because Lee had my seed inside of him, I could follow him and shared the story of the next few weeks with him. They became telescoped in my mind, as time does bending through space.

He went back on the MT and in an area near Hollywood quickly found a place where he could unload the drugs. Undesirable men tried to rob him, cheat him, kill him. But nothing came of this. He was protected, because he had protected me and had given me to my mate. All in all, he made ten thousand new dollars from the sale of the items in the bag. He set himself up in a beautiful apartment and people trusted him and came to him. When all of the drugs—some of which approximated the depths of the seed of the Egg, but

126

never approached its power and sublimity—were gone, he knew that he had to leave. Loneliness suddenly hit him: he was without me, his son and lover. The completeness that had come after I had shared my seed with him left. It was sad for me to see this, but I'd expected it. I knew that completeness for too long can be dangerous, producing its own form of a vacuum. One day, he took a drive through Los Lingos and passing through the devastation that had taken over so much of the city, he headed for a wild canyon, edged with cliffs, next to the coast.

He got out of the car with every intent not to go back to Massachusetts, but to end his life there. He had brought the mini-dissolver with him, and was going to shoot himself. He parked his car in a canyon, carpeted with thickly flowered desert plants whose blooms seemed to make a music of their own, of intense color, in the air. He walked out over the cliffs towards the water, and there he spotted a small, redheaded boy of six, lost, wandering by himself, away from the devastating wreckage of a burned-out car.

Lee picked the boy up and held him. Then he took the child back towards the car's smoking hulk and saw within its destruction that there were two people inside. The boy screamed and Lee held him. The two were burned almost beyond recognition. Surrounded by charred icons and power emblems of the WCP, they had both been shot dead by bandits. I saw this directly through my own eyes as both Lee and I realized, exactly, what had ended there, on this cliff: this was the boy he and Sandy had produced, stolen by the hospital staff in Orleans, secreted off to a White Christian couple in California, whose own story had ended at that spot—on this wild cliff next to the Pacific.

Lee crouched down. "What is your name?" he asked the child.

"Albert." The boy suddenly hugged him.

"My name is Lee." Lee began to cry. "I want you to know that I'm your father."

The boy too cried. "What about Mommy and Daddy? Bob and Marjorie?"

"They took care of you until I could find you. Do you believe me?"

The boy looked into his eyes. He stopped crying.

Lee took his hand, and they went back to his car, and began the trip back to Massachusetts. In Provincetown, he presented Albert to Sandy and Carol. Sandy realized that he was theirs. She felt the connection between them—it was unexplainable, but real. Carol was skeptical; she was sure Lee had merely fooled them again. First he had gone off with their own son, now he had presented them with another. She never accepted the second boy and told Lee that she wanted the child out of her house. "You're only breaking

Sandy's heart," she shouted.

So Lee kept Albert with him, and Sandy came often to visit. Sometimes she felt as if she were Lee's estranged wife, since leaving the two of them, especially the boy, was heartbreaking to her. Lee had to provide for the boy and he did this alone. He loved him immensely. Sometimes his feeling for the small redheaded boy reminded him of the loss he felt for another Albert, the beautiful man from Ki who had come to him in the most unusual way. He had never thought that the child he and Sandy had given birth to would end up solely his. But he was overwhelmed with love for his young Albert, a love that could be only fatherly and in no way that of a lover's.

CHAPTER 12

"Where is Lee?" Laura asked the next morning at breakfast. Vincent and I were sitting on a terrace in the back of the house. The mood from the beach was gloomy and fog ridden, but I was sure that it would lift. My own mood was different—although not that much different—I felt happy but lost; suddenly alone now without Lee. I looked into Vincent's face and smiled.

I explained to her that he had to leave. She asked me where, and I told her that he had gone back to where it had all started.

"Never a bad idea," Jennifer said. She looked very beautiful, her hair gray but still streaked with spots of gold; her face looked amazingly calm and serene. "I want us to go back up North. I want you to see the place where Nick and Reuvuer are buried. It was hard getting them back up there, but I wanted them buried together and I found this gay cemetery in the most beautiful place. I think you should see it—both of you."

In the afternoon we piled into Jennifer's PT, an old Japanese import, from the early twenty-tens. It only had some radar functions, so she had to do most of the driving, but it was in good condition. She joked about being the "little old lady from Pasadena," a joke that meant nothing to me but made Vincent laugh. We got off the main highlane and then took turns driving. We went straight through San Francisco and then up the Coast and headed off towards Guerneville. It was in the middle of the night by the time we arrived. Guerneville was small and filled with rustic-looking stores and restaurants. "This is an old gay resort," Vincent told me. "Guys have been coming here since way back in the old century."

"Girls, too," Laura said. "It actually has a lot more women than men. It's really more queer now than gay. There are even straight queers who come here; the old drug people who dropped out of the WC culture. I love it here. Mother and I come back about once a year."

It was too late to go to Still Waters, so we stayed at Clyde's Hotel, a strange structure that looked like some kind of fortress back on Ki, all log corners and gables with high-pitched roofs. Vincent and I stayed in a room by ourselves down the hall from Laura and her mother. I did not feel tired at all. We walked outside and smelled the fresh air, scented with the sharp tang of redwoods. Vincent took my hand. "I could never have done before what I did in your hotel room," he said. "You've changed my life."

I told him that he had changed mine.

"Is it possible," he asked, "that you can just find someone, and he can change everything about yourself?"

"It's possible, if you allow yourself to," I said shyly. "I realized you were the one I was supposed to have when you gave me this pendant."

He shook his head. "I'm still so confused about all of this. When I was a kid my Mom always warned me about following strangers home, and now I've really done it . . . except that I'm not sure where home is for you."

"Just believe it's an awfully *long* way from here."

We wandered away from the town and into the woods that edged up almost to the main streets. We started making love; I saw that stars were shooting over our heads. Naked, we rolled in the grass, only aware of each other's body. Then I blanked out, went on "automatic," feeling Vincent's mouth and hands all over me, and I realized that I was in the room again in the Temple of Ki, where Enkidu and Albert—*himself*—awaited my return. Now both had arisen from the slumbers of death and were watching me, watching Vincent make love to me in the fields of their own death-dreams, through an immensity of space.

I felt like a tiny child again. I wanted to be left lone with Vincent, and I knew I could not be. Enkidu's eyes and the eyes of the Albert I had been on Ki would follow me forever. I could never escape what I had been. Vincent sucked passionately at me, holding my third ball, the Egg I had inherited from a thousand years of Kivian Same-Sex men, in the palm of his hand. He had to have it, and now I was frightened of giving it to him: if he took more of my seed what would happen to him? Could he become like Greeland, ambitious, blind to others, bloodthirsty . . . and yet so attractive to me that I would crawl on my belly through razor blades to get to him?

I let him have the seed, letting it burn through his body with the force of an electrical storm. He jerked several times. The muscles of his arms, chest, and face knotted. I kissed him and thrust my tongue and then my whole mouth into his. He wrapped his hands around my throat; I thought he would strangle me in his intensity. Finally he released me. His breathing, which had been violent and hard, calmed down. "I can do anything now," he said quietly. "Anything that is necessary to be with you."

We did not see Jennifer or Laura until four o' clock the next day. The hotel had a swimming pool and a hot tub and sauna and we had a nice time lounging around, just being in this beautiful, peaceful place, full of sun and shade and a type of air that seemed, after Los Lingos, drinkable. At four o' clock, showered and refreshed, we met Laura and her mother in the lobby. They were dressed in long, simple white robes. I had no idea how they knew to dress like this, but Laura resembled completely the goddess I remembered from Ki. I told her this; she smiled. Was it possible that somehow she had envisioned herself in the same manner that Enkidu had?

The cemetery was in a shallow valley, miles off the main road, surrounded by woods and streams. Waters gurgled down the creek beds and over the rocks as we drove in. "Still Waters is one of my favorite places," Jennifer said. Laura parked the car, and Jennifer took out a picnic basket filled with California champagne, some fruit and cheese, and crackers. "We always have a picnic here when we go see them."

We walked slowly among the graves and urns. Many of them had men's names in pairs or trios and foursomes, like family plots. Then, at the farthest end, surrounded by clipped, sorrowful myrtles, were the graves of Nick and Reuvuer. I noticed that the death date was the same and they were close in age. We rolled out a picnic spread and sat down. "Mother never deserted them," Laura said. "Grandma wanted her to remarry. . . ."

"I thought about it," Jennifer interrupted. "I did; I wanted Laura to have a father, but I thought I'd have to hide all of this from her if I did, and I just couldn't make myself do it. So, instead, I got deeper into mysticism and the gay community. I don't live in a gay reserve, but I wanted Laura to know that her father was gay and that he was murdered because he was gay—I'm sure of it."

"It's only a guess," Laura said. "This whole thing—that he was killed trying to assassinate Rich Quilter when he was vice president—always seemed like a pile of crap to me. I can't believe that my father would have done that. It doesn't make any sense."

"Maybe he was under another influence," I said. "Something he couldn't control." I looked over at Vincent. He smiled at me, then he added: "History is just full of that—people do things that seem insane, and then it's just accepted. Wars. Invasions. Who's to know what's at the bottom of it all?"

"Exactly," Jennifer said. "*Exactly* . . . I think we should try to find out now." I asked her what she was talking about. "How about some of the champagne first?" She uncorked it expertly with her thin, veined hands and poured out glasses for all of us. Vincent, who knew booze, pronounced it great, and we soon had another. The sun began to set, edging all of the trees and leaves with a cool, quiet light that became a liquor of its own. The light, 131

I knew, was slowly draining way. "Now, let's join hands," she said. "And close our eyes, and I'll talk. Quietly. And we'll see what happens."

We held hands; I took Vincent's hand and Jennifer's and closed my eyes. Jennifer began an invocation that seemed mostly gibberish. She said it was a spell—it had worked in the past. "I've contacted them through it."

I had no idea what she meant. If she *had* contacted them, didn't they tell her what really had happened? I opened my eyes. Vincent was looking directly at me and shaking his head. I knew nothing was going to happen, then I suggested that I take Laura's hand instead, and then—I knew I had to say something—I said that I wanted us to take our clothes off. "I'm an old woman!" Jennifer objected. "I wasn't raised to take my clothes off in front of—"

"Oh, Mother!" Laura said "In that case, just keep them on!"

The three of us took our clothes off. Laura was really beautiful—she seemed younger than either of us—and I could not get over how right she and Vincent and I looked together, naked and pure, sitting on a spread next to the graves of Nick Lawrence and Reuvuer Svoizhe. "Suppose someone finds you?" Jennifer protested. "In a cemetery—naked!"

"Nothing will happen," I said confidently.

"It won't work, Mother, unless we *are* this way; I know it."

Jennifer bowed her head. We promised not to look at her, and she took her robe off, too. Now sitting on the spread, I could feel a warmth traveling through us as I took Vincent's and Laura's hands in each of mine and they in turn took Jennifer's. "*Father,*" I said. "*I know that you want to show me so much, and we have all come to learn.*"

Night settled in. A premature night: the night that guards death. I became aware of being pushed over, although I was still sitting up. My equilibrium was destroyed; my stomach traveled up to my head and I wondered why I'd had the champagne. I knew Enkidu was talking to me. I was merely mouthing his words, bringing them back from Ki.

I will take you down, he (I) said. *Down into the depths, the strange world we see as night, that only poets, children, and the Others who cross and come back see. Beware my beloved son: not everyone will come back.*

I squeezed Vincent's hand. Suddenly I was frightened for him. Suppose I caused *his* death? No! I whispered, but the whisper was lost, because I knew that the three of them were now under, and were traveling with me and with my father Enkidu as our guide.

CHAPTER 13

We were in a large, dark room without any walls or windows. Only light divided us from the Eternity of silence and twilight beyond us. The light poured in on us, as Vincent, Laura, and Jennifer woke up and were now clothed in the light that seemed glowing and solid, like pure ice: crystal clear. Nick and Reuvuer were there, too, sitting and holding hands, naked on the floor. The four of us watched while the two of them kissed, endlessly it seemed, and words poured out of them that we could hear distinctly.

"Jennifer," Nick said. "I'm sorry that I never really got to know you. I was your husband, but I could not know you at all. I think I loved you as much as I loved Reuvuer, especially after I knew that you had given me a daughter—"

"Oh, I told him that!" Enkidu appeared. "I said that Laura was going to be the Goddess of Ki. Imagine, Nick, your daughter would be the Goddess of a planet!"

"A planet that *I* saved," Reuvuer insisted. "Only because I loved Nick so much—and that strange third Egg."

"This is very nice," Laura said. "But I still don't know how my father died."

"Your father," Enkidu explained, "and I once shared the same identity. On Ki, where I come from, this comes from the Egg of the Eye. I'm afraid the only way Nick could escape the bind he was in—being two things at once—was to kill."

"We'll make it simple, young lady," Reuvuer explained. "Your daddy and I attempted to kill Rich Quilter. We were led to believe that if we brought Quilter back to Ki, we might save the planet from its own tribal hostilities. Totally nutty idea, but no more so than most nutty ideas. At the time, it seemed right. What we did not know was that Quilter was much more evil than we thought, which of course—as anyone can tell you—is the reason he's around today."

"God!" Jennifer exclaimed. "You *did* try to murder the vice president!"

"No. . . ." Nick said.

"Yes," Reuvuer said. "True. And I would do it again to save Nick's life. 133

Even then it seemed crazy, but suppose it had worked? Quilter has been President now for ten years; he's made life Hell for people like us."

"I would have done the same," Vincent admitted. "To save Albert's life."

"But you can't just kill. . . ." Jennifer said sobbing.

"You don't know what pressure we were under," Nick tried to explain. "A whole planet was in the balance—and only through our own deaths did it ever go right."

"Yes," Enkidu said. "You two were a part of it all: the balance of Ki was achieved. A balance that has never, ever existed on Earth. And for a while the Same-Sex men of Ki were a part of this balance; they saw their places in it restored. For this I thank you, Nick and Reuvuer; and I grieved for you all the time I was alive."

"It has taken my whole life to understand why you both died on the same evening," Jennifer said. "None of it made any sense before."

"They were desperate," Enkidu tried to explain. "Something that Quilter understood perfectly: all Earth politics operate under desperation. But that is not important now; something else is at stake. My son Albert must return to Ki, with the mate promised him."

"Is he talking about me?" Vincent asked.

"We shall see," Enkidu said. "I want you both to come with me."

"You're leaving?" Jennifer cried. "You can't leave—please!"

"He cannot stay," Enkidu said, looking away from her.

My father took my hand and I took Vincent's, and we walked away from the light, leaving Nick, Reuvuer, Jennifer and Laura in the room which soon fell into darkness. I could hear Jennifer sobbing to herself as we left; I felt terrible about leaving her, but I knew that I had to follow Enkidu. The light disappeared. Winds started to howl. I felt vulnerable and exposed. I wanted to cling to Vincent but every time I got closer to him, he would shy away from me as if in fear. We walked through a huge, dark forest, but one without leaves: only hacked-off bare limbs and exposed trunks; with brambles and thorns at our feet. My feet became bruised and started bleeding. In the dark I became battered by the stumps and low shoulders of trees. The wind raged harder, flogging my skin with its whip. I looked at Vincent. He looked older and worn. He shied away from me every time I tried to touch him. "Where are we going?" I asked Enkidu. "This is horrible!"

"A little farther," he said. "Just a bit more. It is normal to be afraid. Many have died on this road and if you look deeper, you will see them. Sometimes they are in the woods and sometimes they *are* the woods."

134   I looked around; he was right. I saw faces like iron, colorless and hard.

There was no difference between them and the woods. We walked on, until Vincent gasped. He collapsed and I got closer to him. I embraced his crumpled form on the ground. He pressed his head to my stomach and began to kiss me softly, crying in a whimper, touching his face and mouth to the hair below my navel—but Enkidu pushed him from me. "You cannot stop," he said and pulled me away from the man I loved.

Then, only a short walk from the place where Vincent had collapsed, I saw it: the *Tree.*

Bathed in light, it glowed in the midst of the barren woods. Leaves sprouted from it in abundance—dark, shiny green, splayed into three lobes, like maple but without a ragged edge. I looked up into its branches and I saw there, hanging limply from each branch, countless numbers of human skins, complete from face to foot. They were hanging limp and flat, without muscle, bones, or skeletons. But each face was fully formed, feature by feature, as if waiting to be inhabited by a single human soul.

I gasped; yet each face seemed calm and at peace. I wondered who had killed them. Then Enkidu said: "They are not dead. Do you see they are only waiting? Many have tried to understand the Tree—what is on it and how it holds us together. Here are the men with their secrets and secret lives: that is why it is surrounded in darkness. It is, you could say, the 'fairy tree.' The Tree of clear spirits—holding our vanished lines: where we all come from and to where we go back. The Tree is our circle forever. All of the Same-Sex men of Ki; Earth; everywhere. Few ever see it unless it is time to return, but I have shown it to you because you are my son."

I smiled. "So was this the Tree from which came Kiwa, brother of Ki, whose sons were the first Same-Sexers?"

Enkidu nodded his head. "It is the Tree of many stories and myths. Four thousand years ago someone must have seen it. Its knowledge has been with us ever since."

I could not keep my eyes off it. I felt stunned and filled with love for the light waiting in its branches. There we were; and there we'd be again. Once, perhaps, this Tree had been surrounded by the first Garden: in Eden. And all the dead trees around it had been alive, pulsing with one continuous life. Suddenly Vincent appeared at my side. I hugged him and tried to hold on to him. But without saying a word, he extended his arms and was pulled into the waiting branches of the Tree.

"I knew it!" Enkidu said. "He could not survive. He is without the third Egg. He has seen the Tree and it has taken him."

"I won't let it happen!"

"Why tears, my son? He has only to wait; he will be reborn again. It is the way: he will wait on the Tree, and then come back."

"But not with me!" I tried to pull him off. Over and over again I kissed his skullless face, as it hanged towards me: a flat mask of empty skin, draped over one of the branches.

"If you pull him off, Albert, you will be the one who *has* to pay. But if you do pay, you will find him to be the *only* man worthy to be your mate."

"Why did you take me here?" I asked, but my father would not answer. Instead, he guided my hand until my fingers, stretching way above my head, touched Vincent's groin. With some effort, I was able to lift him, gently, by the scrotum back to the ground. There he became alive, filled with breath once more, and he embraced me. "It's my turn," he said, whispering hoarsely into my ear. "Now *I* will avenge Nick and Reuvuer." His lips brushed my neck, and he said: "And *I* will bring the balance of Ki finally to the planet Earth."

His words rang in my ear. "What are you saying?"

"Look back up on the Tree," he commanded, and he twisted my neck until I was forced to see there in its branches the boneless skins of Nick and Reuvuer and with them, at last, my father Enkidu; his skin empty, finally lifeless. My face fell. I was wearied and sad. Then in the dark fields around us, I turned and saw rows of other faces: one row following another, and all of them sleeping. Rows of dead Same-Sexers. Their faces illuminated only by the light from the Tree. Suddenly they awoke and they stared back at Vincent and me, and I knew who they were—the past going back forever; the future forever giving birth to itself. Both lines were indistinguishable: now they were one and they were watching us, as witnesses.

They knew what had to be done: I saw it in their rapt faces.

Their faces quickly vanished, but the Tree remained. Again on its lower branches I saw the skins of Nick, Reuvuer, and Enkidu. The same terrible sadness overwhelmed me. Did I have to look more? But Vincent made me, gripping my neck with his hand, forcing me to see once more the boneless skins of the men in the Tree until, with both hands, I withdrew his fingers from my neck. I placed his hand tenderly on my face and felt its warmth streaming through me. I kissed his palm and saw that his hand, only lightly covering my eyes, had dissolved into the star-brilliance of the Tree, glowing in the darkness.

I opened my eyes into the dense, clear night. The sky glittered with stars, and the moon was round and full up above us. Laura was sitting next to me, her robe back on, crying. "What have we done?" I looked at her, puzzled; the whole thing had been too puzzling. "Mother's dead," she sobbed. "She never woke up."

But Vincent, though, was awake with his clothes back on. He looked very determined. I quickly got dressed and went to him. "You're in grave danger," he said and hugged me. "I know it. There are forces out to destroy you and they are worse than anything in Lingo Santos. Albert, I love you. And I know that I must kill Rich Quilter."

"Why?"

"Not just to avenge Nick and Reuvuer, but for your sake, Albert. You'll never be safe as long as Quilter and his forces are around. None of us will ever be."

"Then you also saw Nick and Reuvuer; it wasn't just—" I hesitated, then said—"some hallucination I had?"

"No. I saw it. And I know they're gone. And as always, only Quilter remains."

I did not know what to say, but I knew there was no stopping him; there never had been. But I had the strangest feeling that someone else was present nearby. This presence terrified me. I didn't know who it was. Woosh? Even the dead themselves . . . but I knew that saving my own planet was paramount, and it occurred to me then that only Vincent could do it: he was ready for it. He would not retreat.

I clutched him to me, kissing him on his cheeks and mouth, and then I returned to Jennifer. She was still naked; I felt ashamed looking at her wrinkled body when she'd wanted her privacy so much. But her face was at peace. It seemed young, dreaming. Then I realized that death itself was probably only a dream that separates us from another life. And if we can step into this dream—if we *can*—we will not be separated from any spirit that we've loved who has died.

Laura and I managed to get Jennifer's robe back on her. We both felt empty with grief. I agreed to drive back to the hotel and get the police. Luckily, Guerneville was part of the San Francisco gay reserve, and the police did not question me with the kind of hostility that would have happened in the White Christian areas.

CHAPTER 14

A gay mortician was brought in, and he prepared Jennifer for burial. We bought a simple pine coffin for her, and a Jewish woman rabbi said some words for her at her burial next to Nick and Reuvuer. When it was over, Laura talked to us in her room at the hotel. "Jennifer told me that no matter what happened to her, you were to have some money. I think she knew that she was going to die here. Where will you go now?"

"We have a task that we have to accomplish," I said. "Or Vincent does." I smiled weakly at him.

"I will draw out a check for you. I wish you would come back to Venice with me. It's going to be terrible being there alone."

I took her into my arms and hugged her. "I wish I could take you back with me," I said.

She smiled. "To the place where I'm a goddess?"

I nodded my head. I knew it was impossible. Now I also felt alone: I knew that I would never see Enkidu again—only in the sort of dreams which I knew were only dreams, but not in his real visits after death. She opened her check book and wrote out an electronic statement, giving me twelve thousand new dollars. The statement, written on my I.D. number, was fully cashable, or I could insert it into a cash reserve machine and take from it whenever I wanted. Then we drove back to San Francisco, and Vincent and I stopped at the dormo in New Castro where Lee and I had stayed, and we said good-by to her there.

At the dormo, now that we had more money, we took a suite. It seemed luxurious, although compared to accommodations in the straight sections of town, especially in the corporate towers along the Bay, it really wasn't very impressive. Vincent was not tired at all, but I felt, I guess the word was more 'lost' than anything else. We turned on the telecom to the newsprint section and read the coming events.

"We have to plan this," he said, and I knew what he was talking about. By any logic, I knew that it was an insane idea: but the whole idea of sanity no longer made any sense, certainly not after what we had been through in the last week. "Quilter and Brother Bob are going to make an appearance in San

Francisco at the end of the week. There's a WCP evangelicals group that loves to come here 'in the belly of the pagan beast,' they call it. First they go down to places like Lingo Santos and gamble and whore, all the time praying and proselytizing; then they come up here for the real high-profile media coverage."

It was night now, and I pulled him to me on the large bed. He was bare chested and his skin was smooth and wonderfully fragrant. Some men just smell good. I started licking his neck and we kissed deeply. "You're just going to dissolve him?" I whispered.

"Too easy," he joked. "I learned a lot working at Lingo Santos, and one of the things I learned about was microdots." I asked him what he was talking about. "They're a very small part of a microchip. There's one that works like a virus; it can transverse from computer to human form. Once it's inside of you, it works very fast, choking off arteries, literally strangling you. I think that the old President is going to find one in a tequila melon when he comes to the Bay Area." What about Brother Bob? I asked, "*Him*, oh yes. He'll think it's the work of the Lord!" Vincent exploded with laughter.

It seemed that there were many other men with the same idea, and it was not too difficult in the various byways of New Castro to find exactly the microdot Vincent told me about. The dots were against the law, certainly. They had to be detonated by a palm screen with the right "nerve material" in it to do the job. Now I could only watch, as Vincent and I began that slip into the unrolling of history itself—that fateful unrolling—that seems always so 'accidental' from the sidelines.

We were going to be assassins, and second generation ones at that. The idea threw me into a kind of nausea. But even I was not free of an abject hatred of Quilter and Brother Bob, of their sugary exploitative "concerns," and their beaming smiles that hid such . . . "animal" teeth.

Vincent was consumed with their destruction and with avenging the deaths of Nick and Reuvuer, events that had happened even before he was born. Was it being up in the branches of the *fairy tree* that had done this? I couldn't say. But I did know this: it seemed that all of modern history has pointed towards the disavowal of magic; yet only what is outside of what we called "reality" can account for the deeper channels of human behavior that direct our actions. Where did these channels stop? Only at the very threshold of magic: for how else could I explain Vincent's enchantment and his need to take on these enemies whose own venom had seeped . . . into him?

"They'll be here in a week," Vincent announced to me breathlessly. "Our boys are already looking out for them."

I asked him whom he was talking about.

He touched his fingertips together and smiled. "My 'gay knights.' They're all over New Castro. They've been dreaming and plotting this for years. They told me they've only been waiting for someone like me to come along. Quilter just watched and smiled during the spread of the plague in the old Twentieth Century while it killed us by the million. He and Brother Bob support the new Dark Ages we live in. Now that I've tasted the power in you and have seen the Tree, I can't go back. I love you with all of my heart, Albert. But Quilter *must* be killed, before I can give myself totally to you."

"It's madness, Vincent. All I wanted was for you to be my mate. Everything that happened years before, while I was still a child on Ki, is coming back to haunt me. Why? Whose revenge *are* we seeking? Nick's, Reuvuer's—or is it Greeland's, my other father, whom I truly loved, but who came within a hair of destroying Ki?"

Vincent smiled. "It's no longer just revenge." He took me into his arms, which seemed bigger and stronger. I knew he'd been working out at a New Castro gym during the day. He had made the progress of a year in single week: his strength came from his own need to be powerful, as well as the nutrient force of my seed, which worked more efficiently than any anabolic steroid. He ran his lips through my hair and whispered, "After I gave you the pendant—and you released your seed to me—I knew we had set into action something that could not be stopped. I must free us, Albert. All of us: the *whole* Same-Sex race from which we've come."

It was impossible to argue. And I realized that if I tried to change him, tried to bridle Vincent, I would only kill him. And then I would be left with nothing: be left to return alone to Ki; and with my own sadness have to face the planet by myself. The thought brought tears to me that I could not show Vincent as he told me the rest of the plan. A huge political rally had been planned for the Reagan Towers at the end of Quilter's Bay Area appearance. The Towers were a showy part of the New Conservatives' corporate system. They were highly techno-advanced with a mega-convention center, a vast auditorium, and telecom facilities. Brother Bob was going to telecom one of his "STF Club" shows that usually came from South Carolina. "Strength To The Faithful" was shown all over the world, with a viewership of more than a billion people. Quilter, as we saw at Lingo Santos, was often a guest on "STF," and this time, word got out, the President was really going to give it to San Francisco. He had been attacking the city as a gay reserve for years, but his new project was to ask for a national referendum to remove its status. The whole country, in short, would decide San Francisco's fate. In other speeches he had said, "This beautiful city is a gift to our entire country, and it's simply *not* fair for it to be the site of 'special privileges' for a few deviates who choose to live outside the normal Christian laws of our country."

Since the telecom would originate at the Reagan Towers, the whole audience would be stacked with New Conservative hacks and WCPers—making viewers worldwide believe that all of San Francisco was in Quilter's favor. Still, getting in, incredibly enough, would not be that difficult. Many of the personnel at the Towers, who worked in catering and the construction shops of the com studio, were from New Castro or its sympathizers. For years it had been a matter of just doing it for the money: giving blow jobs to the enemy if you had to. But now people were boiling mad. I could tell this from the stream of men who met Vincent. They spoke to him with all the passion of their souls, with the anger that had been dammed up for years by collaborating gay politicos who were content with a few crumbs, a few rubbers, AIDS shots, and sex clubs, thrown to them by the Northern California WCP machine. Now these same-sex men were for Vincent; a new leader had been chosen. Some pledged their lives to him immediately. This inflated Vincent even more to me, making him more attractive, yet worrisome. I wanted to give in to my own weakness and seduce him away. But I knew I could not. He was stronger than I—always my fathers' spoiled son from another planet—had turned out to be. At moments when I felt my determination weaken, all I wanted to do was get him away from San Francisco—and back to me, on Ki. Alone.

I injected him with my seed late each night as we had sex in our suite. He became so powerful after each climax that momentarily I was *sure* I was back on Ki and was having sex with another man from some other past—Vincent, his chest twice as broad, his shoulders, arms, and calf muscles massive—was he now Greeland? Or one of Greeland's hunter forebears? "After we kill them, I will be in line to lead us," he whispered into my ear, following the words with his large, wet tongue. Sometimes he had my sperm down his throat and other times in his bowels, on the way to his gut. "You are transforming my heart," he confessed. "Albert, do you understand the power you have in you?"

I shook my head. In the dark I did not. I was only a conduit. A dumb ridiculous person placed in the most unexplainable position: and it seemed now that my only power was to thrust Vincent, the man I truly loved, into the corridors of death.

Getting into the Reagan Towers was easier than even I had thought, as we mixed with thousands of black-suited, faceless men and overdressed women with tense smiles set like fresh lipstick on their faces. To make matters more interesting, the afternoon, which started out fairly warm in mid-November, turned into a raging rainy evening. I was with Vincent and we were both dressed for the part, in identical "Jesus suits," black polyfiber outfits with crosses subtly woven into the fabric. We were both glad-handed and back-slapped countless times, and told, "Christ is glad to see ya," a greeting which we managed to parrot back. There was an electronic weapons check, administered to the audience and the handscreens carried by the press, military agents, and corporate executives who stayed in contact with their "soldiers" at all times. The check though could only detect certain software; ours passed easily. In addition, we had cards barcoded that said we were from a group called "Nazareth Communications." This brought instant smiles all around, and guys came up to us and said they'd heard what good work we did, and weren't we the ones in the Amazon last year who had cleared out most of the forest to make way for a WC theme park down there?

Getting through the auditorium, then underground, and to the backstage area was the difficult part. At New Castro we got enough corporate ID to get us through most of the checkpoints, but at the final one, only a few yards from a press area where we could see Quilter and Brother Bob at a pre-show interview, we were given a red light. "Sorry, guys, this area is completely off limits. The President and Mr. Dobson are giving an interview for Russian telecom. No outsiders here at all."

"Too bad, friend," Vincent said, looking straight ahead. "Rich needs these briefing papers for Berlin tomorrow."

"Rich?" the guard said. "Do you have ID for this?"

Vincent took out a holographic ID, and the guard tried to decode it. As he was doing this, Vincent took out his handscreen, pretending to be casually studying it. He pushed a small slide on it and immediately the guard stood, board-straight, paralyzed, smiling blankly. "How did you do that?" I asked him.

"It's a little trick one of my knights taught me. A new function on my screen. Works like a charm."

Once past the guard, soon we were in sight of Quilter and the portly Dobson, who looked, in their makeup and toupees, like two plaster puppets. At this point, I saw a waiter go over to them to offer something from a tray. "Would you gentlemen like some refreshment?"

"What have you got?" Quilter asked.

"I don't care," Brother Bob cut in. "I'm as parched as the Sinai Desert." The waiter offered them two fruit drinks. "Any chance of any tequila in that?"

"It's already in, Brother Bob," the waiter said and smiled.

"Good for you!" Dobson said. "A little libation in the name of the Lord is precisely called for."

We could hear every word they said. Although both Quilter and Brother Bob wore ear inserts to get briefings and amplify the voices of others, like so many old men who were losing their hearing, they spoke very loudly. Brother Bob, who was used only to speaking in public, whose every word, in fact, was accepted as a public utterance, spoke at what normally would have been a shout level. I could see that Quilter had a hard time keeping up with this. He was not a shouter. But after being known for years as a man who once could not say a word publicly without stepping all over himself, he framed each word, syllable, and consonant precisely.

"It's in them," Vincent whispered to me. I asked him how he could tell. "I just can. I don't know how. I don't even have to look on my handscreen—it must be some kind of vibration."

The interview was over. Vincent walked up to them. In the glare of the telecom lights, with dozens of aids and production people staring right at him, he shook Quilter's hand. Quilter looked at him like he was a long lost cousin, the old politician's "I-know-I-know-you-I-just-can't-place-you" gaze that in the past I'd even seen on Enkidu. Vincent was smooth; I had some idea what he was saying since he'd been rehearsing it to me. In a nutshell, he was presenting himself as a "gay conservative," part of a low-key group of closet WC gays who were not in favor of "special status for anyone." "We want to be treated like other people," Vincent was saying. "Keeping San Francisco as a gay reserve is not fair to the silent majority of good men and women who are not part of the promiscuous San Francisco gay culture."

I saw Quilter grab Vincent's arm and pat him on the back soundly.

"Love the sinner, hate the sin!" Dobson broke in. "You deserve the same rights as anybody else! The loud deviates, the drag queens, the rowdy gays— let me tell you, they undermine your rights. And the most important right you have, right now, is to worship Jesus Christ just like anybody else. I had a meeting with the new Pope himself last month and he said he was going to reverse a thousand years of Catholic policy. He wants to embrace you gays in the Church, because he said, 'only there can they be changed.' And the Holy Father is correct. Let me tell you, Christ never said a word about homosexuality—He was above that kind of thing. He was a man of the common people, not the special people. But homosexuals, for some reason, seem to want to be treated like they're plain different."

"Not all of us," Vincent said. "Some of us want to take our places in the WCP, just like anybody else."

144   "That is something," Quilter chimed in, very seriously, "I, for one, have

always wanted." A makeup man came in and fluffed up the President's toupee and brushed some more color on his ancient face. Brother Bob pretended to wave him off—"They're gonna have to take me warts and all, just like the Lord will"—he joked, and then submitted to the same treatment Quilter did. "I want you," Quilter said to Vincent, "to be sitting up front at this telecomcast. And I—*personally*—I want you to say in front of a billion people what you just said to us right here."

Vincent bowed his head. "I am prepared."

Vincent and I were seated in the "live" audience for the show. These were several rows of chairs set up within camera range on stage. They were usually for kids who had thrown away their crutches at the insistence of Brother Bob or heathens who had given up Shiva, Buddha, or drugs and the new "bangbutt" music, that could not be played on the mostly WCP-controlled radio, for the sake of Christ. The show began with a WCP version of the "Star Spangled Banner" sung by the hundred-voice "STF" Chorus ("Oh, say can you see, through the Christ's perfect Light/ by the Cross we will stand/ in the twilight's last gleaming. . . ."). Then the "Up With Goodness" dancers came on dressed as life guards, cheerleaders, Girl and Boy Scouts, and other exemplary adolescent types. The boys looked really sexless and "wholesome," like they'd just been formed out of some lo-cal butter substitute and were ready to be spread on toast.

After the dancers, the whole hall darkened. Then accompanied by a gasp, a mountainous 3-D holographic image of a young blond Christ floated above our heads. His snowy white robes rippled in the darkness; a make-believe wind parted them just enough to reveal his smooth, seductively chiseled chest. "Christ must have joined the NFL," Vincent whispered to me, as His sandals passed over us. I wasn't sure who the NFL was, but the audience "oohhh!"ed it up. Lights were again raised and an announcer with a twangy country accent took over. "Friends and neighbors all over the world, the Strength To The Faithful Club is here this evening in San Francisco, a pretty lady by the Bay but with some ungodly habits, that we want Jesus to take care of right now! So here for your spiritual growth is our own BROTHER BOB DOBSON with his guest, J. RICHLAND QUILTER, President of the UNITED STATES!"

Dobson got up from his plush chair and shook hands with Quilter and they hugged in that way telecom men did, with their fists clenched, and then Quilter sat down quietly and Brother Bob began his talk, introducing the subject of sin, concentrating on homo sin in San Francisco. He repeated many

145

times that, like God, he loved all people, and had a very close place in his heart for repentant sinners. I looked over at Vincent and saw something in his eyes I had not been prepared to look at: it was revulsion mixed with the reflection of power itself. The reflection was flat, without a hint of compassion in it. He was looking directly at Quilter and Brother Bob, and absorbing their coldness at the same time. It was inevitable, but it made my stomach turn and made me want to get this over with. I moved my hand to his, and cautiously touched it. He recoiled. "When will you do it?" I whispered.

Vincent looked straight ahead. His face chilled me. What had I done to him—and to myself? I wanted to get out of there; I hated these people so much that even killing them did not seem good enough. He turned his head a few degrees, then whispered to me. "You are in my thoughts right now, Albert. Don't think you aren't."

Then Quilter got up to speak. After praising the decent people of San Francisco, the WCP, and Bob Dobson many times, he announced: "Now, folks, I want to introduce a young man who comes from a different point of view. All this talk about 'gay reserves'"—hissing and boos from the audience—"I know, friends, this is not a pleasant topic among Christians, but we have to face it. This young man wants the New Conservatism to embrace homosexuals and allow them in, as long as they give up any special status. What do we think of that?"

"NO QUEERS!" rang out from the audience. "No Queers in the WCP— Christ does NOT bless QUEERS!"

The din went on for several minutes. Dobson and Quilter looked at each other and slowly nodded. Quilter knew that it was time for Brother Bob to say something instructional. He backed away and Dobson said, "We Christians listen to all sides, don't we? Don't we always say 'Love the SINNER, but hate the SIN!'" Steady rhythmic, clapping went up; Brother Bob smiled. He nodded his head, then added, "But remember this, friends and neighbors: *Hate in the name of Jesus is better than Love in the name of anybody else!* That's something I am not ashamed of, and I call that the truth!" A huge cheer followed. "Now, let's hear once more from Brother Rich, who is still, with *our* help, the President of this Christian country!"

For a moment Quilter looked dazed; almost off balance. Then he called Vincent forward to the camera area. "I want to say," Vincent began, "that a lot of us are not in favor of *any* special rights. We don't want *special* rights at all. All we want is to be able to live our lives with the same dignity that everybody else wants. We want to be able to walk down the streets without fearing abuse and we want not to *have* to blend in—that is, we don't want to have to fear just being ourselves. We don't feel these are special rights, just *human* rights—the right to have our own families, the right to love and be cared for—these are not special rights. They are only human rights, or you can give them any other name you want."

"You stated your point well, brother," Quilter chimed in. "And I'm sure you *don't* want 'special rights.' But, remember, the true family values of Christ and these United States do not recognize your desire for what you call 'human' rights, either. That's part of the old humanism, and look where that got us!" (The audience began booing again.) "Our Christian world, brothers and sisters, wants Christian rights, not 'human' rights!" The audience began to cheer, and Quilter added: "Especially, if those same rights lead *only* to your own *selfish* happiness!"

The audience booed again . . . without a single cheer. It went starkly quiet. For the first time, Quilter looked disturbed, even slightly bilious. He'd wanted them to cheer, and he didn't like at all what Vincent had said. Indeed, Vincent had surprised him. The President put on his best, pasted-on smile, which, truthfully, he knew he had never been able to do as well as Dobson. "We're going to give up this godless idea of *happiness* for real GODLI-NESS, aren't we, Brother Vincent?"

A few scattered, reassuring cheers went up and Quilter once more shook Vincent's hand. He gave him the clenched fist hug. Then he made sure that Vincent was escorted out of the camera area and back to his seat, as immediate pandemonium broke out in the audience.

"NO QUEERS FOR JESUS! NO GAYS IN THE WCP!"

This time it did not let up; the roar was earsplitting. Even when Brother Bob got up and lowered both of his hands from above his head, his old gesture for quiet, the chanting and shouts did not stop. "NO LOVE FOR QUEERS! HATE IN THE NAME OF THE LORD!"

The smile left Brother Bob's usually genial face. The ghost of panic rattled Quilter's tight nervous features. Guards in the hall went up, trying to sit people down again. Flyers, buttons, and wet soft drink cups were hurled towards the stage. The "STF" Chorus came back on, and began a medley starting with "That Old Rugged Cross." But the noise in the hall did not abate, and two security men, both of whom looked like armored tanks, approached us.

Vincent's hand reached into his jacket pocket. He pulled out his palm screen and casually glanced at it. He moved a slide on the screen's face and then, barely in a whisper, said to me: "Now, see why we had to do this?" The screen fell back into his pocket, as I felt the grip of one of the security goons pull me from my seat. Vincent smiled at the security team, which was met by four others. "I'm glad you guys can get us out of here alive!"

Wordlessly, we were escorted out of the "live area," while every face in the hall followed us. I had never felt such cold-blooded hate before. It emitted a sound of its own: a rattling thunder that got louder and louder, peaking into another wave of homophobic chants ("DEATH TO QUEERS. DEATH IN THE NAME OF JESUS!") until security on the stage realized that Quilter, who had started to weave about, had fallen to the floor. His tongue rolled out of his head. Only the whites of his eyes showed. Shock spread through the audience, followed by a rush towards him. The chants gave way to stunned disbelief.

We had passed already through the door to the underground corridor out of the center and were on our way down the passage, when a voice announced over a pocket radio: "The President has collapsed." The security team disappeared, rushing back towards the hall. We were left alone in a dim, low-ceilinged waiting room in front of the last door to get us out of the Towers. Over our heads were tiny watchful cameras. "What about Brother Bob?" I whispered.

"He'll be *over* in a few more minutes. It was planned to go slower on him."

"And us?"

"A cleaning company van's waiting. We'll be out of here in a second."

We were almost at the door, when I saw something accumulate in the shadows at the edge of the room. It seemed to come out of the air; its movement was not human. It passed silently towards us. I felt my body stiffen. Fear froze through me. I became aware of the pendant quivering and moving on my neck. A vision flashed to me of the two snakes: they were hissing and twisting in the dark. The shadow blackened, and my eyes met two narrow eyes in it. I could not utter a sound as the snakes twisted faster and faster. Then a dissolver was aimed point blank at Vincent's head.

He could not be dead. *No!!*—I was screaming. But not a sound came out of me. I tried to grab it; this thing that was not human. "You're mine," it told me. "*Go back with me.*"

Then it grabbed me. And only later do I remember, somehow, waking up.

CHAPTER 15

I have no idea how I got back to the suite and ended up on the bed in the darkened room. I had been sedated—an injection quickly shot into me. A man in a loose white suit was sitting over me. I could not see his face, but thick, hairy hands were gently stroking mine. I thought I'd had a dream that Vincent had been murdered and we were leaving this long hallway and just before, right as the door was opening, leading to freedom . . . the snakes opened their mouths and swallowed each other. . . . I squeezed my eyes shut as hard as I could to squeeze the scene out of my mind. It was too painful. "It's time to go home," he said. His voice was soothing, like the voice of Enkidu . . . but it was not like the voice of Vincent. "You have done everything here that you intended to do . . . you have done all the necessary work."

I was still out of it from the sedative. I felt terribly alone; not frightened, just empty inside. I remembered the screaming and craziness in the convention hall, the chants of hate that came from the audience. There was a knock at the door. A man came in—I had no idea who he was, but he said, "You're going to have to get him out of here as soon as possible. Can he travel?" The man in the white suit nodded. "They're doing a house-to-house search in New Castro. The WCP has started burning some buildings, but the gay reservists are fighting back. The Army's been called in. Both Quilter and Dobson are dead—they finally figured out it was done through cyber poisoning. It just went through them and stopped all their functioning. They found Vincent Lanier, but the cameras were not able to pick up his assailant."

"It's okay," the man in the suit said, hushing him. "Albert and I will be ready to leave shortly."

The man walked out of the room, and then the other man locked the door. He came back to my bed. I was only in my underwear. My hands reached up for my neck and I realized that even through all of this, I was still wearing the snake pendant. He started to stroke my body. "Let me take this off you," he said, kindly, trying to remove the pendant. But it would not budge. Every time he tried to remove it, the chain shrank from his hands, skittering across my skin, as if the chain itself had become a snake and were alive.

"It does not matter," the sweet voice said. "I will let you keep this, Albert

". . . always." I turned my head away from him. Bitter tears of gratitude clouded my eyes; I did not see him take his clothes off and get into bed with me. At first it felt only as if some sort of rushing fog had entered the environment of my most immediate senses: a larger darkness. His body: immense; hot. He put his mouth on mine and then reached into my briefs. He knew exactly where to find the Egg. "You will give this to me now," he said. "I allowed you to keep the pendant." I knew it was true. I could not fight anymore. I held on to him and closed my eyes as he drained me completely, sucking the seed out expertly, eating me with his deft tongue and lips, oiling me with the smoothness of his mouth and warm throat. My seed emerged in long coils of light and smoke. "It's sweet," he said, now back at my face, his mouth dribbling saliva over my neck. I touched his large blunt penis, that seemed weirdly cold—not a bit human—and big as a bull's.

"You know how to get back?" he asked.

"No. . . ."

"It's simple. Do you know who I am?"

"No."

"Yes, you do," the soothing voice said. "I am the thing you most feared, with whom you must now merge yourself: I, who allowed Vincent to kill Quilter, who was . . . you should know . . . one of us."

". . . one of *you*?"

"Yes, Lord Albert. Quilter came from my tribe: we were both creatures with the souls of animals: unmoved by the pain of others. Basically . . . *dead*. That is how he was once able to murder Nick and Reuvuer. His blood lacked warmth. But now, Albert, it is time for you to mate with me and I will have your own sweet warmth as I want—and all of Ki will be free."

I bolted out of the bed.

"*Noooooo!*" Now I knew who he was. But before I could escape, his hands had grabbed the pendant at my throat, gripping it until I felt the two snakes constrict as they wrapped themselves around my neck, causing the veins there to pop out of my skin. Then with his hands around my neck, his dead cock sprang to life and he fucked me, holding me down, until my short hoarse screams ceased and I realized, exactly as he had said, that I *had* merged with him: the brute animal within me . . . had come out. I could feel it: a strange, brainless inner movement, going through its own inverse evolution. Monkey; marsupial . . . amphibian; all the way down . . . until I knew this hairy creature on top of me was only sticking his hard, wet, male organ into something that had *once* been me, but was now disconnected from my real soul. I had become as low as a bottom-feeding mud worm: a lowly, slime-slick fluke wriggling mutely within his arms.

There I was: returned to shit-sweetened, primal ooze. I'd willed *not* to offer my body to him, but he'd taken it violently anyway; and me with it. I should have felt guilty but he had brutalized me past guilt. Past any glimmer of the light of self-awareness: to pure animal existence. But even there a sudden spark of nausea hit me. I threw up all over him, but that did not stop him. He merely brushed my vomit aside and continued. Certainly, I will never recall again the *total* horror of what he did to me. Because whatever mercy he had shown to me in our merging came only by delivering me from my real human form. And only thus had I been spared the *total* knowledge of the degradation he'd inflicted on me.

His cum roared inside of me, as intense as anything that had ever come out of me. I could feel it speeding and exploding. A storm of wild raging sperm, gripping the essence of time and space with it. It was pulling me— *grabbing me*—as his hands encircled and squeezed my throat, pressing hard the pendant with the two snakes until an impression of them burned their way right into my windpipe, leaving the boy Albert, who had been born in Massachusetts, dead. Suffocated. Only then did I know that the gruesome slide I had taken part in, the slide out of humanity's reach and into the animal chambers of a man's darkest brain, had left me—finally—mated with Nafshee.

Part Three

CHAPTER 16

The process reversed itself: the third Egg (my "special nut" as Lee used to call it) withdrew, invisibly, from my scrotum. As a variation of gravity, it began its spin back away from the dark room in San Francisco where Albert Lee lay lifeless. The Egg, which had once settled in Sandy Feltner's womb in the dark waters at Cape Cod, emerged into twilight: there it floated for a measureless second in the immensity of space. Time and Space folded: then passed themselves in opposite directions. I "awoke" on Ki, with the inert body of Enkidu lying on its bier next to me and Nafshee holding my cold hand. My only feeling as Albert, still a child of this planet, was that I had been napping. Briefly.

"He agrees now to MATE with ME!" Nafshee announced wildly. "Our Lord Albert agrees! In fact, *gladly*, he gave to me himself! And I *myself*—" he had to regain his breath—"as the Blue Monkeys do, will bear our son!"

"As I thought," Hortha said, bitterly. "You got to him on Earth, correct?"

"My son," Woosh suggested. "Is not to be castigated by you."

"Shut up!" the Elder Priestess hissed. "You hate your own child, anyway."

"Not anymore. He is even *more* ambitious than I."

Anvil looked at me, his wary reptile eyes sparkling. I looked around: we were all there again in the Temple. M'raetha, my sad old mother, and Dyla, the young, blond priestess.

I saw disappointment all over Hortha's wrinkled face. "We send you over to find a decent mate, and you end up with *Nafshee*? How did this ever happen?"

Anvil and Woosh joined hands. "We did not think you had it in you," Anvil gloated to Nafshee. "We did not think you were man enough to grab what should be yours!"

"He is *not* 'man' enough!" Woosh corrected. "He is a Blue Monkey like I am, or at least the best part of him is."

I sat up on the bier of death where I had "slept," while the real part of me was on Earth, for what had been on Ki a much shorter duration of time. I stretched my arms that still felt heavy. "Now is the time to take Enkidu into

155

the Cave of Mysteries," I said, sleepily. "As the Lord of Ki, it is the first thing that I want to do."

"That is only right," Woosh said, still smiling. "Anvil and I will see to it immediately—we shall arrange the burial of the Lord Enkidu in the Cave."

"*Not so!*" I snapped back, as if my ears had lied to me. "Just because your son tricked me—and murdered the man I loved and would have brought back to Ki, the man who shared my seed and my Egg—that does *not* mean that you and Anvil will *ever* control life here."

"Is this true?" Woosh asked. "My son . . . resorted to trickery? I am shocked by the very mention of it. *Shocked!*"

"Do not listen to that old monkey," Hortha retorted. "He is merely shocked that his son, who he thought was a fool, could do anything so impulsive. These two have been waging their own war—and fouling up the planet in a way that will take us a lifetime of Ten Moons to clean."

"Nobody likes a bitter old lady," Woosh reminded her, wagging his dirty index finger in front of Hortha's face. Hortha lifted her hand as if to slap him for his effrontery. "It seems that Nafshee has won Albert's hand and heart— if not his sweet soul—fair and well. Now we will take Albert back with us, and we will build a new palace in our own part of the planet, away from the Dark Men from whom Enkidu came. These forest men do not have the future of Ki in mind. In fact, they have no future at all. Correct, Anvil?"

"Absolutely, according to my plan and Woosh's." With these words, a group of Anvil's men broke into the Temple of Ki. They marched past the statue of the Goddess Laura, who looked even more familiar to me than ever. They pushed Nafshee as well as the women away, then surrounded me. Thick leg irons and handcuffs were snapped onto my ankles and wrists; I was grabbed to my feet and taken away with force.

"You will not get away with this!" Hortha screamed until her voice cracked. "Albert will always be Lord of Ki—I swear to you!"

Woosh bowed lowly. "Right you are, dear Sister: Albert shall be Lord." He rose up to his full height. "It is just that in our own *humble* way, we will advise him."

"Yes, that is so," Anvil said. The baron began to cackle to himself. Then he broke into a full blast of laughter, which Woosh, strangely enough, did not join in. "Come, Woosh," Anvil said, smiling through his rotten teeth. "Once more Albert is ours to do our bidding. I think it would be a pity to murder him, after all of this, especially now that your beloved Nafshee is mated with him."

"Shhh," whispered Woosh. "No talk of murder." Even I, fresh from my "nap" on Earth, could see that Hortha's presence inhibited Woosh. She looked directly at the old monkey. Suddenly she spat right into his face. Then, with Dyla and M'raetha, she walked out of the room.

Nafshee looked stricken, as if all of his animal courage had turned to sugar water in the face of his father's power on Ki. I caught his eyes as I was led away. "I *would* have shared myself with you," I called back to him. "The mate I wanted from Earth would never have allowed this outrage to happen—but you are powerless here, Nafshee. But remember this: if they do kill me, you will be left with nothing. *Nothing!*"

I was brought back over the dung-colored plains of Ki to Anvil's busy, glowering fortress. There I was kept under continuous guard. At the drop of night I was promptly violated over and over again by Anvil, then beaten and threatened with death; while by day the people of Ki came to me, petitioning, making me their lord, "free" to rule them. A mock court was set up and the people were eager to see me, Albert, Enkidu's son. The Off-Sexers came with their disputes over land and inheritance, and I settled them, and each time Anvil raked off a big portion of each settlement: profitable parcels of land, jewels, precious metals, provisions and animals, all of this he claimed for the "Court of Ki," which in fact was none other than himself. He set himself up as my sheriff and bondsman. I became more and more dispirited. My stomach turned as I realized that as the days dragged on, my own presence became a farce, while he became ever more powerful. The only Kivians who stayed away were men from the Same-Sex enclaves, my own brothers, whose absence remained a mystery to me: could they see—did they know, instinctively—what was going on?

Sometimes, after Anvil finished, Nafshee came later at night to me, engaging in what he called in his own tender, stupid way "sex," but which in fact was no more than another rape. He fucked me like a dog, making me squat with my shackled wrists and ankles on all fours, while he entered me from behind, pushing and plowing through my unlubricated rear, making me scream from pain as his swollen poker of ape equipment thrust into me. He apologized after each event. "Was I too rough, Lord? You obtained no satisfaction at all?"

I could only laugh. At one time I had been an unmarried prince who had taken the form of a childish but dutiful son; now I was a prisoner who had taken the form of a king. My only comfort was the pendant with the two snakes that never left my neck. It appeared gleaming in the first shit I had taken back on Ki. I had pulled it out from my own feces and then carefully washed it (mindful always of the strange powers it had) and then placed it back on my neck. I knew that it would never leave that place again. I touched 157 it whenever I felt my resolve to survive fading, and at those moments when either Anvil or Nafshee "had their way with me" I would touch it again and feel the power of the twin snakes revolving in my hand.

Anvil did not resent Nafshee's sexual attentions towards me. He welcomed them, personally leading Nafshee into my cell; they only added to what the warlord thought was my necessary daily dose of humiliation. Nafshee thought he was making love to me in the most noble way he could, but Anvil knew that Nafshee would never be able to free me—could never make me totally his own. Nafshee was too afraid of Anvil's whiplash anger, which, allied with the power of the Blue Monkeys—led by Woosh—kept him always, once outside of my cell, weak and intimidated. The three of them seemed to be in a pattern of their own, corrupting and polluting all of Ki as they kept me a pawn and a prisoner.

I watched over the next several Moons as Anvil's power mushroomed and Woosh (who, with his Blue Monkeys, stayed aligned with Anvil) remained ever "innocent," pretending always to be on the side of our Same-Sex brothers and the ancient "balance" of Ki. With the bounty he had been able to extort from the Court, Anvil proceeded to build my "castle," which actually was to be his own. Skeletal palatial rooms grew up before my eyes—I could see its structure taking shape from the small cell in which I tried to sleep.

I could take it, finally, no longer. I began to make sly coded messages in my pronouncements. In the midst of a law suit over land rights, I hinted: "Take care not to see *red*, when you leave here." To a condemned murderer, I smiled and said: "Take heart, friend. You are less a prisoner than I, your own king." With Anvil at my side, telling me which decision I was "free" to make, I rebelled, eventually siding even with the guilty to thwart him. "You are signing your own death notice," he whispered at my right hand, as I let a group of accused thieves, who were only poor farmers who had attempted to steal food from Anvil's rich estates, free to return to their meager farms.

When I was alone in my cell one night, after a dismal visit from Nafshee, there was a knock at the door. Anvil entered with Torahn and Ola, two of his lieutenants. They were both burly and knuckleheaded. They seemed even more apelike than Nafshee, although by their birth documents they were both human. They began to spit and jeer at me, until Anvil restrained them. "Enough! Our Lord Albert is to be respected; is that not so?"

"He is a slack-off!" Ola growled. "With no sense of justice. He sides with the weak and pathetic against the right. Ki will fall into rebellion unless Albert is curbed, Lord Anvil."

Anvil smiled. "So what should we do?"

"It is up to you, Lord Anvil," Ola said. "But if it *was* up to me, I would

call for a trial now. We would put *him* on trial for mating with that ape
Nafshee. And for letting thieves and murderers loose."

"But," Torahn smartly observed. "Mating with Nafshee was the best thing
he ever did. Mating with Nafshee delivered him right into *our* hands."

I watched all of this mutely, close to tears, and wished that I were simply
a boy back on Earth. And not a "king," on Ki.

"Shut up, fools," Anvil warned. "We shall put him on trial, that is the
truth. But we can not do that for 'letting thieves loose.' The people will not
stand for it. There will be an insurrection; there has been word that the Same-
Sex bastards are banding together. The forests are starting to teem with them.
As much as we try to keep them in a state of warfare ourselves, if they band
together and ever ally with their Off-Sex cousins, all will be over. No, we
will have to do something a little more"—he stopped, then said—"clever."

There was a pause; my gut feeling, since they'd finally stopped keeping
me shackled in my tiny cell, was to want to raise my fists and strike Anvil
dead.

"What are you talking about?" I asked. I reached under my loose shirt and
secretly touched the snake pendant. I knew I'd never get out of the fortress
alive; its dark halls and crude barrack rooms were crawling with Anvil's
thugs. But suddenly the ugly, crippling shame that had stalked me like a
shadow left; and the threat of death meant nothing to me, only rejoining
Vincent, whose spirit was within me as his pendant vibrated with a life of its
own close to my heart. But I realized death would mean deserting my brothers in the forests; it appeared that very soon they would need me.

"Pay it no mind," Anvil snapped back at me. He began to chuckle. "Have
fun with your *ape*-mate!"

This last insult did it; I could control myself no more. I'd paid enough for
every humiliation. Both of my fists slammed straight into Anvil's teeth:
bull's eye; he reared back, knocked flat to the floor. Torahn and Ola grabbed
me. But kick-jamming with my left heel, I rammed into both sites of their
balls and then used my fists to do as much damage as I could. Anvil slowly
hoisted himself up. With his men restraining me, he hit me hard in my face,
chest, belly, and groin. But I would not be stopped. Even though lights were
blinking above my head, I called on the power of the entwined snakes and
shoved his two goons off me. Then I grabbed Anvil again. Torahn rushed out
for reinforcements, and five guards came piling in. I knew they had me now.
"Try to murder me!" I warned, out of breath. "You will NEVER get away
with it!"

Anvil stroked his jaw where my fists had hit him. There was blood in his
mouth; he spat a brownish red mess into my eyes as his guards held me.

"Murder you, King? Never!" He and his men left the cell, locking the door behind them. I sat in silence on my hard cot and wondered what their plan was. I looked up. From the small peephole in the door, I saw a pair of smiling lips. "Murder the king?" Anvil taunted. "No, dear Lord. That bitch Hortha would never allow such a thing . . . but any problems from you and we *are* going to try you—for the *murder* of Nafshee."

CHAPTER 17

The murder of Nafshee . . . my repulsive mate; enemy; on Earth, some-times . . . savior. The archfiend who had raped me and brought me back to Ki, alone, without Vincent—the mate I loved. This was a total declaration of Anvil's power: that after such a trumped-up trial, with Hortha kept at a dis-tance but Woosh presiding at the baron's own right hand, my head would end up rolling across the executioner's floor. So the only thing keeping me alive was . . . Nafshee. What an revolting thought, as I mulled over it that night. I felt furious, alone, and angry. If *only* Vincent had been there. If *only* I'd been able to take him back with me, instead of being raped and forced back against my will by Nafshee, who—as forceful and evil as he'd been on Earth—was as of late impotent against Woosh on Ki.

What could I do? I jumped out of bed, and looked over at the door. I knew they were watching from the peephole. I was naked; the only thing I wore was the pendant. But it burned with an odd cool heat on my bare chest, reminding me of its remarkable presence. It had become as much a part of my own life as the Egg of the Eye, violently twisting in my scrotum. My anger only made me feel more frustrated, more a prisoner. I banged on the door, and saw an eye darken the space behind the hole: "Sir?" I shouted for him to *Get Out!* "Get your wormy *eye* away from me!"

The guard only laughed. "Get used to it, Lord!"

I got back, seething, into my bed. When I'd felt frightened and hopeless the situation did not hurt so much; I had been too saddened even to *think* about my liberation. But now, something different was in the air . . . and even I, from the bleak confines of my cell, felt it.

The next day another case was brought before me. For the first time, a Same-Sex couple was brought before my court. They were renegades, them-selves outlaws: Rakdu, a tall dark handsome man, with muscular arms and shoulders and large hands and feet, and his partner, Norland, a smaller, inter-esting fellow; lean, bright-eyed, intense. It seemed that by accident, they had wandered from the wet forests of the Same-Sexers and found themselves trudging the endless rolling distances of the Off-Sex plains. This had happened ten Moons ago, and they decided to stay there. Exactly why was hard to say: perhaps they were tired of the infighting among their own people or was it just adventure; the search for something new?

They took on a clandestine career of poaching late at night and hiding during the day. They avoided the armed Off-Sex patrols and lived by their raw wits. Finally after chasing some small game through the territories of Othar, another greedy baron who had aligned himself with Anvil, they were surrounded and caught. They admitted in front of me that they had pursued some small buck deer onto Othar's reserves, "But," as Norland said, humbly, "Lord Othar is not interested in these animals; his farms provide well for him." Othar, a porcine, suet-bellied man, was not interested in their excuses. He whispered something to Anvil who stood, as always, at my right. "Kind Lord Othar demands *blood*," Anvil said to me coldly. "Blood coming . . . from their severed heads."

I cringed. Othar's thinking—I was sure—was why not start at the top? A more usual sentence would have involved some sort of restitution . . . most probably hard labor. The free labor would have benefited Othar and more than made up for the small animals lost from his lands. But there were principles involved here: that Rakdu and Norland had breached the laws of Ki, had left their own brothers in the forests, and were now wandering freely through a territory of rich Off-Sex vales. Suppose the two men had actually decided to settle there and then bring in others? The mixing of the two tribes—Off-Sex and Same-Sex—did not set well on our planet. Anvil looked at me and smiled. "Allow our friend Othar to exact a heavy sentence, your Lordship. We must show this scum that boundaries must be respected on Ki."

"Exactly how heavy?" I asked innocently.

Anvil looked at Othar and they both grinned. "If you will not agree to their lives, we will accept fifteen years' hard labor on Othar's lands—instead of their heads." Othar bowed his head, satisfied.

I pretended to think on it. The whole court was silent through this charade. Usually, I would mouth as a puppet simply what Anvil had dictated.

"I am easy," Othar said, licking his rubbery lips. "I will go with twelve years' *very* hard labor, your Lordship."

"Not enough," Anvil corrected. "Too generous. *Fifteen,* at least."

"Agreed, not enough!" I ordered. The whole startled court turned, unbelieving, to me. An uproar went up. I called for order and put out my right hand. "Their heads . . . exactly as Othar requested."

Othar bowed at me. "Lord Albert, that is *most* generous. You are persuading me to give our Lord Anvil an immense bounty for such a just sentence—"

Rakdu began to cry. "Lord Albert," he sobbed. "Our heads for a few stags? I do not understand—who was your father? Did he not come from our people?"

"Justice must be served," I said calmly. Othar looked jubilant; Anvil scowled, while Norland looked calmly at me. I could see in his bright eyes a premonition. "Take them away," Anvil ordered his sergeants. "Prepare them for execution."

"Wait," I demanded. "One small condition." With the attention of the whole room riveted on me, I cleared my throat. "The sentence must be carried out only in the Six Moons." The Six Moons were weeks—reckoned on our rather clumsy Kivian calendar—away; we were only in the first days of the Fives.

"*Why?*" Anvil demanded; but Othar put out his hand. "Allow the King his wish," suggested Othar, satisfied in his need for blood.

"They must meditate on their crimes," I explained. "They must understand their *significance.*"

"The King is right!" Othar agreed. "What is the use of a punishment if the criminal does not understand the crime?"

"Yes," I said. "And I want them to realize how painful their deaths will be." Anvil nodded his head at this. He raised his eyes in a revolting, triumphant grin. "So," I added forcefully, "*I* will remind them of it every day. I myself will instruct them *each* day in the right attitudes of Ki."

"You are indeed," Othar said smugly, "the wisest king Ki has ever and *will* ever have."

I thanked the greedy baron, then placed my gaze on the two attractive Same-Sex prisoners. Then, casually, I added: "But, to do this, properly, they must sleep in *my* room while they think about their misdeeds."

Anvil looked up, jolted out of his triumph. "Impossible!"

"Very well," I assented. "As you wish, Lord Anvil." I turned to Rakdu and Norland. "If the court cannot comply with my order, then I order that you both be released. You, Rakdu and Norland, are therefore free to go."

"Wait!" the baron said, "Agreed!" He took out a fat gold chain from his pocket and stuffed it into Anvil's hand before Anvil could say another word. "Their heads, on the Six Moons! I, myself, will ensure, Lord Albert, that they are kept exactly as you wish. I will even *pay* for the condemneds' provisions. Justice will be served on Ki!"

I looked at Rakdu and Norland as they were led away in chains. Radku turned his sorrowful head back at me, his tall body trembling. I wondered how they would feel, the two of them, trying to figure out what I was doing. The picture this brought to my mind was not pleasant, but it was much better than any alternative Anvil or Othar might have suggested for them.

At the end of a long day, I was led into a larger cell where the three of us would sleep. As soon as the guards left us and the heavy door was slammed, I told them how happy I was to see them. I kissed them both on the lips and started, as much as I tried not to, to weep. "But you condemned us to death!" Rakdu cried. "You are a king and yet you live in a cell with prisoners—why?"

I told them then my own story, about Anvil and Woosh taking me a prisoner, about the ape Nafshee's mating with me, and Anvil's plan to have Nafshee murdered and to try me for it. "In short," I ended, "we are all renegades. The three of us are now outside of the law, although I am supposed to uphold it; that is why I need you to help me."

"We will," Norland swore. "For a long time the Dark Men thought you had deserted us. You did not mate with one of us and you lived in a castle, away from us. We knew that Enkidu, your father, had mated with an Off-Sexer and we felt that you, too, had left us."

"It is true," I said sadly. Then I explained that had I chosen a Same-Sex man as my mate, the jealousy of others from my tribe would have left Ki in turmoil. "I wanted to mate with someone else," I confessed. "A man from far away."

"How far?" Norland asked. I told him the truth: Earth.

Rakdu looked confused. "*Earth*? That is way beyond the Tanna." He was referring to the great muddy river that ran through our wet forests.

"Yes," Norland smiled. "Earth is very, very far; it is another planet. There have been ancient stories of some of us who went there and there met other Same-Sex men. You met such a man?"

"Yes. I wanted him as my promised friend. He was full of courage and daring. He tried to solve the problems of his own people. But," I could not help my tears again, "Nafshee murdered him."

"Perhaps death on Earth is not the same as death here," Norland suggested. "Perhaps there is a way of getting him back."

The three of us looked at each. "The Tree!" Rakdu exclaimed. "I have seen the Tree!"

"You have?" I asked.

"Yes," he said, nodding his head. "I am only a simple hunter, but once you see the Tree you are never the same. One day, perhaps six Ten Moons ago, while I was out with Norland, we became separated—"

"I remember," Norland said.

"I fell into a deep pit. I was sure that I would die. I saw animals walking along the edge of it; animals I had never seen before. Animals not on Ki— huge, like big deer and woolly things with long noses. They appeared to me as if in a dream."

"You never told me this," Norland said.

"You would only think me stupid. I thought I had gone crazy. Then I started to wander off—or maybe only my mind did, as in sleep. I came to a forest, filled with sad dead trees. In the middle was this huge tree, green and full of light, and on it were the empty skins of—"

"Us," I said.

Radku bowed his head. "Yes," he said, humbly. "I realized they were *our* skins."

"The Tree is hidden from us," Norland declared. "But you—Rakdu!—have seen it." Tears filled Norland's eyes. He kissed Rakdu tenderly.

It was late. I expected a visit from Anvil or Nafshee soon. But no one came. Perhaps they realized that since I was no longer sleeping alone in my cell, no longer could they could come and go as they pleased, doing what they wanted to me. I went to the door and put my ear to it. I heard nothing at all outside. I turned to Radku and Norland. "I promise you this: neither of you will die. No matter what."

Then we heard the peephole of the cell door snap open. I could see Anvil's fishy eye swim back and forth behind it. A guard unlocked the door. "A regular henhouse," Anvil observed, stomping in. "I would fuck all three of you, but I would not give you vermin such pleasure. But nor shall you give it to each other. Henceforth, an eye will be behind this door, spying on you all night."

He left, slamming the cell door behind him. The peephole was open. I went over to it, and saw another eye staring directly at me. We stripped off our clothes and went to bed, the two of them sharing one small cot and I in another. I tossed and turned, watching the two of them holding each other. I got up several times and looked directly into the peephole and saw the eye there. Finally I went back to my cot and realized that I lusted for the two men who slept next to me, wanted to have them in the worst way, wanted to experience sex with another man who was not a monster.

The White Star came up and the eye was still there. I was sure that the eye must have been very sleepy, even more sleepy than I. The next day Anvil's guards came back for me, and I went out to pretend to be king again, while Rakdu and Norland remained prisoners in my cell.

Anvil met me in his dismal court chamber. "I trust my lord has slept well," he said winking. "You must be very frustrated having two such handsome men next to you." I told him on the contrary, that I had slept perfectly. "Good, my lord! Because an eye will always be kept on you. If we see any foolishness going on in your chamber, I personally will come in and kill those prisoners. After all, our bargain said that you would personally *instruct* them, not fuck them!" He laughed till his sides hurt.

All day I could think of nothing except Rakdu and Norland, who waited in my cell. But the question was how could I keep the cat-like eyes of my jailers off us. I thought about it steadily while a parade of disputes came before me, and Anvil whispered into my ear what decisions should be made. Frankly, I cared little what the outcome would be. I thought about sticking a finger into the eye, but knew that the jailer would only scream and bring in more guards; then Rakdu and Norland would surely be killed. Now I felt bad about what I had done; the pleasure of having them with me was diminished. The only good thing I realized was that if Anvil would stay away from me, so would Nafshee; I began to look forward to returning to my chamber that night, the thought of being with the two renegade Same-Sexers warming me, even if their sweet bodies could not.

Then just as the day of court proceedings ended, Nafshee appeared. Suddenly I found his presence a little less repulsive. "I am told that you no longer sleep alone in your cell, my mate and lord. That two others are in your room." I told him this was true; he bowed his head. "Then I will not come in for sex with you until the night of their deaths."

I could not help but smile.

"You realize, Albert, that as a Blue Monkey, *I*, Nafshee, still bear your son."

It was a sad fact but true. By ingesting my seed, he had impregnated himself—this was the distinction of his vile tribe: that indeed, even the males could bear young. The thought of having a son with him revolted me.

"When will this thing be born?" I asked.

"It is not a thing; it belongs to you and me, Albert. It will come in the Sixth Moon—just in time for the deaths of your friends."

I bowed my head. The smile fell from my face; but what took its place was an iron determination. If I had to, I would die with Radku and Norland, rather than be alone with Anvil and Nafshee. I wondered what this strange ape-issue from us would be like. I had heard of such monsters before, strange freaks of nature born from the mating of two species. My distaste for it must have shown on my face.

"You look pained, Lord Albert," Nafshee noticed. I did not answer him. "I am sorry for your pain. Anvil has told me you are being watched in your cell each night: to make sure there is no sex between you and these 'friends.'"

166

"There is none," I assured him and asked him to leave. The sight of him was starting to repulse me again. Suddenly I felt that if Anvil did want to murder Nafshee and cast the blame on me, then I would only too gladly accept it—just to be rid of him.

"Alright, Albert, I will tell you: if I find out that you and these men are doing sex with each other, then *I* shall kill you."

I started to laugh. "Fat chance of that!" I howled and spat right into his face.

"You HATE me!" he screamed, turning away from me. His body began to shake. I was puzzled: how could a thing so powerful as he had been once on Earth be so weak on Ki? The riddle amazed me. I wanted to kick him hard and end, somehow, this strange child he bore with me. I grabbed his shoulder and pulled his foul-breathed face to mine. "Watch yourself, Nafshee. Anvil has promised me that your days are numbered. You may not live long enough to bear this strange fruit you have promised me."

Nafshee wiped his swollen eyes with a thick leathery hand. "So Woosh will have it," he confessed sadly. "That is *his* power; that even in my death, *he* will take our child."

He walked away from me. I felt that I would never be off the hook. But, at least—with the Goddess's help—I would decide *whose* hook I would rest on.

CHAPTER 18

Again the hours drifted by that evening, while the three of us knew we were being watched at every moment. Norland decided to play a little game with the jailer. He went up to the peephole and stuck his eye into it, so that our jailer's eye from the other side met his. We heard a big belly laugh from outside, and Norland winked. The door unlocked. The jailer, another of Anvil's brainless minions, whose breath stank of cheap barley beer and rotten teeth, giggled. "Making winkies at me, you fairies!"

Norland smiled demurely. "I thought, your lordship, you would be amused. I see you are a right striking figure of a man!"

"My name is Balbus," the jailer said, sticking out a shapeless, greasy palm. "Few around here treat me kindly, but like anyone else I can appreciate a gentleman who recognizes quality."

"You are of the highest quality of any of our jailers," Norland observed. "And my eye will always be upon you, sira."

Balbus's head bowed. "If it were up to me, personally I would thrash you both soundly." He bobbed his head in profound self-satisfaction. "But I would *not* ask for your heads."

"You are kind," Norland said. "And we will consider you our friend."

"That, sir, you cannot do. Anvil would have *my* head, if he knew I was friends with sorts like you." He snapped his toes and knees together, almost crippling himself in an attempt to appear in command. Then, as his bovine, swaying rump disappeared from our faces, he slammed the big door behind himself and ceremoniously locked it.

After the door was locked, Norland resumed looking through the peephole, snorting sometimes, while Balbus laughed as well. This continued deep into the night, until I fell asleep from exhaustion. Suddenly I was woken by a hand, gently touching me. A soft, moist pair of lips touched my own. It was Rakdu, big and naked, and now slipping into my cot. He whispered into my waiting ear: "Norland has his eye on the peephole. The pig behind the door cannot see as long as Norland does this."

I opened up my arms and pulled Rakdu closer to me, feeling his large male piece touch mine. I knew that I could not share seed with him, he had been promised, after all, to Norland; but the feel of his warm sweet body next to mine was like food and drink to the starved. "I have not held a real man in so long," I whispered. "Only these animals, who come at night to shame and rape me."

"If they should dare, my King, I will kill them," Rakdu said sincerely, pushing his tongue into my mouth to taste there the very desire I had for him. I was sure that I could contain it no longer, as he began to stroke my male organs with his hands and then lovingly explore them with his mouth.

"No," Norland whispered to us. "You must stop. The jailer is getting angry." Rakdu tiptoed back to his cot, and Norland left his place at the door. We could see again an eager eye peering in at us from the other side. I wondered then what Balbus really wanted to watch, and if his most sincere desire was to catch me having sex with my two friends.

This strange charade went on for a week, with Norland spending time at the door, peeping through the other end of the peephole and Rakdu stealing into my bed and offering his body to me. I wondered if Norland was jealous of this; and if he was, how did he contain it. But having Rakdu close to me, kissing and holding him, getting me hot almost to the point of explosion was just reward for the days I spent in Anvil's corrupt court. I had to be careful though that Anvil did not see it, that I looked well-rested, as if nothing had taken place. Then, at the end of the week, after a grueling day of making settlements, I returned to the cell, and saw a different look on Norland's face.

"We have succeeded," he said. I asked him what he meant, and Rakdu answered: "My friend today asked them for paper, pen, and colored inks. Show the King what you have made."

Being careful not to let the spy behind the door see it, Norland showed me an eye, totally lifelike that he had drawn. It resembled his own in color and size. He had pierced small holes in it, so that light passed through it, as would a real eye. "I have even made some paste from the flour that remains on the doughy bread they feed us and water," Norland said. "So tonight, we will test out the eye; then the three of us will go on a forest journey."

That evening when Balbus came on duty, Norland again began his winking game. We could tell, though, from the loud yawns from the other side that our piggish jailer was tired. He laughed some, then told Norland to stop. But Norland did not, and soon both of their eyes were staring quietly from either side of the heavy door. Then Rakdu handed Norland the drawn eye and the paste and Norland pasted the eye to the door.

We waited to see if the jailer could detect this, but he did not. Norland stripped his clothes off and joined Rakdu and me in bed. The two of them started to make love to me at once, with Norland seizing my male-pipe and sucking it until I was sure I could not hold back my seed any longer, as Rakdu kissed me and held me in his large hairy arms and caressed me. Then, just as I was ready to explode into orgasm and could hold back no more, Norland took my organ from his mouth and pressed the thickened tip of it with his fingers. The two of them began kissing me and touching me at once. They knew exactly how to touch, kiss, and hold me. I felt off balance, as if I were being sucked back into a peculiar void: perhaps it was the void of the orgasm that did not come, but I realized immediately that I was someplace I had been before, traveling a distance once more of many light years.

Earth. At the moment of Vincent's death.

The thing that had appeared in the hallways was raising the fatal dissolver to Vincent. But I, under the influence of Rakdu and Norland, was no longer helpless. I had achieved the power that I had wanted to escape Nafshee's guile. I put myself between his weapon and the Earth being I loved. I could see Vincent's face now, terrified. *No!* he screamed as Brother Bob's security force ran back towards us. "They need a killer, Albert. Let it be me!"

"You will not die," I said as Nafshee's face became more distinct. I pushed Vincent away; at that moment my head was directly in the path of the dissolver.

"You cannot die here, Albert," Rakdu interceded—thrusting his thoughts into my mind—"Let what must be happen. *They want a villain and Vincent has agreed to be it.* Remove yourself!"

I did.

Again, the scene: the strange shape behind the dissolver. Fire, brilliant, sharp as a laser's eye, cutting through Vincent's beautiful face, piercing to the core of his brain. He crumpled—and the dark form grabbed me, trying to snatch me away. But Rakdu would not allow it, I was in his muscular arms this time as Norland sucked me, slowly, replaying the scene again, but now—as I had not expected it—differently. The orgasm he had withheld happened. Without my control; without my attempt to thwart destiny. There, at the dim edge of consciousness, I felt my seed reeling out softly, like a glowing filament of light twisting through dark space. And the seed itself—with its light shining all the way through Norland—was leading me and these two men back, through that same barren forest Enkidu had revealed to me, to the Tree.

The *Tree*; filled with the skins of our brothers. Empty skins waiting to be filled with souls. There hung the skins of Enkidu and Greeland, their boneless fingers touching each other's hand; and of Greedu and Nick and Reuvuer, and below, on a lower limb was Vincent. His sweet body that I had loved was slack and empty, like a sail devoid of wind, or an evening when, unexpectedly, you remember someone who's gone and time stops right there.

Suddenly it was apparent to me what Vincent had been on Earth: he'd come to show me the way to my own completion—my adulthood—but had been killed by Nafshee's animal force before I could arrive at it. The three of us, Rakdu, Norland, and I, gazed at him in a rapture of recognition; they knew that he was my promised friend, for whom I had gone to the Earth. Norland whispered something into Radku's ear and the two of them lifted me up to him. I attempted to bring him down, as Enkidu had once guided me. But this time all I could do was nuzzle his face with mine; he was *too* far up for me to pull him down. My hands could not reach beyond his navel. All was silent. I looked down anxiously at my two friends from Ki; I wanted to ask for their help but could not. The Tree seemed so much bigger, filled with even more skins than I'd remembered. I wondered where they had come from. And faces: countless faces, even new faces that took me farther back through history. Then, as I looked at the faces, I realized that I was far away now from where Radku and Norland stood.

I looked again at Vincent. His boneless skin face was smiling. Did he really want to be there? "What should I do?" I called down below to them.

"One of us must clothe himself in his skin," Norland called up to me. "That is the only way."

"How do you know?" I asked.

"He knows!" Rakdu shouted. "He is much smarter than I."

"I will do it," Norland volunteered. "I have had your seed; that will protect me. And I hold you to your promise, Albert, that we will not die."

I carefully got down, and then we hoisted Norland back up. He seemed to do it easily. He knew exactly what to do, peeling Vincent's skin from the Tree with no effort at all. Then he pulled it over his head as if it were a nightshirt, and soon he disappeared under it.

Vincent's green eyes again looked at me as I brought him down into my arms. "You have done it," he said, and kissed me, passing his tongue, it felt, all the way into my brain. I held onto his hand, solid now, interlocking my fingers with his. It was real. He was solid flesh between my fingers. The "fairy tree" shimmered above us. Its light reflected across every waiting face. Then suddenly it became darker, as an aggressive darkness on all sides embraced it. "Let's go," Vincent said. "Take me out of here."

There had been nothing—*nothing*—I'd wanted to do more.

It was over.

My eyes opened. I looked into the cell and I saw Radku weeping next to me, as the jailer Balbus stood over Norland's dead body. "The little cheat! I wondered what kind of game he was playing with me. So I thrust my knife into his eye—it was only paper! I opened the door, but you three were so busy in repulsive sex with each other that you did not notice when I took my revenge on this little fairy!"

"Just like I take *mine!*" another voice intruded. Nafshee, his large knife drawn, lunged at my nude body. "Anvil told me to see you tonight. He said maybe you are in 'danger' from your visitors. He knows I am jealous. Now I see he is right. I was going to do sex with you, Albert, even with them in the room. Why not? You reject me so much—nothing bothers me. Let them watch; I do not care! But what do I see? The three of you in this *orgy!* Only my jealousy can make me kill you, Albert—and the time for that is now!"

But he was wrong . . . *this* time.

Something pushed Norland's still warm corpse aside. It appeared out of sheer air; out of nothing. It was Vincent. At first sight of him, Nafshee began to blink his eyes; then tremble. He looked as people do when out of fear they can no longer control themselves. His body stood frozen, yet softly twitching. It turned from its usual bluish-brown cast to dead white as his blood ran to his feet. All of his anger and jealousy and the courage that went with them disappeared. Only his eyes moved, shooting first left, then right, then bulging from his head.

Vincent put his hands around the blue ape's throat to choke the life out of him. Nafshee was too frightened even to scream; Balbus stood transfixed, not knowing where Vincent could possibly have come from . . . and not realizing that Radku had circled behind him and now had him by the throat. The jailer, surprised, dropped his knife, and I used it on him. What pleasure I took pushing it all the way up into his guts, while Radku's grip prevented any sound from escaping Balbus's piggish throat. His body fell with a graceless thud to the floor. Nafshee started jerking back and forth as Vincent choked him harder. But I stopped him. "Don't kill him," I ordered. "He's powerless on Ki. We'll take him with us."

Radku and I pulled our clothes back on—I threw Vincent a shirt to wear—and then we tied Nafshee's hands with the leather cord that had belted the jailer's waist. I stuffed a dirty toilet rag into the ape's mouth and with his own gleaming knife pointed at his throat we led him by his chest hairs out of the cell and down the murky halls of Anvil's dungeon. The beams overhead were thick with cobwebs and rang with the shrieks of bats. Startled rats and water bugs chased from our feet. Four armed guards carrying knives, lances

173

and spiked clubs appeared from around a corner. But the three of us, using only surprise and two knives, were able to get the best of them. With Vincent by me, I was now without fear. Moments later only one of Anvil's guards, barely conscious, was alive, and we had the weapons that we needed. I knew how to follow the back underground passageway, usually used by the condemned, up to the court chamber. The spiked door was unbolted; the chamber empty. I looked around at the low-ceilinged room that seemed forever in twilight. *How many times had I been forced to sit there?* I hurried to the wide entry door, the one leading outside to freedom, to the planet beyond Anvil's glowering fortress.

It was locked. Then from the other side, I heard footsteps. I turned to Radku and Vincent and shushed them with a forefinger to my lips. They nodded.

"As I said," Anvil told Woosh, as I heard a key turn inside a clanky lock. "Your son tonight is with Albert."

"But he promised me he would not go near Lord Albert, as long as others were in the room."

"Yes, but he is foolish and jealous."

"I am afraid so," Woosh agreed. They entered the chamber, as Vincent, Radku, and I ducked behind an ugly, wooden prisoners' bench. My knife was poised at Nafshee's throat, but I took the filthy rag from his mouth. "Listen," I whispered. I wanted Nafshee to hear Anvil's words and those of his own father. "He is an idiot boy and a failure to our Blue Monkey tribe. My disappointment in him has been immense. This rapture he has for Albert—there is no accounting for it."

Even in the dark I could see Nafshee's face as tears welled in his eyes.

"A disappointing son?" Anvil asked innocently. "What *should* we do with him?"

"He will die soon enough," the old wizard said. "Right now, inside his loins he bears Albert's son. But after this sorry freak is born, I have plans to get rid of Nafshee. What do you say, Anvil?"

"Why not cut off the heads of two birds with one stroke?"

I looked up from the back of the bench that hid us. The smirk on Anvil's face was too beautiful to miss. He thought he had it all; I was sure of this. Woosh asked him what he meant. "Simple. We will go down there and kill your son now. I know that you can take their child away from him, Woosh, and finish the gestation. That is a talent of you Blue Monkeys, right?"

"Certainly, but it would be better if Nafshee bore the thing—wait," the old ape opened his mouth and bared his dirty, razorish teeth. "Now I see it. If we kill Nafshee, we will control the whole planet. Is this what you are saying, Anvil?"

The baron nodded his head. "My thought is that we could try Albert for the death of our poor dear Nafshee. Do it, in fact, right here in this room."

Woosh began to laugh. I took my knife away from Nafshee's throat, and cut the cords at his hands. I put my lips to his ears: "Your own father betrays you. He mocks you, Nafshee. If all your courage here on Ki comes from Woosh, if *that* is the reason why now you are so powerless, you *must* kill him."

"Like I said," Anvil said, his voice ringing through the damp, cold air of the court chamber, "cut off the heads of two birds with one stroke!" He laughed, holding his belly, and then invited Woosh to come with him through the other door leading down into the dungeon passage to my cell. "We'll kill Radku and Norland as well. You as a witness will see that they tried to harm their king, who has condemned them to death."

"You are brilliant!" Woosh said. "We shall kill all the little birds at once." Woosh collapsed into a belly laugh and then reached out his arms to embrace Anvil, but was stopped in mid motion by a strange dark form he could not recognize. It seemed to glide in pure air towards the old monkey and the baron. Vincent and I looked and could not believe what we saw: it was the same creature that had killed Vincent on Earth, that had no relationship to Nafshee, the pathetic ape-son on Ki. Using the knife I had given him, he pushed it through the throats of both his wizard father and the hideous red-faced Anvil, in one unwavering lunge.

CHAPTER 19

"You have done so well," Hortha said to me, "I feel that now I can die. It is silly to live so long." Radku, Vincent, and I had come to her to tell her the news, as Nafshee had gone immediately into hiding.

I told her that I had done almost nothing. Nafshee had killed Anvil, as well as his own father, Woosh. Her face quivered as soon as I mentioned Nafshee's name. I could tell that she would never approve of him. But I wanted something else: I took her wrinkled, pale hand in mine and asked her to bless Vincent and me. She took my hand and trembling closed it upon Vincent's. Suddenly she started crying: "You will never be able to produce a son, you know, with each other."

I realized what she was saying was the truth: Vincent did not have the third Egg. We would never have a son, produced from both of our sperms.

"You will be like your father: you will die alone, in a terrible, premature flowering of your old age, without the replenishment of seed from your partner."

"But you knew that when you sent me to Earth," I said.

She nodded her head. "Your only son will be that of Nafshee's. Now I wish that both he and his father had died. What use is Nafshee to us, an ape who bears your son?"

I clung to Vincent. How wrong the old lady was—I was sure of this. "I shall still mate with Vincent," I told her. "He will still be my promised friend. And if I have to die to keep him alive, as he died for my sake on Earth, then that will be enough."

The other Sisters gathered around Hortha. They made a circle around Vincent and me while Radku looked on shyly from the side; they began singing softly a song that I realized was an old wedding hymn to the Goddess Ki. Hortha spoke close to my ear: "No more of this talk of dying, my son. Ki must be safe and only you can guarantee that."

The Sisters continued to circle us, and garlands were placed on our heads, robes placed over each of us, and in sparkling white we were led in front of a multitude of people into the courtyard of the Temple. The throng cheered to see me safe again. Word spreads quickly on such a small, talkative planet and already the people knew that Anvil and Woosh had been "disposed of," and now I, alone, had power on Ki. A path was cleared for us through the crowd, and Vincent, Hortha, and I walked behind a group of Sisters clad in either pure white or black leather. Behind us was Radku, and further behind him was my mother, M'raetha, who occasionally caught my eye as I turned back to look at her. She looked both radiant and tearful, a look that I realized was partial to women at weddings. In the middle of the courtyard, Hortha began a speech that I was sure she had been preparing to make for many Ten Moons. "We are gathered here together to celebrate the promising of our Lord Albert and his mate," she paused, then went on: "Vincent, a man from far away who is new to the ways to Ki, but not new, we are sure, to Albert's heart."

"Then neither shall he mate our king!" shouted an army of loud male voices. I turned to look beyond Hortha. There, striding into the Temple grounds were hundreds of Same-Sexers, in a column as far as I could see, in pairs, linking hands, armed with knives and maces. They pushed aside the frightened throng that had gathered for our mating ceremony, and made a circle around me, tightening it until I was separated from Vincent. Suddenly Nafshee appeared. "I have come to claim what is mine," he said. "To take you back. You will not live anymore in a castle, but we will live in the forests of your brothers. And you will return there to your roots. . . ." A huge cheer went up from the Same-Sex men. "And from there," Nafshee said, "rule Ki."

"How can I rule Ki," I asked, "if it is forbidden for me to have the man I love?"

Silence fell. A stony, thoughtful silence. The men dropped their hands.

"You have been promised to me," Nafshee declaimed as loudly as he could so his words filled the walls of the Temple and the pathways of its grounds. "I bear your son. Your only son."

"That is not true!" Radku protested. "I—I—" I told Radku to be quiet. He had given up too much already. But he refused, and spoke anyway: "Our Lord Albert and his promised friend Vincent will have a son, through me. I shall give up my Egg for Vincent. Even though I know it will mean my life to do so."

A great wailing went up; the men gathered around Radku, nodding their heads and offering him consolation. Suddenly a very old man appeared from out of their ranks. "I am Aawkwa," an old, wrinkled face said. "Sira Albert, I knew both of your fathers, Sira Greeland and Sira Enkidu. I knew how much Greeland loved Enkidu, but he could not hold back the troubles within himself. He led Ki into war and Enkidu, to his great regret, had to kill him.

Therefore I say to all of my brothers here, we must allow Sira Albert to mate with his own heart and not force him to mate with Nafshee of the Blue Monkeys, no matter what. But we only ask of you, Sira Albert, not to forsake us and live away from our forests. Come back to the forests with us—"

"Then how can I rule Ki?" I asked. "From the forests?"

Hortha nodded her head. "The King is right. This is a difficult question."

Then Vincent spoke up: "I get it, why don't we bring the forests to Albert? And every few weeks a different contingent of you forest guys can come to the castle and see what's shakin' and then report back to the other guys there and—"

A buzz of questions went through the crowd. "What?" Aawkwa asked, puzzled, "is 'contingent' and 'forest guys'? What does all that mean?"

"Sira Vincent still speaks as an Earth person," I explained. "He is trying to say that we will invite you to come and visit us at my new court often, and that I promise you all, as I promise Vincent, to go back into the forest at least once every new Moon—and I shall never stay away from you again as my father did."

A great cheer went up and I thought for a moment that all was settled, until I realized that Nafshee was now standing immediately behind me . . . and aiming the cruel edge of his knife at my throat.

CHAPTER 20

"One move from you," he said loudly, "and I shall do away with you the way I killed my father and Anvil."

Now the crowd, both from the Temple and the Same-Sexers, was stunned into silence.

"Nafshee," Hortha said. "It is one thing to be an ape and another to be an idiot! Ki will collapse without Albert. We know this. What plan can you possibly have for him?"

"I will rule with him," Nafshee promised. "I took on all of my father's powers—and his desires for Ki. Woosh saved Ki many times, and I will do the same. You will see: I do not even need a knife to possess Albert."

With those words, he dropped the knife that had been aimed at my throat and in the next moment I found myself going into a profound sleep, as the two of us—Nafshee and myself—disappeared.

When I woke up—and I have no idea how long I was unconscious—I was deep in the magnificent coiled chambers of a cave. The setting seemed vaguely familiar. I looked up: torches blazed through the gray misty air. My eyes stung from the fumes of their burning pitch. A low voice, tense with tenderness, said: "You are mine now." A leathery palm explored my face; then Nafshee emerged, out of what had been only the damp, chilled air. He kissed my lips with his animal mouth. "You must love me, Albert," he confessed. "Or I will die."

"Why?"

"You are the *only* lord I know. I will keep you here in this cave forever."

I got up and saw a deep, rock-bound pool of blue and white water in front of me. "This is the Cave of Mysteries," Nafshee explained. I told him that I'd been there once before as a child; also that Greedu was buried there. "Then you know it goes deeper—much deeper. I can keep you here by my own power. You will never see the light of the White Star again. Do you see how serious I am, Albert?"

I told him I did. "What about our son? Will he be a prisoner here with me?"

Nafshee nodded his head. "He is being born now."

My eyes panicked. What was the ape talking about? The son . . . now? Nafshee began to twist about in a convulsive, circular motion, his hands stroking his chest, stomach, genitals, and then his anus. I had no idea what to do. I could only watch while he howled and screamed, both in pain and ecstasy. "It is almost here," he cried. "Almost. . . ."

Something bulged out from his lower body, just below that place where humans have their navels. I could see another form, another life. But it seemed trapped, unable to emerge. "Help me," Nafshee whispered. "You must help, Albert."

I asked him what I should do. He told me to take my hand and stick it slowly up his anus, until I felt the thing within him. With much trepidation, I did this, slowly pouring my hand, first as a spaded fist, then as a slightly open palm, up the furry canal of his rear opening. At first I thought I could get none of my hand in. Then he began to breathe deeper, with long, slow breaths, and he opened up for me. I was able to go all the way up there, almost to my elbow. Finally I felt the thing alive in my hand—it felt soft and firm, smooth, the head round, covered with fine silky hairs that waved about my fingers, like the waving tendrils of weeds in a river. His breathing became faster and deeper. "What now?" I asked.

"It is what *I* will have to do," he warned me. "But first, you must begin to pull him out—slowly."

I did this, as carefully as I could. I was afraid I would hurt it—the child—even inadvertently strangle him. The whole thing seemed so odd and miraculous; a male creature giving birth—this way—was it possible that he would just come out Nafshee's anus?

"You will have to cut it open," Nafshee said, and handed me a small, razor sharp knife.

"Where?"

"Just above my testicles, there is a place only we Blue Monkeys have. It is soft and pliant, and extends just enough to get our sons out."

"Why don't you do it?" I asked.

"He is your son, too."

"But this is dangerous," I whispered. "Suppose I. . .?"

"Kill me? Yes, Albert, it would be possible for you to kill me. And take this creature that is ours away. But I think that I have loved you because you are a noble man, and you will not harm me."

I took the small knife and made the incision, even with my other hand still in him, still moving the child towards its birth. Blood poured out; then it stopped. It—or he—emerged. Gray, slimy. Its face wrinkled into a snout. He opened his mouth, already filled with small, pointed teeth. The mouth of a puppy, a wolf kid . . . or an ape. But the body was closer to human. I could see it. It had no navel at all, but as I picked it up and began to examine it, I realized that our son, amazingly, did have the third Egg.

"See," Nafshee said, his face wringing wet with sweat, his voice a bare whisper. "He will be the Lord of Ki."

He took the child from me and together the two of us waded with it into the water, the "Pool of Mysteries." The pool was warm and intensely comforting. I felt relaxed in it; I let myself go and felt as if I were being held up by invisible hands. Then I realized that in another chamber of the Cave both my fathers were buried along with generations of Same-Sex men. Their spirits must have been in the pool, holding on to me, touching me and making me feel at ease. I looked over at Nafshee; he was glowing as he held the small creature he—or we—had just given birth to. The water had turned the small child from an ash gray to another color: the palest, most radiant blue, shimmering with light.

"We will call him 'Alfee,'" Nafshee announced. "Because he came from both of us."

I nodded my head and smiled. I felt dreamily happy. Now I did not care if Nafshee and I lived in the Cave forever. I had my son—strangely endearing and peculiar looking as he was—and Nafshee would give me everything that I wanted. I felt tired. Lifeless. Suddenly my head shook, and I realized what was happening to me. The longer I stayed in the pool, the more in Nafshee's power I would be. But I was incapable of moving. A few moments longer and I would become like a vegetable, completely in Nafshee's control. I looked over at him; he smiled at me, baring his animal teeth. With Alfee in one hand, he swam easily towards me and began to drag me out deeper into the pool's lovely, deadly waters. "Nice, is it not?" he asked softly. "You will have a whole lifetime in this pool. I will bring you here every day—and you will be mine."

"No. . . ."

"Yes," he whispered and put his vile mouth to mine. I withdrew in disgust and with every stroke of energy I had started to swim away from him, struggling so hard against Nafshee that he had either to let me go or else drop the child into the water. He began to swim after me, then stopped. He looked at me and said, in a voice as warm and gentle as the pool, "You must swim back to me, Albert. I am your mate."

I wanted to say something, but could not. My mouth could not open— could not utter a word—I was trying so hard to get away from him. Then I heard loud words reverberate through the walls and chambers of the Cave. "NO, Albert is NOT YOUR MATE." I looked up and there, at the edge of the pool, were Vincent and Radku, holding out their arms for me.

"He cannot keep me away from you!" Vincent said.

I tried to reach him, but I could not. Nafshee's power was too much; he kept repeating for me to come back. "I am your mate. I have your son." I was now stopped within a few arms' lengths of Vincent; then I realized that my body, almost lifeless, had started to draw back by itself towards Nafshee. It seemed impossible: he would have me in the pool forever. He could drown me if he wanted to. Vincent saw me, and I witnessed the terror and anguish in his face as I began to drift back, uncontrollably, towards the blue ape and the odd, shimmering creature we had produced.

Vincent had no choice. He dove into the pool, and with long, quick strokes swam out to me. But now I was in Nafshee's arms, and I knew that he would gladly even give up Alfee to keep me. The child was dangerously floating, by itself, as Nafshee tried to take me away.

"He will not get you!" Vincent screamed. "I will kill this child before I will let him have you."

"Take it!" Nafshee called back. "Take the damn thing as long as I have Albert!"

I looked at Vincent, and realized that now, he, too, was powerless. The same force that had effected me in the pool began to work on him. All he could do was take the infant Blue Monkey and hold him up in the water while he swam away from us. I watched Vincent, as he disappeared into the thick white mists that began to blow over the warm waters. All was lost. Nafshee would have me forever; I had no idea what power had brought Radku and Vincent all the way over to the very lips of the Pool of Mysteries, but I knew that surely it had its limits and Vincent would never find me again. I began to sob uncontrollably in the warm, hateful waters, only to see that they were covered in blood. Behind me, Radku had jabbed the same knife I had used to deliver Alfee into Nafshee's nostrils. With one elbow around Nafshee's throat, he was twirling the knife up, directly into the ape's brain.

Nafshee's body fell below the warm waters as his blood bubbled up to the surface. With his strong hands digging into my shoulders, Radku pulled me to the edge of the pool where Vincent, out of breath but safe, waited with Alfee.

"I would not let that thing take you, Sira," Radku said. "I may not be smart, but I knew that he was going to take you away from Ki. You went away once, King, but not again." He smiled and kissed me, and then Vincent took me in his arms and kissed me even more. We got up and left the Pool and wandered through the Cave of Mysteries. I found the chamber where Same-Sex men had been laid to rest in pairs for generations. Vincent, Radku and I looked in on it, a room full of skeletons and pale, waxen folds of mummified flesh. But we were not horrified, for we also remembered the Tree that grew in the barren forest and which held the skins of these men, waiting to be reborn. Finally, we got to the mouth of the cave and there were met by Aawkwa and Hortha.

"I am getting too old for these things," Hortha said. "But I could not let Vincent come here all by himself."

"He knew you were in here," Aawkwa said. "I have no idea how—he has never been here himself."

"I can't help it," Vincent said. "I guess I'm joined to you, so you just can't get rid of me."

"What did you say?" old Aawkwa asked. "What is *rid*? This man's language is very strange to us."

Hortha noticed Alfee. She knew instantly what the creature I carried in my arms was. She took him from me, and started to coo and smile. "I'm afraid he looks like his father—I mean the other father, Nafshee," she said. She looked closer into his tiny face, and then noticed something: "He is blind. The small thing is blind!"

I took him from her and knew she was right. His eyes were opaque; pale as milk, with almost no pupils at all. Now I was glad that we had saved him. I wondered if Nafshee realized the child's blindness, then I remembered how quickly Nafshee was ready to sacrifice his own son for me.

Vincent took the little boy from me and kissed him. "Strange critters you got here," he said, as Aawkwa tried to figure out what he was saying. It was night and dark, as we walked back towards my father Enkidu's castle, where I knew that Vincent and I would live, hopefully for the rest of our lives. I looked up into the sky. There were the Six Moons, the Moons in which Norland and Radku were to be executed. At the door before my father's royal bedchamber, I said goodnight to the Elder Priestess, to Aawkwa and Radku, and a whole group of servants and retainers who had come back to stay with me. We decided to let Alfee sleep in our room, on a small pallet of fur. "What will he eat?" Vincent asked, as we took our clothes off and got into bed.

I told him I had no idea, but I was tired and the little boy was not crying or asking for food. A few moments later, nestled into each other's arms, a most welcomed sleep fell on us both. I felt so at home, so happy. Everything

I had really wanted had happened. Then suddenly I felt very badly for Nafshee. His desire for me—the obsession of his life—was a painful thing to watch. He had never been treated right by Woosh or by any of the other inhabitants of Ki. A hand started to run itself softly across my shoulder. With a chill chasing down my spine, I woke up.

"I must feed him," a sad, broken voice said. I looked up. It was Nafshee.

"I thought you were dead?"

"You cannot die in the Pool of Mysteries, Sira. It is one of the first rules of Ki. But how can I live without you, Albert?"

I got up and watched him scoop Alfee from his furry bed. "How do you feed him? *What* do you feed him?"

"You will see." He lifted his robe and pulled his long dark penis out from between his hairy flanks; from its flaccid shaft, a soft, white milk came out. Alfee greedily lapped from it. "See, I must have him. I will take him with me. You are indeed, Albert, the mate of Vincent. I am afraid I know this now. Nothing will every come between the two of you. Even death. All I ask is one thing."

"And what is that, Nafshee?" I was ready to go back to sleep. It was cold in the royal bedchamber, as often such imposing places are, and I wanted to be back in the arms of the man I loved.

"That you will honor the promise that you made to me on Earth. That you will share yourself with me, even though you are not promised in any way to me. And that you will recognize your son, not as your heir, but as our child."

"I promise you this," I said firmly, and drew him towards me. I kissed him on his hard, animal mouth. "Take the boy with you—only you can feed him. And every third Moon, I will visit you and give myself to you as I have promised."

His face fell. "Every *third*?"

"Yes," I said firmly. "So don't ask for anything more."

He nodded his head. "I was just trying. . . ."

"Try your way out of here," I ordered. "Remember, every *third* Moon."

"Not every *second*. . . ."

I grabbed his arm and, wrapping Alfee up in a blanket, gave the boy to him. I walked them both to the door, and said, "Now, get out!"

"Alright," Nafshee said as the door slammed behind him. "The third . . . *third*."

I sighed a deep sigh, and then got back into bed with Vincent. He opened his eyes. "Don't these people ever leave you alone?"

"'Fraid not," I said. "That's the *trouble* with being king of Ki."

CHAPTER 21

Six Ten Moons went by. I had been able to consolidate my power, and, in fact, had become used to it. Something that I learned quickly enough is how easy it is to get used to real power. Of course I'd had to change many feelings about myself. I was no longer simply Enkidu's son, thinking only of myself, often feeling sorry for myself—and hiding from real adult problems. I admit that I'd once been that way, living only for a good time: hunting with my friends, the times spent with my father in his library or talking with him until late into the night about abstract things. I realize that there are many men who live this way and their lives become frittered away, by not dealing with who they really are. But Vincent would not allow that to happen. He was, as they say, "down to Earth," although he had his own thirst for power, and even I could see it. "If I came all the way over here to another planet," he announced to me the first week of our life together, "I didn't come, honey, just to be *Mrs.* King of Ki."

I asked him what he wanted.

"I want to be in charge of something. Back home we have these women called 'First Ladies.' You ever hear about them?"

I told him in truth I'd not. "First ladies of what?" All I could think of was that they got to try on the new dresses first. We were getting dressed for a state visit. Hortha, Nohnie, Dyla, and a platoon of other Sisters were arriving at my castle to present a plan. I was not sure what it was, but I had a feeling that it had to do with Dyla's investiture as the next Elder Priestess. Of course it was all supposed to be a surprise to me—women always have this idea that you have no idea what they're thinking. But I knew that Hortha had fallen in love with Dyla, in the way of Sisters, and that she wanted Dyla to succeed her in only a few Ten Moons, when Hortha was sure her time would come to go back to the Goddess Ki Herself. This was our idea of death, that in death we simply return to the Goddess and to the planet Ki which She represents. We are only borrowed from our lovely planet; death "recycles" us, you might say.

"No!" Vincent said firmly. "I'm supposed to wear this damn thing?" He was trying on a heavy purple sash that somehow my chamberlains felt looked royal. "It makes me look like one of those telecom stars from way back. You know, Joan Collins!"

I had no idea what he was talking about. Certainly on Ki I had never heard of John Collins, whoever he was. "So tell me about these first ladies."

"They're the wives of the Presidents. Rich Quilter had already outlived his wife by a long time—the thing is in America they aren't going to allow a woman to be President, not the New Conservatives, anyway, so the most you can be is First Lady."

"But you can't be," I said. "You're not a lady."

He took off the sash and tried on a small chain, that actually looked nice on him. He sat down and looked at me seriously. "That's not the point. The point is, I *have* to have position of my own."

So I made him in charge of all of my dealings with the Temple. He also became my ambassador to the Off-Sexers, who seemed to feel more comfortable with him. He looked more like them than I did. I was dark and resembled the ancient Same-Sex men of the wetlands, whereas he was taller and lighter skinned. His sense of humor helped with them, too. For the most part, he could not take their warring and intrigues seriously. In one of his first meetings with the Off-Sex lords, they started squabbling in front of him, and Vincent pulled out a sword and said, "Now just get over this!" Immediately Kandon, the youngest lord there, a blond man with a beard, tried to jump over Vincent's blade. This only proved to Vincent that the Off-Sexers took everything literally. "Damn!" he said to me one night after dealing with them all day. "These people drive me into a rage! All they ever think about is themselves and their kids!"

"I guess it's their children," I said. I pulled him closer to me and took off his top piece, which on Earth might be called a shirt. I smiled. I was very much in love with him and hoped he felt the same way about me. Even being promised to some one does not stop their mind from wandering; I knew that it was possible for him to find some of the Off-Sex men handsome. Some of them were extremely attractive. "When you have children," I said, "all you think about is yourself and them."

"Yes," he said, seriously. "I guess that's why the world—I mean the Earth—is so screwed up. All those people having kids and all they can think of is . . . their kids. I'm glad, sometimes, that we don't have kids."

I looked directly into his eyes: he was telling the truth, and yet it was not completely the truth. He was glad that we did not have kids, because we *could* not. But if we could, he wanted kids; I knew that. "We're different," I said softly. "I mean, even in the forests, the couples who have kids—the two guys who get together with an Off-Sex woman—their kids kind of belong to everyone. They don't just keep them to themselves like the Off-Sexers do. They're part of our tribe or enclave."

"Then why don't we have one?" he asked.

"You mean just 'borrow' one?"

"I'm not sure," he said. We were both naked, and he started to massage my scrotum, feeling the soft beauty of the Egg revolve in his hands. He put his mouth softly to it and then said to me, "If I had one of those, we could have a son together, couldn't we?"

"We could."

He touched the pendant that he had given me on Earth. I'd had an identical one made for him. He kissed me softly on the lips. "I know I can have one," he said. I asked him what he was talking about. "The third testicle; I can have it."

"But you were *not* born with one. I accept that in you, Vincent. We cannot share seed—I will die early because of my love for you."

"How about your consort Nafshee?" Vincent asked angrily.

"He's not my consort."

"Sure, but I know what you do with him."

I pulled my promised friend closer to me. "I have to see him every third change of the Moons. It's an agreement that I made. I also see our son Alfee."

"Who is not, *by the way*, my son. How is the little monster?"

I did not want to talk about Alfee. He was blind but amazingly intelligent. Frankly, I loved him and I guess that's why I felt so tenderly but embarrassed about him. His blindness might keep him from becoming a monster like Woosh, but he did have Nafshee's strange soulfulness, that amazingly loving nature. "He's an interesting child," I said. "One day I must bring you to meet him."

"Sure, then Nafshee can try to kill me again. No way!" Vincent turned away from me. I could see how angry he was. Sometimes he reminded me, interestingly enough, of Greeland. It must have been Greeland's seed coming through me to him. "I wish you never went to see them!" he exploded. He looked directly at me. "If you have an agreement with Nafshee, why don't you ever hold Radku to his! He promised that I could have his Egg. Remember?"

I buried my face in his handsome chest. "I cannot hold him to that; to do so would kill him."

He got up. His male-pipe was quivering, semi-erect. We were both turned on and ready for sex; I knew it. He knew that I was hungry for him. That I   189 desired his male-pipe, his loins, his face and mouth. I grabbed him, pushing him, dragging him back into the bed. There were marks on his body where I had dug my fingers into him. "I want you," I said.

"I will not give myself to you, Albert, until you agree to it."

"Then *you* will drive me to Nafshee!" I was sure that the chamberlains could hear every word we said in our closed bedroom. I felt terribly ashamed; I could not help crying. He pulled me to him and stopped resisting me. I was all over him, pushing my mouth into his, following it with my male-pipe which he took willingly. I grabbed his beautiful, silken black hair and pushed my pipe down his throat until it could go no further. Then I turned him around, biting him, clawing him, scratching him, until I took his. I was shaking with rage and sorrow and abject desire for him. We ended up blasting our seed into each other, though his would do me no good. "I will do anything for you," I said when it was over. "I can deny you nothing." I felt humiliated. I had not wanted to hold Radku to his promise; it pained me to do it. I owed him my life but now he was an older man and Vincent was still young; and Radku was yet without a mate, since the murder of Norland. I tried to balance the elements in my mind. It would be Vincent's life for Radku's . . . then Vincent said: "I have brought it up already with Dyla. She is the Elder Priestess, and even she believes that this is the best course."

I hung my head in sorrow. "When will it be done?"

"The Sisters have taken Radku into their custody. Tomorrow I will go to the Temple and I want you to go with me."

I pulled his neck to my lips and kissed it softly. How could I love another thing as much as I loved him? Even if we had a son, it would be impossible to love the child as much. "Did you think that I would stay behind?" I asked.

That night I had a dream. You could call it a premonition. My life would be very happy, but under it would always be a great sorrow. Already I had given birth to a son who was a strange but soulful monster. I knew that Vincent and I would have a son, but only through the death of Radku. Suddenly my eyes opened and I looked at my promised mate. He was sound asleep. I felt terribly alone, ashamed of my own thoughts and fears. I pulled him closer until his warmth spread through me. Then I was able to go back to sleep, dreaming of the child we would have and, also, of Vincent and the first time we'd made love on Earth.

The next morning we woke up before the White Star appeared. There were eight Moons out, not a very good sign I thought, but I knew that this had to be done. We bathed and put on light robes and then began the walk over to the Temple.

"We are ready for you, Sira Albert and Sira Vincent," Dyla said after we had entered her private quarters. She smiled at Vincent. "This has been a long time coming, has it not?" She seemed still so young and yet I remembered her when she was only a blushing novice. Hortha had died three Ten Moons ago, and I remembered Dyla's investiture. Her parents had been there, no longer ashamed of the tomboyish daughter of theirs who had run off to join the unmarried Sisters of Ki. They were very proud of her, now that she had more power than any other woman on the planet—and any other man except myself, although I feel always that my power is only an illusion. For some reason the people believe that I hold the planet together, when in truth only Vincent holds me together. Now I realized what he had done.

"Where is he?"

"He is in the operating room, where we do the implantations," Dyla answered. "Normally, we do not allow men in there, but for something like this—well, we must make an exception!"

She seemed almost gleeful. I found it odious. I think she liked the idea of what she was about to do. It was certainly an exercise of her own power. I asked if I could see Radku before it happened, and Dyla agreed. "We will give you a short time with him and then Vincent, the two Sisters who will assist, and I will join you."

Dyla led me down several flights of winding stone stairs to an almost buried chamber. She unlocked a heavy wooden door. I entered, and she closed the door behind me. When I heard it clang, a shudder rang through me. The clang reminded me too much of the prison in Anvil's fortress in which I had been locked. Then I realized that *I* had been in this large clean room before. I turned and there in the middle of a it, lit with rows and rows of small lamps, was Radku.

He bowed and kissed my hand. "Thank you, Lord Albert, for coming to see me."

I bade him get up. "I am to thank you," I said. Tears collected in my eyes and I looked at him through their watery prisms. He seemed so old now, ages older than he had been only six Ten Moons ago.

"I do this gladly," he said.

"But it is giving up your life."

He shook his head no. "You, Albert, have given up your life for us. For Ki. I promised that Vincent could have my Egg."

"But I was not going to hold you to that promise," I wept. I knew there was nothing I could do. That all of this had been arranged behind my back, and if I tried to stop it, my own power on Ki would be over—too many people already knew of it and Vincent would never forgive me. He would take up with an Off-Sex man; I could see that in our future and it would kill me just as I would have to kill him if he did. "Is there anything you want to say to me before this is done?" I asked.

He shook his head again. "No. Only that I will join Norland on the Tree and that," he paused, then said, "I want you not to forget me, Sira. I have always loved you as my lord and king. I am not a very smart man, not like Norland was, but my heart is deep."

I smiled. It was true. There were distant small windows at the top of the room, and from these I could see the first light of the White Star. Dyla and the two Sisters came in, wearing pure white smocks. Vincent followed them. "It is really very simple," Dyla explained. "We will give them both something to sleep. Of course there is always the chance that the Egg will not take in Vincent's scrotum—unless he is by some stroke of nature primed for it. I mean he did not originate on this planet." She let out a little giggle, which brought a similar response to the other Sisters.

I asked her if I should leave, and she told me no. "Take Vincent's hand," she ordered.

"No," I said. "I would rather take Radku's."

"You *are* a noble lord," she said. "Perhaps you can take both."

I did as she suggested and both of them were brought within my hands' reach. Then both were given an herbal potion and some strong berry wine to drink with it. The Sisters began to rub the foreheads of the two men; I could feel Vincent becoming drowsy. I knew that I had to make a choice at that moment: whose hand would I keep? Vincent looked at me and clenched my hand and then released it, so that, if I preferred, I could have stayed with Radku; but I did not. I let go of Radku's hand, just as he softly dropped onto a waiting table, where Dyla arranged him as if he were a floppy doll. She exposed his male parts and applied a salve to them. "This will not hurt him in the least," she promised. "He will feel nothing."

I held on to Vincent as the conscious life in him left. He collapsed into my arms and the three Sisters picked him up and put him on another table. I watched them also expose him. I looked at the two men lying there, so vulnerable; worthy of my pity. It had not even occurred to me that Radku's Egg might be rejected by Vincent—the thought suddenly crippled me with fear: suppose Radku will die in vain, and Vincent will be condemned for life without the Egg he wanted so much?

"How will we know if Radku's Egg takes in Vincent's anatomy?" I asked
Dyla as she began to prepare for the operation, first by cleaning her hands

well.

"You will know, Lord Albert. That is why I wanted you here. You will know even before Vincent awakes. Believe me, you will see. You know, Sira, this is the first time I have ever done this. I am sorry that our Lady Hortha is not here, but she told me how to do it before she herself passed into the arms of the Goddess Ki."

"You seem *happy* to do it," I said, gritting my teeth. There was something almost a little too gleeful about her attitude, as if removing the Egg of a noble, dying man delighted her.

"Sira, you know what they say about Knowledge and Power? The two go hand in hand—and being Elder Priestess I can use all the Power I can get!"

"Is that why you and Vincent conspired to do this?"

She looked at me seriously. "Conspiracy is a harsh charge, Sira. Radku knew what he was saying when he made his promise to give up his Egg; correct?"

"He is a simple man, who will do anything for me."

"So, we have put him to the test. But I know, as surely as you do, that if Vincent does *not* have his Egg, strife will again break out on Ki. And this time, even you, Albert, may not be able to settle it. We have a few moments before the drugs we have given our friends truly work; they are only starting to dream now. Tell me about the time you spent on the planet Earth. What did you learn there?"

I looked into her clear blue eyes. She seemed eons away from me. It was not so much that we came from two different tribes as that we came from two different times. She was part of the new Ki; one that would work, I was sure, with a terrible efficiency. And I was part, somehow, of the old one, the one still attached to Enkidu and Greeland. I left her gaze and looked over at Vincent, the only man I would ever love, as dangerous as that promise is. "I learned," I said, "that Evil exists in a much more terrible form than strife. That the balance we prize so much here on Ki, sharing power among the Same-Sexers, the Off-Sexers, and the Sisters, does not exist there. But the intelligence of Earth people seems to necessitate the kind of violence that we despise here. There they pretend to despise it, but in reality they love it. Nothing seems to make them so happy as shedding blood in one way or another. Or hating anyone who is truly different."

"So people lie to each other often?"

"Yes, and they smile when they do it. They tell huge lies on these devices that reach the entire planet, and they smile. They make up characters that they worship—as we do our Goddesses—who also, in fact, lie. It seems that their whole existence is lies."

"It sounds terrible. It makes me happy to live on our small planet, as difficult as life is here . . . since we have such limited territories in which to live. I think they are ready now."

She went over to Radku's table, where the two other Sisters waited, smiling. She took a thin, sharp blade from a white tray and made a small, deft incision into his scrotum. He jerked violently. The two Sisters had to hold him down. A noise came out of him, like a horrible whimper, a sigh of misery. I had to clench my fists to keep from going over there and stopping Dyla. "I thought there would be no pain?" I cried.

"He is only feeling this as in a dream," Dyla explained. "Look at his face."

I went over to him; she was correct. He was smiling now. The dream had passed. She finished the incision and with steady hands parted Radku's scrotum, revealing the Egg. It glistened and pulsed in the air, like a beating heart. I gasped, as she delicately cut it away from the surrounding tissues, and then tied off what she had left of the dense tubing that connected the Egg both to the inner workings of his male parts and to his brain. "I have to do this quickly," she explained. "Hortha told me that speed is necessary. She did this operation many times in the past; mostly as a punishment. It seemed that *some* of your forefathers were very *irresponsible* with their Eggs."

She hurried over to Vincent, who did not even flinch as she made a similar incision in his scrotum and then using part of Radku's own tube reconnected the Egg in its proper place. I thought I would faint watching her; her blithe attitude amazed me, as if she *had* done this many times. She turned to me before she sewed up the sac. "I always wanted to be an animal doctor," she explained. "But of course among my people a woman would never be allowed to do that. For them it was always just babies!" She made an ugly face at the words, and then said, "Before I sew it up, I want you to put your hand under Vincent's sac."

I felt nervous; queasy. She had used a wad of white gauze to soak up a small pool of warm, glistening blood that had oozed out from Vincent, but I hated the sight of the wound she had caused. It is one thing to watch the blood of your enemies and another to see the blood of a loved one. "How will I know this will work?"

"You have to feel it pulsing, Albert. I must tell you, Sira, that if it does *not* work, I will reconnect it to Radku."

I cupped my hand under his scrotum and waited. I watched Vincent's face; a terrible grimace chased over it. What pain and fear was he going through? Was it a preview of death itself?

194   "They are only dreams," Dyla said, reading my mind. "Have you ever

watched the face of a blind man dreaming? It seems like all of life is written on that face—the same with your friend here. The herbs have done that to him. They are powerful; one must know how to use them."

I waited for something to happen. As I did, I heard more groans coming from Radku. He started calling out for Norland, and the two Sisters went over to him and held his hand and kept him from moving. His scrotum was still cut open, and I realized that his other two testicles were still exposed. Nothing happened. I felt awful. Why was this happening . . . would I be able to keep myself from crying? *Please*, I said to myself. *Let this end!*

"You must be strong," Dyla said. "You must let him know that your strength is with him—he will know this, even in his dreams. Talk to him."

"What should I say?"

She shook her head at me. What a fool I was, as if I did not know what to say. "You are my promised friend from Earth," I said. "I can never love anyone else but you. You must take this Egg, and it will join the two of us." I leaned over to his mouth and put my lips on his. I could feel the air passing slowly out of his nostrils. I paused and realized that his breathing was slowing; it was too slow.

"Oh. . . ." Dyla said. "I forgot to tell you—he could die. I mean if the Egg is too strong for him—Hortha once warned me—well, he might reject it; it might simply kill him."

I stood up, but with my hand still cupped below Vincent's sac. "If he dies, Dyla, I personally will kill you. I swear to the Goddesses Laura and Ki!"

Dyla rubbed her hands together. "I am afraid not, Sira. To kill me has never been in your power. Even Woosh understood this: that is why he feared the Lady Hortha. So, *if* Vincent dies, the Sisters will take over the planet. Right, Sisters?"

The other two women smiled. I felt crushed from all sides, but I knew that what she had said was correct: if Vincent died, leaving me, without a partner, without an acceptable heir—they would take over. What a mess I had I got myself into, and now it seemed that only Vincent could pull me out of it. I steeled myself as much as I could; I prayed softly that my beloved friend would take the Egg. I looked up. Dyla put her hand close to his nose. "I think Vincent's breathing has stopped. I had better take the Egg back."

She began to point her blade over his scrotum, but I pushed it aside. "Wait."

"It is poisoning his whole system, Sira."

"I *told* you to wait."

"As you wish."

I thought my own heart would stop; the silence within me became unbear- 195 able. My hand did not leave the underside of his sac. I cupped it with all the tenderness and strength that I had. The only words I heard were from Radku, calling softly for Norland. The sound tore my heart to pieces, but I knew that every hope I had must be for Vincent to live.

"I think he has left us," Dyla said, her face looking cast in iron, completely determined.

"No!" I protested. "He cannot. Vincent, you cannot leave. Please hear me!"

I wanted my own heart to stop so that I could feel every movement within him. His breathing had ceased, but his heart was still faintly beating—working, despite everything.

Then I knew something.

I could feel it through the barest tips of my fingers: the Egg moving; the movement vague, faint as a distant breeze, but definitely there. I exhaled . . . huge grateful tears fell from my eyes as I realized that Vincent was breathing again, steadily.

"Well, he scared us!" Dyla proclaimed. "It is now time to sew him up. Sisters, a little thread, please!"

One of the Sisters brought her a needle and thread. Dyla sewed up Vincent's scrotum. She did this with my hand still below it, although now I was exhausted from fear, worry, and even anger. When she was finished, I removed my hand and watched Vincent's eyes. The lids drew up slightly; I could see their beautiful green fields as dreams passed through him. Then I went over to Radku. The other Sister was sewing him up, quickly but obviously without the tenderness Dyla had used on Vincent. "He is leaving us," the Sister said.

I knew it was true as his breathing slowed; he no longer called for Norland. I took his right hand and kissed it softly. "Good-bye," I said, as tears flowed down my cheeks onto his fingers. I felt a slight pressure from them, and then that was gone. His heart stopped, but for a second the glow of life remained on his face. It was followed by a terrible jerking that ran through him; then a coldness that made his body seem like stone. I kissed his lips and felt as heavy as if a thousand pounds of weight had been put on my head.

"I did not expect him to go so fast," Dyla said. "But I am sure he is happy now. He is with his promised friend, and he has given his Egg to you and Vincent. You will have a son, I know. You will be greatly happy." She turned her head away from me. Something was wrong, I knew that, too. I asked her what was the problem. She turned back to me, her face now clouded with tears. "You will not be alone, but I will be, Albert. All the power that

I have here will not assuage the loneliness I feel."

I hugged her. "You will never be alone as long as I am here."

She pulled away from me. "You must not embrace me. The Sisters must align themselves with no one. That is our strength, our destiny, and our . . . sentence . . . here on Ki."

She walked out of the room, followed by the other two Sisters, and I stayed. I wanted to be in the presence of Radku and Vincent one last time. I pulled a stool over to Vincent and sat holding his hand, until his eyes opened completely. "It's there, isn't it?"

I told him it was. He smiled. "I wish I could make love to you right now." I told him no, he had to let the stitches heal. "How is Radku?"

"Dead."

He nodded his head. "We will name our first son after him."

"No," I said. "We shall name him for you both."

CHAPTER 22

Two nights later we brought Radku's body into the Cave of Mysteries, and then I went back to Vincent and we made love, as the Same-Sex men of Ki do, for the first time. I shared his seed and he shared mine, and I felt for the first time in my life completely exultant and happy, as if I had been on a long journey and had finally returned: to myself. We lay in each other's arms afterwards smiling, and I realized then, at that very moment, that we were both thinking the same thoughts. At the same time.

We were back on Earth, traveling even faster than light, borne on the flash of the power of the Egg. I could see the Earth through Vincent's own eyes, years later. Most of the worst had happened, only mitigated by a little of the best. After the incident at the Reagan Towers, the assassinations of both Quilter and Brother Bob, a firestorm of riots, repression, and marshal law was ignited. The White Christian Party began to harden, taken over by its most benighted elements, the lowlife and small criminals who used the assassinations as excuses to destroy anyone and any degree of freedom that stood in their way.

Vincent saw this and cringed. He had wanted to avenge the deaths of two gay men, but his action, which he thought would galvanize the gay community of America, only led to a wave of immediate death for many of our Earth brothers. They were rounded up and executed, often without trials. The White Christian Party used the paranoia following the assassinations to bring another, scorned part of the population under its wing. A new "Rainbow Coalition" arose. It came from the new "technopuppet" blacks who had just emerged from the underclass, clawing their way into the old (formerly white) lower-middle-management "elite." This segment, an always ready market for most consumer advertising, had been made up of those who pushed phony data through the country's various information systems or the immense "ant army" of skilled workers who repaired its machinery.

The Coalition took in other minorities trying to survive in the shadows of the New Conservative power works, such as lower-class whites living miserably on government subsidies or emerging pockets of violently conservative, fundamentalist Hispanics. The "Rainbow" pledged itself to rid America of "anti-family perverts and scum." Linking arms, uncomfortably, with the WCP, the "Rainbow" put on huge rallies that labeled any pro-gay feeling as "anti-minority." Thus it seemed that for the first time in American history a true melting pot had been formed, and for the first time the face of America seemed uniform. No one could publicly question the Coalition and the WCP. Since all telecom media was controlled by the New Conservatives, it simply reported that on such-and-such-a-day so many "enemies of the people and of Christ's Word" were being "Re-Processed," which meant they were either in prison, controlled in mental facilities through the use of cyberdrugs, or had been destroyed by legal executions.

Vincent looked at all of this and his face fell. Tears gathered in the corners of his eyes; then, suddenly, I saw him smile. Something truly liberating, changing, appeared. Even we could see it as we stood invisibly at the edges of nighttime cities. A genuine underground was formed; not everyone's mind had been shackled. Those who really knew what was going on learned to find each other. For them, words from the old "liberated" twentieth century meant nothing. "Gay," "lesbian," "queer"—black, white, Latino, minority, marginal, multicultural, conservative, liberal—the list went on; the words ceased to have any meaning as terms of kinship, cohesion, or strength.

The old identities had become only so much advertising copy: worn-out labels for selling worn-out ideas. The only "issue" (another worn-out term) had become psychic survival: how to preserve a sense of your own being, dignity, and hope. How *not* to be "sold" simply as another product, or bought simply as another "consumer." Psychic survival drew on the power of thoughts to take form, to hold others close, and not to be enslaved by the manipulations of the New Conservatives, the White Christian Party, or the Rainbow Coalition. Same-Sexers were becoming Out-Sexers, out to themselves, out among themselves, and *out* of the mass public culture that ran the world. They were no longer ashamed, gulled, or passively ready to die. We went to meetings, and saw households of "queer families," many of whom passed in the daytime and wrecked damage on the system at night. We went into the country and saw children who looked individual and happy, who were not afraid of every adult, and who could be trusted not to turn in their parents. It was very much like being on Ki.

"Are you ready to go back?" Vincent asked me. He was ready to return to Ki, but I wanted to see one more thing. Still Waters; almost sunset. Laura was there by herself. We were invisible to her. There were now two more places in the same plot where her mother Jennifer, Reuvuer, and Nick lay. The places were not for graves, but for marble urns. I looked at the inscriptions on them. One said "Albert Lee." I smiled. I had always liked the name;

I looked at the other. At first I could not believe it. "Vincent Lanier *Lee*," it said.

"She gave me your name," Vincent said. "God, I wish I could thank her!"

"You can," I said. She was wearing a dark, simple dress. With my hands, I closed her eyes. She smiled and I made her see both of us at that very moment with her eyes closed.

"Thank you," Laura said. "I know you're here."

How will this all end? Vincent said to me, running his thoughts through me. We knew that this would be our last time on Earth.

One of us must come back, I said to him.

Not one of *us*?

No. Not one of *us*, but another generation. Then, a man from Ki will be born on Earth just as I was. And he will make a difference. His thoughts—his words—will move the Earth ahead; if they will listen and not destroy each other in the process.

"And you think that will change the world?" Vincent asked.

I was not sure.

Vincent and I looked at each other as we watched again the struggles going on on Earth. Perhaps the answer was on Ki; it seemed to be within us, within the power of the third Egg and the strange, recurring vision of the Tree. To convey a consciousness of Same-Sex thought, of our own bonding and closeness, to Earth. Through our rituals and actions, outside of sex but held together by it, we on Ki had produced a balance—as fragile as it was. But would the Earth ever allow such a thing? I was not sure. Perhaps balance would never—*could* never be—a part of the real nature of the Earth.

Vincent's eyes reopened. Ki was all around us—this magnificent, quiet, small planet that I had inherited from my two fathers and a mother who had been unknown to them. He went over to a window in the simple room we slept in in my father's castle, and looked out and smiled. "Boy, am I glad we're here and not there. For a second, I thought you told me that one of us would have to go back there. What a thought!" He came back to bed with me. "When do you think this guy from Ki's going to end up on Earth?"

"Don't have a clue," I said. When we were together I often lapsed into Earth slang. "Beats me. But I know it'll happen. Maybe it'll be our own son. It seems that my fathers and I couldn't seem to stay away from the place."

He sighed and came back and kissed me. "Well, as long as it's not you, Albert. Now that I've got this Egg, I want to use it. We'll have several sons and I want to enjoy my life *here* with them. None of this going-back-to-Earth business for me. Being a Same-Sexer on Earth just doesn't cut it—not after I see what's happening there!"

Vincent was right. We did have several sons—three in fact. The first was born from a mother who had actually been a cousin of my Off-Sex mother M'raetha. She was a sweet young woman named Raena, and we got to know her and she allowed us to name the boy Vinku, after Vincent and Radku. Vinku was good-looking and a hunter. Sometimes he seemed more Off-Sex than Same-Sex. He seemed to exist only in the nuts-and-bolts here-and-now and resembled my memories of Greeland, as well as Radku himself. If I'd met him in a crowd, I wouldn't have called him a brainy sort. But he was an affectionate and sweet kid, without a bit of guile to him. He protected his younger brother Alvin, named for me, Albert, and Vincent. I could tell that Alvin was intelligent—he could outread me very quickly—but he never seemed to be able to do anything. He was always living in his own dreams that never came up to reality. Most of the time he stayed with his own Off-Sex mother, a young, unmarried woman named Norah, who volunteered to bear him, thinking that it would be the greatest honor of her life. Then she spent a great deal of time complaining to everyone what a pain having him had been, how no one cared about her, and how she regretted ever doing it. I'm not sure how much of this rubbed off on Alvin, but he always chose to be with her, and I did not fight it. In the new Ki, Same-Sex boys were given this option, and sometimes I really wondered if it did not disrupt the whole balance of the planet.

Our third son though was the enchanting one. I had never thought that we would be allowed a third son. The strangest thing was that I did not know his mother. Dyla came forth to me and told me that a woman had wanted to bear him. "She refuses to name herself," Dyla confessed. "She has always loved you, so for you to know her would violate her own modesty." She gave me a small crystal jar. "Bring the seed to me, and in the space of two Ten Moons, I myself will return to you with the child."

I went back to Vincent and he was jubilant. Same-Sex couples are rarely allowed to have three sons, since population control on our small planet is paramount. The decision is always in the hands of the Sisters and the final say would be Dyla's herself. "The old girl must really dig you," he said smiling.

"*Dig?*"

"Yeh, Dyla's always had a twinkle for you," Vincent observed. "Of course I would never share you with her; I know the Sisters all started off as Off-Sex girls, but, believe me, she's never going to get you!"

I thought he was crazy, but that night we pulled our seed out together into the crystal jar and I myself brought it quickly over to the gates of the Temple. A Sister whose face I could not see snapped open the peephole within the huge gate of the Temple walls. I told her who I was. "We know who you are—and why you have come," she said. I did not recognize the voice. Her hand reached out and took the jar. I felt strangely cold, uncertain, once it had left my hand. Where was it going? Who would bear this next child?

I wondered about it for the next two Ten Moons. Then one morning I saw the most unforgettable procession from our window. It was as if royalty were coming from the direction of the Temple to our castle. From the distance emerged a hundred people dressed in robes of sparkling white; some were in festive red. There were scores and scores of Sisters, followed by their maids, servants, gardeners, and retainers. They passed through the gates of our castle. I hurried down to meet them in the courtyard. I had been given no word, so I was uncombed and unbathed from sleep. Vincent soon followed behind me.

I asked who they were, and then I heard Dyla's voice: "Your son is here—to live with his fathers."

I rushed towards her and then my feet stopped dead. Her face, which had been so lovely and young, was veiled. She wore a white robe, edged in gold, and over this was a hood with a veil attached that kept my eyes from her. "He is yours," she said calmly. "But we have given him a name ourselves."

"And what is that?" I asked.

"He will be named Ki, for the whole planet."

She presented a wriggling bundle to me and I took it. He was lovely, with platinum hair and immense blue eyes. They were so blue! I looked into them: they were of the same clarity and depth of color as Vincent's green ones—but blue. As for the hair, I had no idea where that came from. "He is yours," Dyla said. Then suddenly her voice sounded strained, as she added: "But remember, he will belong to the whole planet."

I smiled and thanked her with all my heart. Vincent was so pleased, but even I, still shocked with delight, could hear the heaviness in Dyla's words as she bade us farewell. "I must leave now," she said and turned from me.

We took the beautiful child up to our room. "The whole thing sure is a mystery," Vincent said. "Suddenly Dyla pops up and we have this kid. . . ."

Then he ran over to our window, in time to watch the procession make its way from our gates back towards the Temple. "Quick!" he called to me. With Ki in my arms, we both looked out. Dyla had removed her veil, and even in the midst of the crowd I saw the light catch her hair, as fine and Moon-pale as our new son's.

203

I wish now that I could say that I have told you everything, and also tell you how happy my life is. But even now I have my moments of fear and doubt. I am afraid that Vincent still has the wandering eye of an Earth man. Or that my children may die. Or that my son Ki will someday leave me and be pulled back into the Temple forever. Although he is still only a small child, already he has turned into the most wonderful son—thoughtful, kind, and handsome. Some of the people of Ki already feel that he is a god. They worship him, which I think is silly, but people are like that. They are always looking for someone who they think is bigger, greater; closer to the inner mysteries of heaven. I have no such illusions about the boy, although his strange thoughtful seriousness, even in a child of only eight Ten Moons, does amaze me. His older brothers will soon have to be promised and what a mess that will be. I myself would like it if they do not complete this action for a very long time, but I know the dangers of remaining single on Ki. You need a promised friend here, because there is no telling, after all, when the planet can kick itself off balance.

But the thing I have not told you is that I have kept my promise to Nafshee: I do see him every three changes of the Moons. He lives in the ruins of Anvil's old fortress and what was to be "my" castle. It is run down and creepy, full of tiny, long-nosed monkeys; scurrying insects; and a tribe of rats who sleep in the same warren of cells where I once slept. It is many days' journey from my own castle, but Nafshee has his old father's power to move me there in the wink of an eye. So I am only gone for a short time and Vincent does not miss me, or if he does has never let me know it. I do not really see this as an act of adultery, since I had once been mated to Nafshee, even if it was *totally* against my will. But Nafshee had saved my skin on several occasions, and so I allow him certainly liberties with it as I had once bargained.

Our sex is not pleasant, since he smells badly and his old bluish monkey hide has become as mottled and ragged as an old fur coat. I tell him he really needs to look after his grooming, and have offered to send over to him a young man I know from one of the Same-Sex enclaves whose duties are to wash and comb out bugs and lice when they appear. "Being handled by a fetching young man appeals to me," Nafshee admitted. "But I have my pride. I want to be loved for myself!"

I laughed when he told me this, since I bear so little love for him as it is. But I do love the strange, freakish thing we had together, our son, Alfee. He is now amazingly grown, almost as tall as Nafshee. His skin is a soft bluish color with very little hair on it, just at his underarms, on his chest, and pubic area. He rarely wears clothes, and walks about freely naked, which I think is beautiful; that he is so pure and unselfconscious. After I leave Nafshee's bedroom—when I desperately need a breath of fresh air—I go out behind the fortress, to what had been once animal stalls, and see him. He can tell that I am there by my smell and he quickly bounds over to me, sometimes ranging on all fours, since he stumbles a bit. He is blind, and I always kiss him on his forehead and nose. He says very few words, not from stupidity—I am sure— but from a natural sense of economy. He knows my name and calls it.

"Albert?"

"Yes."

"*Happy?*"

I tell him I am.

Sometimes we sit together in the dirt and I look out at the new Moons as they come rolling softly in the dusk tides of light, as the great White Star that rules daytime on Ki wanes. It is then that I tell him the story of my fathers and their fathers before them and how at one time the Blue Monkeys and the Same-Sex men of Ki were partners and that the Same-Sex men of Ki have cousins thousands of Star years away on Earth, and how we are joined together. But exactly how, no one is sure.

The End

A Note About Ki and the "Egg of the Eye."

Many people have asked me about the third Egg, or the *Egg of the Eye*, the powerful third testicle that Kivian Same-Sex men possess which distinguishes them from their Off-Sex "cousins." Sometimes the question is does it have its equivalent or origin in human organs? One friend asked me if it could possibly be the prostate gland; another suggested the perineum. The closest I can say is that the Egg is the physical manifestation of an inner primal communication and understanding between and among gay men: a communication often necessitated by our own outcast status and demonstrated under trying circumstances—such as chance meetings, signals and glances of the "Eye" itself. By the "Eye," I mean an ability to see inward and beyond oneself. I consider this a strangely modern "gay" characteristic, one that many of us are blessed to have in a time of deepening psychological and spiritual deprivation and confinement. The third Egg, then, on a physical level, is the charge, or battery, of the love we have among us. Unfortunately the passion of this love, when compressed by oppression, can create terrible mutations of itself. It can twist and fire into rage and hate. But conversely, the charge can grow and diffuse into insight and compassion, feelings which are suspect among "normal" men who for the most part can see each other only in terms of indifference and competition (or "cannon fodder," as I call it).

How does a Same-Sex couple produce a son with a third Egg? Same-Sex sperm travel in pairs, in tandem, and when the combined sperm of two mates is used to inseminate an Off-Sex woman, one sperm becomes the third Egg of their son, which will determine most of his psychological and spiritual traits, and the other sperm will contribute the major physical characteristics of the child. Of course some physical characteristics will be contributed by the genes of his mother, who for thousands of Ten Moons, according to the ancient Agreement of Ki, had to be unknown to the male pair whose child she bore. This unknown woman was chosen by the Sisters of Ki, who decided the number of Same-Sex men on the planet. Since the woman was already married to an Off-Sex male, who was obliged to "loan" his wife to the

209

Temple, her bearing this child was part of a couple's obligation to the planet. However, a year after the child's birth, if his mother refused to give the boy back to the Sisters, who would then deliver him to his two fathers, her husband's obligation was over and he would have the right to kill the boy—who definitely was not his.

Some of these customs were changed by Enkidu, who said that Off-Sex women could later know their own Same-Sex sons. No longer would they be lost forever to them. However on a planet whose balance was as fragile as Ki's, it is easy to see that any tinkering with the original Agreement holding the planet together might be dangerous. On Ki all three of its population groups had places in its balance; there was rarely a desire to overlap or exchange roles. The most dramatic change was having a Same-Sexer as King—or even having a King—since a position of this much power was considered wasteful on such a small planet.

While the Same-Sex population was kept in control by the Sisters of Ki, whom these men served (although not always willingly) as acolytes during rituals to the Goddess, Off-Sex numbers were kept in check by war. These feudal-type conflicts were not discouraged by the Sisters, unless they began to involve the whole planet and upset its balance. But by keeping themselves in a constant state of hostility, the Off-Sexers also kept the planet in a state of anxiety—and feudal control; conditions which can be seen in any region on Earth where nations are in ritualized conflict. This anxiety could be eased only by the Sisters themselves. They positioned themselves above the conflicts of their natural Off-Sex families, just as they had counted for thousands of Ten Moons upon peaceful Same-Sex enclaves for their support in bringing spiritual and political balance to Ki.

PB

Perry Brass

Although Perry Brass was born in Savannah, Georgia, he has spent most of his adult life in the North East. He edited *Come Out!*, the first gay liberation newspaper in the world, published by New York's Gay Liberation Front, and with two friends founded the first health clinic for gay men on the East Coast. His poetry and essays—some of the most influential in the early years of the gay movement—were published in alternative papers here and in Europe. His work has been included in *The Male Muse*, *Angels of the Lyre*, *The Penguin Book of Homosexual Verse*, *Gay Roots*, *Gay Liberation* (from Rolling Stone Press), *Out of the Closets*, *The Bad Boy Book of Erotic Poetry*, and the new Columbia University anthology of gay writing and literature.

His 1985 play, *Night Chills*, one of the first to deal with the AIDS crisis, won the Jane Chambers International Gay Playwriting Contest. He has collaborated with many composers, including Chris DeBlasio who set *All The Way Through Evening*, a song cycle based on five poems from which "Walt Whitman in 1989" was spotlighted in the ground-breaking *AIDS Quilt Songbook*, recorded by Harmonia Mundi France; Christopher Berg who set "Five 'Russian' Lyrics" for the group Positive Music; and famed jazz artist Fred Hersch who set "The Brass Songs." His first book of poems, *Sex-charge*, was published in 1991. *Mirage*, his gay science fiction thriller, was nominated for a Lambda Literary Award for Gay Men's Science Fiction. Its sequel, *Circles*, was described by *San Francisco Bay Times* as "a shot of adrenaline to the creative centers of the brain."

Perry Brass currently lives in New York City. An accomplished reader and exponent on gender and gay-related topics, he is available for public appearances.

Other Books by Perry Brass

SEX-CHARGE

AN ACCLAIMED COLLECTION OF POETRY

" . . . poetry at it's highest voltage . . ." Marv. Shaw in **Bay Area Reporter**.

Sex-charge. 76 pages. $6.95. With sensitive male photos by Joe Ziolkowski.
ISBN 0-9627123-0-2

MIRAGE

ELECTRIFYING SCIENCE FICTION

On the tribal planet *Ki*, two men—in the spirit of an ancient pact—have
been promised to each other for a lifetime. But a savage attack and a blood-
chilling murder break this promise and force them to seek another world
where imbalance and lies form Reality. This is the planet known as Earth, a
world they will use and escape. Nominated 1992 Lambda Literary Award for
Best Gay Men's Science Fiction/Fantasy.

"What we've got here is four characters in two bodies . . . a startling his-
torical perspective on sexual politics . . . intelligent and intriguing." Bob
Satuloff in **The New York Native**.

Mirage. 224 pages. $10.95
ISBN 0-9627123-1-0

Works

AND OTHER 'SMOKY GEORGE' STORIES
EXPANDED EDITION with a new introduction by Brandon Judell

"It is this element of realism and fun, not to mention the author's talent,
that sets *Works* above the average . . . The writing is good, the characters are
interesting and the plot gets us off . . ." Jesse Monteagudo in **The Weekly
News**, Miami.

Works and other 'Smoky George' Stories 184 pages. $9.95
ISBN 0-9627123-6-1

CIRCLES

THE AMAZING SEQUEL TO *MIRAGE*

"Brass' prose slides gracefully from down-to-earth plain talk to a richly metaphored language that recalls his roots as a poet . . . the world he has created with Mirage and its sequel rivals, in complexity and wonder, the fantasy creations of such greats as C.S. Lewis and Ursula LeGuin." **Mandate Magazine**, New York.

Circles. 224 pages. $11.95
ISBN 0-9627123-3-7

OUT THERE

STORIES OF PRIVATE DESIRES. HORROR.
AND THE AFTERLIFE.

". . . ghosts, reincarnation, insanity, other-worldly revenge, and demonic possession of dolls, people, and/or souls. Recommended to horror fans who happen to be gay. And especially perfect for reading aloud to a cheating spouse." **Lambda Book Report**.

". . . we have come to associate [horror] with slick and trashy chiller-thrillers. Perry Brass is neither slick nor trashy. He writes very well, indeed, in an elegant and easy prose that carries the reader forward readily and pleasurably from one episode to the next. I found this selection of his work to be of excellent quality." **The Gay Review**, Canada.

Out There. 196 pages. $10.95
ISBN 0-9627123-4-5

At your bookstore, or from:

Belhue Press
2501 Palisade Ave., Suite A1
Riverdale
Bronx, NY 10463

Please add $2.00 shipping each first book, and $1.00 for each book thereafter. New York State residents please add 8% sales tax. Foreign orders in U.S. currency only.